ALONE AGAINST EVIL

"Little father, you can't leave now," Remo said to his Master Chiun. "The world may go up."

"The world is always being destroyed," replied Chiun. "Look at Ninevah. Look at Pompeii. Look at the Great Flood. The world is always being destroyed but gold goes on forever. And the ancient treasure of the House of Sinanju, which has survived catastrophes without number, may well be in danger."

That was that. Chiun was going. And Remo was left to go one-on-one with Kathleen O'Donnell with all the great strokes that Chiun had taught him, but without Chiun's wisdom to guide him.

The trouble was, Kathleen O'Donnell had her own use for those strokes—and he didn't know if he could resist giving her what she lusted for . . . even if it turned the Destroyer into one more weapon in the arsenal of the woman who already was mistress of the most deadly weapon on earth. . . .

THE DESTROYER #63

THE SKY IS FALLING

The Destroyer

THE SKY IS FALLING

WARREN MURPHY & RICHARD SAPIR

A SIGNET BOOK

NEW AMERICAN LIBRARY

For
Cara, Michael, Pat, and
Jim Morris, starring Michael

NAL BOOKS ARE AVAILABLE AT QUANTITY DISCOUNTS WHEN USED TO
PROMOTE PRODUCTS OR SERVICES. FOR INFORMATION PLEASE WRITE TO
PREMIUM MARKETING DIVISION, NEW AMERICAN LIBRARY,
1633 BROADWAY, NEW YORK, NEW YORK 10019.

SIGNET TRADEMARK REG. U.S.PAT. OFF. AND FOREIGN COUNTRIES
REGISTERED TRADEMARK—MARCA REGISTRADA
HECHO EN CHICAGO, U.S.A.

SIGNET, SIGNET CLASSIC, MENTOR, PLUME, MERIDIAN and NAL BOOKS
are published by New American Library
1633 Broadway, New York, New York 10019

First Printing, January, 1986

1 2 3 4 5 6 7 8 9

PRINTED IN THE UNITED STATES OF AMERICA

They couldn't see it. But it could blind. Normally they couldn't feel it, but it could kill. They couldn't touch it, but it could turn human skin to an especially virulent and burning cancer. It could destroy crops, flood the cities of the world and turn the earth into something that resembled the moon, a barren rock waiting for life from elsewhere some aeon hence.

That, of course, was the downside.

"There's got to be some way we can make a buck on this thing," said Reemer Bolt, director of marketing for Chemical Concepts of Massachusetts, who didn't see why they shouldn't push it through Development. "We'd have to work out the bugs, of course."

"I'd say that not destroying all life on this planet is bug one," said Kathleen O'Donnell of Research and Development.

"Right. A major priority. I don't want to destroy all life. I am life. We are all life. Right?"

There were nods all around Conference Room A of Chemical Concepts headquarters, situated north of Boston on high-tech Route 128.

"We are not here to destroy life," said Bolt, "but to protect it. Enhance it. Make Chemical Concepts of Massachusetts a viable growing part of that life."

"What are you talking about?" demanded Kathleen O'Donnell. She was twenty-eight years old, a tall woman with eyes like star sapphires and skin like Alpine marble, white and placid. Her hair, brushed straight off her cool forehead, was a delicate reddish-gold. If she were not always getting in his way, Reemer Bolt, thirty-eight, would have fallen in love with her. Or tried. He'd tried several times, in fact. Unfortunately, there was a problem with beautiful Kathleen O'Donnell, Ph.D., MIT.

She understood him.

Reemer Bolt was glad he was not married to her. Life for a man married to a woman who understood him could be hell. Reemer should know. He had had three of them before he found himself a paranoid shrew. Paranoid shrews were the easiest to deal with. They were so busy chasing their nightmares that you really could do anything with them. With Kathleen O'Donnell, he could do nothing. She knew what was going on.

"I am talking about the basic inalienable priorities," said Bolt. "Life, living life, is important to me." His voice ached with indignation.

But Kathleen O'Donnell did not back down.

"I am glad to see that the survival of life on this planet is one of your priorities. But which priority? Number fifteen, after whether you can sell it to a Third World country or if it can be marketed in Peoria?" asked Dr. O'Donnell of those heavenly blue eyes and the steel-trap mind.

"A major one," replied Bolt. And then, in a deeper voice: "A damned major one. Damned major." Heads nodded around the conference-room table.

"Number one?" asked Kathy.

"I don't know. I said major," snarled Bolt.

"Might survival of life come after say, cost factors, general marketability, use in an oil-rich Third World country, and the possibility of an exclusive patent?"

"I certainly would not discount an exclusive patent. How many companies have poured millions into developing processes and products, only to find they were stolen by others? I want to protect all of us." Bolt looked around the table. Heads nodded. Only one remained still. That coolly beautiful troublemaker.

"Gentlemen," announced Dr. O'Donnell in an even voice. "Let me explain what we are dealing with."

She held up a pack of cigarettes taken from an executive sitting next to her. She tilted it so that the side of the package floated at eye level. It was scarcely wider than two fingernails.

"Around the earth is a layer of ozone, no bigger than this," she said, outlining the side of the cigarette pack with her finger. "It protects us from the sun's rays—the intense ultraviolet rays, X-rays, and cosmic rays. These are all rays which, unfiltered, could obliterate life on our planet."

"They also give us nice tans, comfortable weather, and a bit of chlorophyll called the building block of life, among other things," said Bolt.

"Not as we plan it," said Dr. O'Donnell. "The whole world is so scared of what might happen to the ozone shield that the only international ban ever respected to my knowledge was the abolition of fluorocarbons as propellent for hair spray."

Bolt had thought of that. He was about to interrupt with a brief he had gotten from the legal department, but Kathy continued.

"As you all know, fluorocarbons are colorless, odorless, and inert. They were the perfect propellant for hair sprays. It was a giant industry. The safest ecological substance since they combined with nothing. And that became the problem, because what we have on earth and what we have in the stratosphere are different things. In the stratosphere, these harmless, invisible fluorocarbons combined with the harsh, unfiltered sunlight that exists beyond the ozone."

Reemer Bolt drummed his fingers as he listened to Dr. O'Donnell explain how fluorocarbons produced atomic chlorine in the stratosphere. He knew that. The technical people who were always getting in the way had told him.

"What atomic chlorine does is eat away at the ozone shield which filters out all the harmful rays. Mr. Bolt is really proposing that we manufacture something that, on a broad scale, could very well destroy life as we know it on earth."

Bolt was a taut man. He wore a tight brown suit and his hair was cut dramatically short because a sales magazine had told him that long hair offended some people. He had dark eyes and thin lips. He understood the broader picture very well. O'Donnell didn't want Concepts capital going into one of his programs instead of her Research and Development.

"I said we had some problems," said Bolt. "Every project has a problem. The light bulb had more of them than you could shake a stick at. How many of you would have liked to own a share of every light bulb in the world?"

Dr. O'Donnell still held the cigarette pack horizontally.

"This is how wide the ozone shield was before the hair sprays," she said. She took out one cigarette and dropped the pack. Everyone heard it hit the tabletop. The single cigarette remained in her hands. Then she turned it sideways.

"NASA has conducted experiments in outer space on the unfiltered rays of the sun. The intensity of those rays in space is frightening. But it will be far worse if those rays ever get through this side of the atmosphere with its moisture, tender cells, oxygen, and the richness of molecules that make life as we know it possible."

"What's the one cigarette for?" asked someone. Bolt could have killed the questioner.

"Because in some places this is how much is left of the shield," said Kathy. With a show of contempt, she dropped the cigarette on the table. "Thirty miles up we have, and I hope we will continue to have, a desperately thin ozone shield between all living things and what could destroy them. It doesn't grow. It can naturally replenish itself if we don't destroy it. I am not offering a choice of life or death. I am wondering why you want to even consider committing world suicide."

"Every step forward has been met with dire warnings," said Bolt. "Therre was a time when we were told that man would explode if he ever went sixty miles an hour. It's true.

People believed it," said Reemer. O'Donnell was good. But competition made Bolt better. A book on sales had told him that. "I am proposing that we step into the future and dare to be as great as possible."

"By shooting holes in the ozone shield with a concentrated stream of fluorocarbons? That's Mr. Bolt's proposal."

"Right, a hole. A window in the sky to give us full controlled use of all the sun's energy. Bigger than atomic power," said Bolt.

"And potentially more dangerous," said Dr. O'Donnell. "Because we don't know what a clear window to the sun's rays will do. Not for certain. Space tests conducted beyond the ozone shield indicate that we might be dealing with something more dangerous than we thought. But what worries me most, what absolutely terrifies me, is the fact that it's been estimated that a single molecule of fluorocarbon sets in motion a chain reaction that will eventually destroy one hundred thousand molecules of ozone. How do we know we'll be opening a window and not a gigantic door? How do we know that a concentrated stream of fluorocarbons won't start an unending tear in this desperately thin layer of gas? And if that happens, gentlemen, all life will disappear. All life. Including anyone willing to buy Reemer's stock options in Chemical Concepts."

There was nervous laughter around the table. Reemer Bolt smiled, too, showing he could take a joke. Reemer knew how to take a joke at his expense very well. You smiled along with the others and then a week later, a month later, maybe even a year later, you did something to get the joker fired. The problem with the beautiful Dr. O'Donnell was that she would always be ready for that. She knew him too well.

"All right," said Bolt. "Are you saying we should ditch two-point-five million dollars in development costs because we're afraid of causing a worldwide suntan?"

"Not at all," said Dr. O'Donnell. "What I am saying is this: that before we punch this hole in the ozone layer, we make sure it's only a hole. I am talking about the safe use of the sun. Priority one. Let's not turn the world into a rock.''

The debate raged in Conference Room A for four more hours, but it was a foregone conclusion. Kathleen O'Donnell of Research and Development had won. The main priority of the Fluorocarbon Stream Generator project would be the survival of life on earth. It won heavily, five to two. Reemer had only Accounting on his side at the end.

And Kathleen O'Donnell had an increased research budget of seven million dollars. It always paid to do the right thing.

Six months and seventeen million dollars later, Dr. Kathleen O'Donnell stood looking at a pile of transistors, computer components, pressurized tanks, and a black box three times the size of a man and as unwieldy as an entire operating room. Priority One had still not been met. No one could predict how big a hole would be opened in the vital ozone shield around the earth. And it was on her research budget. She had gone to Bolt's office. She went with her best little-girl-coy look and her womanly perfume. She announced that she had come to discuss the project, and she wanted to do it in Bolt's office—alone.

"We can punch the hole, and I think it would be just a hole. The probability is that it would be a hole. But, Reemer, we can't be sure,'' she said.

This time her argument had force. She said it in the proper way, on Bolt's lap, playing with the buttons of his shirt. She said it smilingly, moving her hands lower down his shirt. She whispered in his ear, creating tingling warm sensations.

"Do you think I am going to jeopardize my position at Chemical Concepts for a tawdry roll in the hay, Kathy?'' asked Bolt. He noticed that the lights were dim in his office. It was very late. There was no one else in the flat single-story concept center that was like so many of the sandstone buildings dotting Route 128. Cars made a blurred procession of lights through the window as they sped by in the rain-slick night. He thought he recognized her perfume. Which of his wives had worn that? Somehow it smelled so much better on Dr. O'Donnell.

"Uh-huh," answered Kathy O'Donnell.

"Not tawdry," said Bolt.

"Very tawdry," whispered Kathy.

And thus on the floor of Marketing Reemer Bolt found himself the sole authorizer of seventeen million dollars in development funds.

But on this day, the very intelligent Dr. Kathleen O'Donnell misjudged the mettle of Reemer Bolt, marketing genius of the high-tech industry, for the first time.

He had the bulky instrument loaded on a flatbed truck and carted to a field just across the state border in Salem, New Hampshire. He pointed it at the sky, saying:

"If I don't make it in this world, nobody will make it."

Dr. O'Donnell heard about the experiment one hour after Bolt and her scientific staff had left for Salem. She flew to her car, careened out of the parking lot at seventy miles an hour, and then picked up speed. She was doing 165 along Route 93 North. In a Porsche 928S, no state trooper was going to catch her. And if one did, no speeding ticket would matter. There wouldn't be anyone to sit on a judge's bench. There might not even be any bench.

She knew where in Salem Bolt had gone. The corporation had a field up there for softball games, picnics, and land investment. When she tore onto the field, tires gouging the soft earth, Bolt was staring disconsolately at his feet with the blank eyes of a man who knew it was all over. His normally immaculate pin-striped jacket lay on the ground. He had been scuffing it with his shoes.

All he said when he saw Kathy stumble out of her Porsche was:

"I'm sorry, Kath. I really am. I didn't mean for this to happen. I had no other choice. You stuck me with a seventeen-million-dollar failure. I had to go for it."

"You idiot! We're all done for now."

"Not you, so much. I was the one who did it."

"Reemer, you have some logic glitches in your mentality mode, but downright stupidity is not one of them. If all life goes down the drain, what difference does it make whether it was you or I who pulled the plug?"

"Seventeen million down the drain," said Bolt, pointing to the blackened metallic structure in the middle of the field. "Nothing works on it. Look."

He showed Kathy the remote console her staff had devised. It had to be remote, because the fluorocarbon generator was so cumbersome that it could only be aimed in one direction: straight up. And that meant the sun's unfiltered rays would return in only one direction: straight down. If everything worked as theorized, the fluorocarbon beam would open a window that allowed raw solar radiation to bathe the earth's surface in a circle thirty meters wide. If it worked. Perfectly.

But now Bolt was punching buttons on a dead board. Not even the On light glowed. The fluorocarbon generator stood silently a hundred yards away. Bolt pounded the console. He hated it because it didn't work. Seventeen million dollars and it didn't work. He hit the console again. He would have killed it if it weren't already dead.

Kathy O'Donnell said nothing. Something was happening in the sky. Set against the clouds was an exquisite ring of blue haze, as though the clouds themselves wore a glowing round blue sapphire. She watched the circle. One of her staff members had a pair of binoculars and she ripped them from his neck. Desperately, she tried to focus on the clouds, on the light blue hazy ring.

"Has it been growing larger or smaller?" she demanded.

"It think it's smaller," said a staffer, one of about twenty people in white smocks or shirtsleeves. They were all looking at her and Bolt with bewildered expressions.

"Smaller," said Kathy O'Donnell. She was speaking as much to herself as anyone else. "Smaller."

"Yes," said a technician. "I think you're right."

Kathy looked at the ground. The grass around the fluorocarbon generator had turned a lighter shade of green. At a distance of about thirty meters, the blades were dark green. Then, as though someone had sprayed a lightening agent, they grew paler, even now becoming a dry whiteness. It was as though someone had drawn the circle of pale grass around the device with a compass. Thirty magnificent, glorious, miraculous feet around the device. It had worked. Perfectly.

"We did it," said Kathy.

"What? The thing doesn't work," said Bolt.

"Not now," replied Dr. Kathy O'Donnell. "But it did work. And it seems our first clear solar window to the sun has given us some interesting side effects."

For the unfiltered solar rays had not only scorched the earth, they had rendered electronic circuits inoperable. The fluorocarbon generator itself was proof. It had been struck and killed by the unfiltered rays.

The eager scientists discovered other side effects. The rays parched plant life, raised the temperature slightly, and burned the skin of living matter in a horrible and unforeseen way. Skin bubbled and blackened, then separated and peeled away. They noticed this when they saw the little furry legs of a chipmunk trying to run out of what was left of its skin.

Some of the scientists turned their heads away. Seeing a poor creature suffer like that plunged Reemer Bolt deep in thought.

If we can make it mobile, and aim it better, we might have a weapons sale, thought Reemer. Or perhaps we could market a screen against the rays. Maybe both. The future was limitless. As bright as the sun.

The budget was tripled and, within a month, they had constructed an aiming mechanism. There was only one small glitch. The fluorocarbon stream could be controlled in the amount of ozone shield it opened, but it could not be aimed very exactly. They could direct the beam elsewhere instead of straight up, but they were just not sure where it would land. Which meant that Chemical Concepts would control this immense new energy source so that life on earth wasn't threatened, but couldn't direct it anywhere in particular. This shot the boards out from under Marketing. It was like owning a car you couldn't steer: if you can't steer it, you can't sell it.

"How far off this time?" asked Kathy. She had once again found Bolt using the fluorocarbon gun, as they were calling it now, without her permission.

"Two or three thousand miles," said Bolt. "I think you'll have to upgrade your targeting computer. I'll help you get more money."

"Over where did we open up a hole in the ozone shield?" asked Kathy.

"Not sure. Maybe China or Russia. Maybe neither. We'll find out when someone's electronics shut down, or if mass skin problems develop somewhere. If it's Russia, I don't think we have to worry. They won't sue for damages."

In his somewhat shrewd way, Reemer Bolt was right. Russia wouldn't sue. It was planning to start World War III.

He was old. Even for a Russian general. He had known and buried Stalin. He had known and buried Lenin. He had buried them all. Every one of them, in some way or other, at some time or other, had said to him:

"Alexei. What would we ever do without you?"

And Alexei Zemyatin would answer: "Think. Hopefully, think."

Even during the harshest times, Field Marshal Alexei Zemyatin would speak his mind to any of the Soviet leaders. He would, in brief, call them fools. And they would listen to him because he had saved their lives so many times before.

When Lenin was fighting both America and Britain on Russian soil after the First World War, and a hundred groups plotted the overthrow of the Communist government, Zemyatin confronted Lenin's worst fears. He was at the time the dictator's secretary.

"I dread the joining of all our enemies," said Lenin. "It is the one thing that will destroy us. If ever they stop fighting among themselves, we are ruined."

"Unless you help them to form a united front against you."

"Never," said Lenin. The one hope the Communists

had was that their disparate enemies would keep fighting among themselves. Otherwise they could destroy the young revolution.

"Then let me ask you to think, Great Leader. If a hundred groups are all working against you, each with a different idea and a different leader, it will be as it was against the czar. No matter how many are killed, the opposition will survive. And then, as happened to the czar, a group will succeed against you one day."

"That will come later, and then only maybe. Right now we are fighting for our lives," said Lenin.

"Later always comes, fool. That is why God gives us brains to plan with."

"Alexei, what are you getting at? I warn you, you are not dealing with a small matter here. Your life is wagered on it."

"No, it isn't," said Zemyatin, who knew that Lenin needed argument in his life. So few now were willing to argue with him, at least not successfully. "Today there are shootings even in Moscow. Your secret police kill one group, but still there are dozens more untouched. Why?"

"Because the sewers spawn different bugs."

"Because none of them are joined. If you have a tree with a hundred branches, every branch will fall when you cut down the trunk. But if you have a hundred dandelion weeds, you will never be rid of them. Forests can be felled. But to my knowledge no lawn, not even that of the czar on the Baltic, was ever free of dandelions."

"But something that strong could destroy us."

"Not if we run it. And who has better knowledge of these counterrevolutionary groups than our own secret police? We will not only join these groups into one strong oak, but we will fertilize this tree. Prune it occasionally. And then, when we wish, we will cut it down with a single chop of the ax."

"It is too dangerous."

"As opposed to what else, my Ilyich?" asked Alexei Zemyatin.

In the years that followed, Zemyatin's strategy proved to be the master stroke of counterintelligence secretly admired by all of Russia's enemies. It was the one move that enabled Soviet Russia to survive, but Zemyatin was never given credit for its formulation. Instead, at Zemyatin's request, credit was given to the founder of what later became the KGB. Nor did Zemyatin accept recognition for saving Russia from Nazi Germany. While everyone else celebrated Stalin's nonaggression pact with Adolf Hitler, Zemyatin told Stalin that these were the most dangerous times in Russia's history.

"How can it be?" asked Stalin, fingering his clipped mustache. They had met in a private room because the dictator was shrewd enough to know that he could not allow any man to call him a fool in public and live. He did not want the brilliant Zemyatin dead.

"The safest times precede the greatest dangers, Mr. Chairman," Zemyatin told him.

"We have made peace with Hitler. We have the Capitalists and the Nazis at each other's throats. We will shortly control half of Poland, giving us more territorial safety, and you tell me that these times are dangerous."

"They are dangerous," answered the middle-aged man with the steady blue eyes, "because you think they are safe. You think that your enemies are at each other's throats. Well, they are. But because you think you are safe, the Red Army thinks it is also safe. The soldiers will sit comfortably in their barracks waiting for weekends in the taverns with whores instead of preparing for war."

Zemyatin's plan was to create another army, secretly, behind the Urals. Let Germany attack. Let Germany have its unstoppable victories. And watch them carefully. See how they fought. Then, with the Nazis rolling toward Moscow, confident of victory, their strengths and weaknesses absolutely clear, Russia would unleash its hidden army. A gigantic trap: a country wide and a people long.

The year of the plan was 1938. Four years later, after the nonaggression pact was proven to be the joke Zemyatin suspected, the Nazi advance was halted with difficulty at a city called Stalingrad. As the Germans prepared to take the city, they were surrounded by fully one hundred divisions: Zemyatin's secret army. The Russians annihilated the

German Sixth Army like locusts descending on old corn, and then marched to Berlin, only stopping when they met the Americans coming from the opposite direction.

Zemyatin, as usual, took no credit, letting the battalion be called Zhukov's Army.

His counsel was passed on from Russian leader to Russian leader like a national treasure. More often than not, he would counsel caution. Alexei Zemyatin did not believe in adventures any more than he believed his form of government was any better than another. He kept his government from war with China. He lectured each new general personally on his belief that so long as Russia did not endanger America proper, there would be no Third World War. He insisted on three safety backups for every Soviet nuclear weapon, his greatest fear being an accident of war. Thus, the entire Politburo was shocked and terrified when it heard that Field Marshal Zemyatin himself was preparing for World War III. This was confided by the Premier to select Politburo members, who later spread the word.

It was autumn, cold already in the country of the Russian bear and Siberian steppes. No one had expected it. No one knew what the danger was or even if there was a danger, just that one was coming. Even the chief of staff was asking: Why?

According to rumors at the highest levels of the Kremlin, rumors the Premier only occasionally confirmed, the Great One, Zemyatin himself, had made the awesome decision to prepare for war in exactly one half-hour. There had been what was termed "minor trouble" at a missile base in Dzhusaly, near the Aral Sea in the Kazakh SSR. Many parts were often faulty, so minor troubles went on all the time. The Soviet Missile Command was used to it. But Zemyatin had always known enough to fear what did not appear dangerous. Often he would make special trips here and there, and then quietly leave. So it was not thought unusual when the General was flown by special KGB jet to the missile base where a strange accident had happened.

The "accident" was that all electronic equipment, from

the firing keys to the telephones, had inexplicably gone inoperative at the same time and needed replacing. This fact had been kept from the higher command for a week because the commanding officer had assumed it was the fault of his men, and had tried to fix it before anyone accused him of incompetence. But a conscientious junior officer had reported him to Central Missile Command. Now the commanding officer sat in a jail cell, and the junior officer directed the missile base.

The junior officer, whose name was Kuryakin, followed Zemyatin down a corridor, talking incessantly about what had happened. The light blue halo that had appeared in the sky, more luminous than the sky itself. The discoloring of the steppe grass. And the sudden failure of all electronic equipment. The junior officer had only heard rumors about Zemyatin—he had never met him. He even suspected that the Great One did not exist. But seeing the way the KGB generals deferred to Zemyatin, the way he would walk into a room and interrupt their discussions, peremptorily dismissing the generals' views as a waste of his time, showed the junior officer that indeed this had to be the Great One.

Zemyatin's face was gnarled like old wood, but his head was bald and shiny like new skin, as if his fertile brain kept it young. He walked with a slight stoop, but even then he towered over the others in his presence. His eyes were a watery blue, somewhat filmed by age. But it was clear to Kuryakin that this man did not see with his eyes.

"And so, sir," the junior officer was saying, "I proceeded to make an investigation. I found animals dying horribly, scorched in their very skins. I found that within a certain radius, the men manning the missiles had become sick. Indeed, they too are now seeing their skin blacken and peel. And all our equipment ceased at once. All of it. When my commander refused to report this, I risked insubordination and my career, and indeed my life, sir, but I reported my findings. This was more than an accident."

Zemyatin did not even nod. It was as though he were not listening. But a question here and a question there showed the old man had missed nothing.

"Come. Let us meet your commanding officer," said Zemyatin finally. He was helped by two KGB generals into the back of a large ZIL automobile and driven to the prisoners' compound.

The commanding officer sat in a single gray cell on a rude chair, his head bowed and his mind undoubtedly contemplating the chances of his spending the rest of his life in a Siberian gulag, or of shortly standing before a firing-squad wall. The man did not lift his head when Zemyatin entered. But when he saw the dark green KGB uniforms behind the old man, he fell to his knees, begging.

"Please. Please. I will inform on anyone. Do anything. Please do not shoot me."

"You disgrace the Missile Command," accused the junior officer. "It is good you have been exposed." To Zemyatin he said, "This garbage must not defend Mother Russia."

"Not my fault. It's not my fault. I am a good officer," sobbed the former commander. Thus began a full hour of obvious half-truths and weaseling evasions, a performance of such abject misery that even the KGB generals were embarrassed for the Missile Command.

At the end of it, Field Marshal Zemyatin pointed to the quivering wreck at his feet and said:

"He is in full command again."

And then to the astonished junior officer: "He dies now. Shoot him here."

"But the traitor and coward was the commanding officer," blurted one KGB general, who had known Zemyatin many years.

"And you, too. You die now," Zemyatin said, nodding to his old colleague. And to the guards:

"Do I have to do it myself?"

Loud shots echoed in the small cell, splattering brain and bone against the stone walls. By the time the shooting stopped, the former commander had to be helped out of his cell, his shirt covered with the blood of others, and his pants filled with his own loosed bowels.

"You are not only in charge again, you are promoted," Zemyatin told him. "You will report everything that happens in this base, no matter how slight, to me. No one will be allowed to leave here. No one will write home. I want to know everything. No detail is too small. And I want everyone to go about his business as though nothing has happened.''

"Should we replace the electronics, Comrade Field Marshal?''

"No. It would indicate that they did not work. Everything works fine. Do you understand?''

"Absolutely. Absolutely.''

"Keep making reports as you always did. There have been no breakdowns.''

"And the dying men? Some of them are dying. Those at the missiles themselves are already dead.''

"Syphilis,'' said Zemyatin.

On the way back to Moscow, the surviving KGB general spoke to Zemyatin as the field marshal drank tea from a glass with a plain dark biscuit:

"May I ask why you had me shoot the loyal soldier and then stand by while you promoted the negligent coward?''

"No,'' replied Zemyatin. "Because if I tell you, you might breathe it to someone else in your sleep. I had the general shot because he did not move quickly enough.''

"I know. I had to shoot him.''

"And you have to do something else. You must assemble a staff to take calls from that negligent coward of a missile commander. He will be phoning me with every little bug that drops out of the sky. But we are looking for only one thing,'' said Zemyatin. "We are looking for anyone or anything inquiring about damage to the base. Do not let the commander or even the staff know that. But if it happens, let me know immediately.''

The KGB general nodded. He had survived a long time, too. While he still did not know why the Great One had promoted the coward and had him shoot the hero, he did understand why he was not told. It was for the same reason that he had had to shoot the other KGB general in the cell, the one who had questioned him. Alexei Zemyatin wanted, above all things, obedience. This from a man who for the seventy years since the Russian Revolution went from commander to commander telling him first to think, then to obey. Now it was the opposite. For some reason, everything had changed in the world.

From Vnukovo II Airport, Zemyatin insisted on being driven, not to the Kremlin, but to the Premier's home, just outside the city. He told the servants who answered the door to awaken the Premier. Then he followed them into the bedroom. He sat down on the side of the bed. The Premier opened his eyes, terrified, certain it was a coup.

Alexei Zemyatin took the Premier's hand and put it on his own blouse, pressing it against something crusty. The Premier's room smelled of French perfume. He had had one of the cheap whores he liked so much again this evening. Zemyatin wanted him to understand the danger. He pressed the Premier's fingers as hard as his withered old hands would let him.

"That is dried blood, the blood of an honorable and decent officer. I had him shot earlier today," said Zemyatin. "I also had shot a general who delayed because he understood correctly how wrong this was. Then I promoted the most craven coward I ever saw back to command."

"Great One, why did you do this?" asked the Premier, looking for his eyeglasses.

"Because I believe we may soon have to launch a missile attack against the United States. Stop looking for your glasses, fool. I haven't brought you anything to see. I need your mind."

Then he explained that some force, probably a weapon, had put an entire SS-20 missile base out of operation. Without a sound or even a warning.

"What has happened is catastrophic, a Russian Pearl Harbor brought about with the silence of a falling leaf. There is a weapon out there, probably in the hands of the Americans, that can make all of our weapons useless."

"We're done for," said the Premier.

"No. Not yet. You see, there is one advantage we still have. Only one. America does not yet know they can destroy us so easily."

"How do you know that? How can you say that?"

"Because if they did, they would have done it by now. I suspect what we have here is a trial, a test. If the U.S. doesn't know that their weapon works, they may not launch the rest of the attack."

"Yes. Yes. Of course. Are you sure?"

"I am sure that if they don't know it works, we are safe. The reason people pull the little triggers on guns is that it is common knowledge that a gun will shoot lead bullets where it is pointed. But if no one knew what a gun would do when fired, my dear friend, they would hesitate to pull the trigger."

"Yes. Good."

"Therefore, I could not allow the one man who had already risked his life to expose the truth to live. He might do something crazy, like warn someone else that one of our missile batteries is useless. Of course, he would do this with the best intentions. But his good intentions could get us all killed now. So I replaced him with the one man who would happily live a lie and command a missile base that did not work as though it did. Then, of course, I had to have shot the KGB general who stopped to think. We need obedience now, more than ever."

The Premier blinked his eyes and tried to organize his thoughts. At first, he told himself he might be dreaming. But even he would not dream of Alexei Zemyatin coming to his bedroom like this.

"Our biggest danger now, of course, is that they find out their weapon, whatever it is, has worked against us. Therefore I have ordered that I be informed of anyone or anything that might be prying into the current ready status of the Dzhusaly missile base."

"Good," said the Premier.

"We cannot waste time. I must go."

"What for?"

"To prepare a special missile for a first strike. Once they find out they can destroy our nuclear arsenal, we are going to have to launch them all or face a certain first strike ourselves."

"Then you wish me to tell no one?" said the Premier.

"I have informed you because only you can authorize a

first strike on the United States. Remember, once they find out how vulnerable we actually are, we must attack before they do. I expect to get more serviceable missiles."

This from the Great One, Alexei Zemyatin, who had dared to call all the Russian Premiers in their times fool, whom history had vindicated as the true genius of the Union of Soviet Republics, and who had now just reversed everything he had been preaching since the Revolution.

In America, the President was informed that the Soviet Union had no wish to share information about a threat to all mankind.

"They're crazy," insisted the President. "Something is disrupting the ozone layer. All civilization could be wiped out, and when we inform them it might be happening over their own territory and that we want to get together on this thing, they stonewall us. Won't tell a thing. They're crazy."

"Intelligence believes they think we're doing it to them."

"To them! What the hell do they think our skins are made of?" demanded the President, shaking his head. And then he quietly went to his bedroom and picked up a red telephone which had no dial or buttons on its face and which connected, when the receiver was lifted, to only one other telephone in the northeast corridor. He said simply:

"I want that man. No, both of them."

"What for, sir?" came back the voice. It was crisp and lemony with sharp New England consonants.

"I don't know, dammit. Just have them ready. You come down here, too. I want you to listen in. I think the world is going up and I don't know what the hell is going on."

2

His name was Remo and he walked among the explosions.

But that was nothing special. Any man could walk safely through this particular minefield. The mines were not designed to kill the person who touched them off. They were meant to kill everyone around him. Guerrillas used these mines, the Vietcong especially.

They worked this way: a company would walk along a trail. One man, usually the one walking point, would step on the buried pressure-sensitive device and set it off. Ordinary mines usually exploded upward, making hamburger of that man. Not this mine. It expended its force outward, not upward, and the singing shrapnel would cut down everyone in the vicinity. Except the one who caused the carnage. A soldier alone, conventional military wisdom said, was useless. No army fought with lone soldiers. Armies worked in platoons and companies and divisions. And if you built a mine that left one soldier standing alone, you rendered him useless.

So the mines went off under his feet, sending pieces of shrapnel cracking loudly along the prairie grass of North Dakota, setting fires where steel spanked off rocks and sending sparks into the dull dry grass. Remo thought that he heard someone laughing up ahead. That was special.

To hear a small sound in a great one was to be able to hear one hoof in a cavalry charge, or a can of beer opening during a football game.

He heard the laughter by not blocking out sounds. That was how most people dealt with loud noise, by defending their eardrums. Remo heard with his entire body, in his bones and with his nerve ganglia, because his very breathing vibrated with that sound and became a part of it.

He had been trained to hear like this. His aural acuteness came from his breathing. Everything came from his breathing: the power to sense the buried land mines, the ability to ignore the shock of the blasts, even the speed that enabled him to dodge the flying steel pellets if he had to. And there, as clear as his own breath, was the laughter up ahead. A very soft laughter coming from the high granite building set like a gray mountain in a plain that had no mountain. From its parapets, a person could see for fifteen miles in every direction. And they could see a thin man, about six feet tall, with high cheekbones and deep-set brown eyes that lay in shadows like the holes in a skull, walking casually across the minefield.

Remo heard the laughter from a mile away, from a thousand yards, and from ten yards. At ten yards, there were no more mines. He looked up at the parapet to see a very fat man with a gold hat on his head. Or a crown. Remo couldn't tell. He didn't care to tell. It was the right fat face and that was all that mattered.

The man yelled down from the parapet.

"Hey, you! Skinny. You know you're funny," said the man.

"I know. I heard you laughing," said Remo. "You're Robert Wojic, the Hemp King of North America. Right?"

"That's legal. And so are the mines. This is my property. I can shoot you for trespassing."

"I've come to deliver a message."

"Go ahead and deliver it and then get out of here."

"I forget the message," said Remo. "It has to do with testimony."

The barrel of an AK-47 poked out of one of the stone slots in the parapet. Then another. They came from both sides of the Hemp King of North America.

"Hey, you're a dead man. No one tells Robert Wojic what to say in court. No one tells Robert Wojic anything. Robert Wojic tells you. And Robert Wojic tells you you are dead."

Remo thought a moment. There was testimony that was needed from the fat man, but what? It was specific. He knew it was specific because he wrote it down. He wrote it down and then he did something with the note. What did he do with the note?

One of the rifle muzzles quivered in an obvious pre-fire sign. The man behind it was about to squeeze the trigger. It was on a white paper that he wrote the note. The rifle fired. It fired a burst that sounded more like a string of firecrackers to Remo, each pop separate and distinct. But his body was already moving toward the castle wall where the man couldn't get a firing angle. The bullets thudded into the ground as the crack of a second burst followed. Another gun opened up, this one trying to comb the wall free of Remo. Making his way up it now, he felt the stone against his fingers. He didn't climb by grabbing and pulling, which was how most people climbed and the reason why they couldn't do verticals. He applied the pressure of his palms to the wall for lift, and used his toes to keep level between hand movements. It looked easy. It wasn't.

He had written the note with a pencil. There were three key points to the testimony. Good. Three points. What were they?

Remo arrived at the top of the parapet and stopped the AK-47 from firing by ramming it through blue jeans into something warm and moist, namely the natural opening into the triggerman's lower bowels. Then he pushed it into the upper bowels and slapped in the man's belly with a hard short blow, setting off the rifle and sending the top of his cranium toward the blue North Dakota sky.

The other guns ceased because the men firing didn't want their weapons muzzled the same way. They dropped them on the stone walkway as they reached for the sky. It was as though the ten men, as one, suddenly became strangers to violence, their weapons foreign objects which had mysteriously appeared at their feet. Ten innocent men with innocent expressions gingerly nudging their rifles away with their toes.

"Hello," said Remo. He had just shown the Hemp King that his military books that asserted a man alone was useless were themselves useless.

"And Robert Wojic says hello to you, friend," said Wojic, looking around at his useless gunmen. They had their hands in the air like a bunch of petrified pansies.

"I need your help," said Remo.

"You don't need no one's help, friend," said Wojic. And then to the toughs he had picked up in the waterfronts of the world: "You there. Put your hands down. You look like you're going to be frisked. You gonna frisk them?"

"No," said Remo.

"Put your hands down. All of you. This whole castle. Everything. Useless. A lousy investment. Listen to me, friend. Robert Wojic, the Hemp King, biggest importer and exporter of hemp rope around the world, tells you here this day: castles suck."

"I need your testimony on three points."

"Oh, the trial," said Wojic, shaking his head. "I got a right to remain silent, not to testify against myself."

"I know, but there's a problem with that," said Remo.

"What's that?" asked Wojic.

"You're going to."

"If you force me, my testimony will be thrown out of court," said Wojic triumphantly, very satisfied with his legal point. He was sitting in a very large chair encrusted with gold. He wore a purple robe trimmed in white ermine, and hand-tooled cowboy boots of Spanish leather peeped out from under the robe. Hemp rope did not pay for all these luxuries.

"I am not going to force you," said Remo, who wore just a white T-shirt and tan chinos. "I am not going to apply any untoward pressure to make you testify. However, I will push your eardrums out through your nostrils as a way of getting acquainted."

Remo clapped both palms against Robert Wojic's ears. The slap was not hard, but the absolute precision of the cupped hands arriving simultaneously made the Hemp King's eardrums feel that indeed they would come out of his nostrils at the slightest sniffle. Robert Wojic's eyes watered. Robert Wojic's teeth felt like they had just been ground by a rotating sander. Robert Wojic could not feel his ears. He was not sure that if he blew his nose, they would not appear in his lap. He did not, of course, hear his own men laughing at him.

And at that moment, Robert Wojic suddenly knew how to help this visitor to the prairie castle. He would give Remo the three pieces of information needed to help the prosecutor in his case. Wojic explained that the three pieces of information had to be the names of three cocaine runners. Wojic's hemp-import operation covered for them, and his international contacts allowed them to move the drug and the money freely. That was how Robert Wojic could afford such luxury from importing a material that wasn't much in demand since the invention of synthetic fibers.

"Right," said Remo. "That's what it was."

And Robert Wojic assured Remo that he would testify to this willingly because he never, ever wanted to see Remo come back for a second favor. Perhaps he would be killed by the angry cocaine runners, but Wojic wasn't concerned. He had seen death just moments before, and the man lying on the parapet with his brains blown out of his skull looked a hell of a lot more peaceful than Wojic himself felt as he checked his nose. Nothing was coming out. Then he felt his very tender ears.

"So long, friend. Will I see you in court?"

"Nah," said Remo. "I never have to go."

Robert Wojic offered to have one of his men give Remo a lift into town. All ten said they would personally have been willing to drive the stranger who climbed up walls, but they had immediate appointments in the other direction.

"Which direction is that?" wondered Remo.

"Where are you going?" they asked in chorus.

"That way," said Remo, pointing east, where Devil's Lake Municipal Airport lay.

"Sorry, that seems to be in the general direction of New York and I'm heading for Samoa," observed one of the triggermen. "I don't know about these other guys."

As it turned out, they, too, were headed for Samoa. Immediately. All of them. So Remo had to walk to the airport alone, back the way he came over the scorched prairie grass where hidden mines were supposed to reduce a company of men to a single quivering human being.

At a push-button pay phone in Minnewaukan, Remo had to punch in a code to indicate that the job had been successfully completed. The code was written on the inside of his belt, along with an alternate code that indicated a problem and the need for further instructions. This was a new system. He was fairly certain the "mission complete" code was on the right. He punched in the numbers, suddenly wondering if Upstairs had meant his right or the belt's right. When he got a car wash, he knew he had copied down the codes wrong. He threw away the belt and caught a 747 for New York City.

On the plane, he suddenly realized that throwing the belt away was a mistake. Anyone finding the belt could punch in one of the correct codes and throw the entire organization Remo worked for off course. But nowadays he wasn't sure what that was anymore. He went to sleep next to a thirtyish blond who, sensing his magnetism, kept running her tongue over her lips as though rehearsing a lipstick ad.

In New York City, Remo's cab let him off at a very expensive hotel on Park Avenue, whose elegant windows now reflected the dawn. About thirty policemen crowded the lobby. Someone, it seemed, had thrown three conventioneers thirty stories down an elevator shaft with the force of an aircraft catapult. Remo took a working elevator to the thirtieth floor and entered a major suite.

"I didn't do it," came a high squeaky voice.

"What?" said Remo.

"Nothing," said the voice. "They did it to themselves." Inside the living room, draped in a golden kimono trimmed in black, his frail body seated toward the rising sun, wisps of hair placid against the yellow parchment of his skin, sat Chiun, Master of Sinanju. Innocent.

"How did they do it to themselves?" demanded Remo. He noticed a small bowl of brown rice sitting unfinished on the living-room table.

"Brutality always begets its own end."

"Little Father," said Remo, "three men were hurled

thirty stories down an open elevator shaft. How could they possibly have done it to themselves?''

"Brutality can do that sort of thing to itself," insisted Chiun. "But you would not understand."

What Remo did not understand was that absolute and perfect peace made any intrusion a brutal act. Like a scorpion on a lily pad. Like a dagger in a mother's breast. Like volcanic lava burning a helpless village. That was brutality.

The mother's breast, helpless village, and benign lily pad were, of course, Chiun, Master of Sinanju, at breakfast. The scorpion, dagger, and volcanic lava were the three exalted members of the International Brotherhood of Raccoons, who had walked down the hall singing "Ninety-Nine Bottles of Beer on the Wall."

As Chiun had expected, Remo again stood up for other whites, explaining away their hideous brutality as "some guys high on beer singing a drinking song," something that in his perverted mind did not call for an immediate return to gentle silence.

"I mean, they couldn't very well throw themselves down a thirty-story shaft with the force of a machine, could they, Little Father? Just for singing a drinking song? Listen, we'll stay out of the cities from now on, if you want peace."

"Why should I be denied a city because of others' brutality?" answered Chiun. He was the Master of Sinanju, latest in a line of the greatest assassins in history. They had served kings and governments before the Roman Empire was a muddy village on the Tiber. And they had always worked best in cities.

"Should we surrender the centers of civilization to the animals of the world because you blindly side white with white all the time?"

"I think they were black, Little Father."

"Same thing. Americans. I give the best years of my life to training a lowly white and at the first sign of conflict, the very first incident, whose side does this white take? Whose side?''

"You killed three men because they sang a song," said Remo.

"Their side," said Chiun, satisfied that once again he had been abused by an ingrate. His long fingernails poked out of his elegant kimono to make the telling point. "Their side," he repeated.

"You couldn't have just let them walk down the damned hallway."

"And brutalize others who might be transcending with the rising sun during breakfast?"

"Only Sinanju transcends with the rising sun. I sincerely doubt that plumbers from Chillicothe, Ohio, or account executives from Madison Avenue transcend with the rising sun."

Chiun turned away. He was about to stop talking to Remo, but Remo had gone to prepare the rice for breakfast, and would not be aware of the slight. So Chiun said:

"I will forgive you this because you believe you are white."

"I am white, Little Father," said Remo.

"No. You couldn't be. I have come to the conclusion that it is not an accident you have become Sinanju."

"I am not going to start writing in one of your scrolls that my mother was Korean but I didn't know it until you gave me Sinanju."

"I didn't ask that," said Chiun.

"I know you have been struggling with how to explain that the only one to master the sun source of all the martial arts, Sinanju, is not Korean, not even Oriental, but white. Pale, blank, blatant white."

"I have not written the histories lately because I did not wish to admit the ingratitude of a white, and how they all stick together even when they owe everything they are to someone kind and decent and mild who thoughtlessly gave the best years of his life to an ingrate."

"It's because I won't write that I'm not white," said Remo. In his training he had read the histories, and knew the long line of assassins the way British schoolboys learned of the ancestry of their kings and queens.

"You said you were raised in an orphanage. Which orphan knows his mother, much less his father? You could have had a Korean father."

"Not when I look in the mirror," said Remo.

"There are diseases that afflict the eyes and make them mysteriously round," said Chiun.

"White," said Remo. "And I know you don't want to leave that in the history of Sinanju. When I take over the scrolls, the first thing I do will be to say how happy I am as the first white to be given Sinanju."

"Then I will live forever," said Chiun. "No matter how afflicted this old body is, I will struggle to breathe."

"You're in your prime. You told me that everything really comes together at eighty."

"I had to because you would worry."

"I never worry about you, Little Father."

Chiun was interrupted from collecting that insult and depositing it in his bank of injustices by a knock on the door, which Remo answered. Three uniformed policemen and a plainclothes detective stood in the doorway. Other patrolmen and detectives were at other doors, Remo noticed. The police informed Remo that they had reason to believe that three visitors to the city, three conventioneers, had been brutally murdered. Something had hurled them down from the thirtieth floor. They were sure it was from the thirtieth floor because the elevator doors on this floor had been ripped open and the cage jammed half a floor up to make room for the falling men. The problem was that they could find no trace of the machine that did it. Did the occupants of this suite hear any kind of machine this morning?

Remo shook his head. But from behind him, Chiun spoke up clearly and, for him, quite loudly:

"How could we hear machinery with all that racket this morning?" he demanded.

The police wanted to know what racket.

"The bawdy screaming yells of drunken brutals," said Chiun.

"He's an old man," Remo said quickly. He added a

little smile to show the police they should be tolerant of him.

"I am not old," said Chiun. "I am not even ninety by correct counting."

In Korean, Remo told him that in America, and the rest of the West for that matter, no one used the old Wan Chu calendar, which was so inaccurate it lost two months in a year.

And in Korean, Chiun answered that one used a calendar for grace and truth, not for mere hoarding of time. Like Westerners so obsessed with each precise day that they think they have lost something if one day disappeared in a week.

The police, confronted with the spectacle of two men speaking in a strange language, looked to each other in confusion.

"Perhaps that loud noise was the machine that killed those men?" asked the detective.

"No," said Remo. "It was people. He didn't hear any machines."

"Not surprising," said the detective, motioning for the others to get going. "No one else heard the machine, either."

"Because of the singing," said Chiun.

Remo shook his head and was about to shut the door when he saw something he should not have seen. Walking through the police line into a murder scene in which Remo and Chiun might be connected was a man in a tight dark three-piece gray suit, with a parched lemony expression, gray hair parted with painful neatness, and steel-rimmed glasses.

It was Harold W. Smith, and he should not have been there. The organization was set up to do the things that America didn't want to be associated with but that were necessary for survival. So secret was it that outside of Smith, only the President knew of its existence. So necessary was secrecy that a phony execution had been staged so that its one killer arm would have the fingerprints of a dead man, a dead man for an organization that could never be known to exist. The fact that Remo was an orphan and would not be missed was a significant factor in his selection. There had been another man who was almost chosen, but he had a mother.

Now here was Smith not even bothering to set up a cover meeting to protect the organization, walking right into the one sort of situation that could blow it all, walking very publicly up to the hotel suite of his secret killer arm, and making himself vulnerable to questioning by the droves of police roaming the halls on a matter of triple murder.

"It doesn't matter," said Smith, entering the apartment.

"I thought you would have phoned to have me meet you someplace," said Remo, closing the door on the sea of blue uniforms. "Something. Anything. Those cops are going to be questioning the cockroaches before they're through."

"It doesn't matter," repeated Smith.

"Hail, O Emperor Smith. Thy graciousness brings sunlight to darkness, glory to the mud of daily life. Our day is enhanced by your imperial presence. Name but the deed, and we fly to avenge wrongs done to your glorious name." Chiun had said hello.

"Yes," said Smith, clearing his throat. He had said hello. Then he sat down.

"Peasants in this very hotel have been defaming your glorious name during the time of transcendence itself. Lo, I heard them this very morning, loud as machines," said Chiun.

In Korean, Remo told Chiun: "I don't think he cares about the three bodies, Little Father."

Chiun's delicate fingers fluttered in the still air, his silk brocaded kimono rustling as he gave greetings. The Masters of Sinanju never bowed, but they did acknowledge others with a tipping of the body which resembled a bow. Remo knew what it was, but Smith couldn't tell the difference and always waited patiently until it was over. Smith had found he could no more stop this than he could convince Chiun that he was not an emperor and was never intended to be. Several times Smith had thought he'd explained the workings of America's constitutional government to the Master of Sinanju, and Chiun had exclaimed that he understood perfectly, even commenting on some of the passages Smith had read him. But always Remo would later tell him that Chiun thought the Constitution merely contained some beautiful sentiments that had little to do with daily life, like prayers or love poems. He was still puzzled as to why America should be afraid to violate its constitutions when any reasonable emperor would flaunt his power to have his enemies assassinated.

"Gentlemen," began Smith. "What do you know about fluorocarbons?"

"They are evil, O gracious Emperor, and were probably behind the desecrators of your glorious name, this very morning sent to their righteous doom," said Chiun.

"They're the things in spray cans, aren't they?" Remo asked. "They make them work."

Smith nodded. "Fluorocarbons are a manmade chemical propellant. Their industrial use was severely restricted almost ten years ago."

"He who would make noise during transcendence," observed Chiun, "would make a fluorocarbon that the whole world despises for its ugliness."

"High in the stratosphere lies a layer of ozone gas. It's only about an eighth of an inch thick, but it performs the critical ecological function of filtering harmful solar radiation so it doesn't strike the planet's surface. Unfortunately, these fluorocarbons rose to the stratosphere and began to eat away at the ozone layer faster than new ozone was being produced up there."

"Our gracious ozone," said Chiun. "The swine."

And to Remo, in Korean:

"What is this man ranting about? Is he afraid of hair sprays?"

"Will you listen to him, Little Father? The man's talking," Remo whispered back in the Korean dialect of the northwest province in which the village of Sinanju, Chiun's village, was located.

"Hair sprays today, poems about people's rights yesterday. What will it be tomorrow? I say now, as I have said before, let us leave this lunatic's service. The world has never had more despots and tyrants, rulers who would not only pay more, but would properly honor a professional assassin with correct employment." This from Chiun, also in Korean.

"Will you listen?" said Remo.

"Yes," continued Smith. "It is a major problem once more because someone, some lunatic, is shooting holes in the ozone layer on purpose."

"What can you expect from violators of transcendence?" said Chiun. Remo gave him a dirty look. Chiun ignored it. If Remo had a flaw, Chiun knew that it was his lack of expertise in dealing with emperors. Remo followed this Smith, still not realizing that emperors came and went, but the House of Sinanju, of which he was now a part, went on forever. To avoid being an emperor's tool, one should never let him know that he, the emperor, was the tool. One did this by pretending loyalty beyond loyalty.

Smith, who had never looked excessively healthy, appeared even more haggard now. His words were heavy as he spoke, almost as if he had given up hope. And Remo did not know why.

"We have not determined who is doing this, but NASA satellites have detected a stream of concentrated fluorocarbons, obviously manmade, collecting through the atmosphere above the Atlantic Ocean. This stream appeared to open an ozone window above central Russia. We are not sure where it originated but we believe it came from somewhere on this side of the Atlantic. Maybe North America. Maybe South America. In any case it opened up that window."

"Of course," cried Chiun. "This is your chance to destroy your archenemy. Find the wicked fluorocarbons, place them in righteous hands, and then conquer the world. Your wisdom transcends Genghis Khan, O Emperor. They will sing of you as they have sung of the great Attila. Praise be that we are at the birthing of this glorious day. 'Sack Moscow!' is the people's cry."

Smith cleared his throat before continuing. "There are two reasons we must locate that fluorocarbon source. One, it may ultimately rupture the ozone shield. Ground radiation levels under the Russian window indicate that the shield closed itself off in less than a day. Provided that atmospheric ozone levels haven't been seriously strained, it will probably be replenished.''

Chuin raised a single finger to his wisp of a white beard and nodded sagely. Remo wondered what he was thinking about.

"The second reason is that when we offered to help the Soviets analyze the damage to the ozone over their country, they acted like nothing had happened. And then we picked up the strangest sort of activity. The building of an entire separate missile command. These missiles are unlike anything we have seen before. And we are afraid these new missiles have only one purpose. A first strike.''

"How do you know? I mean, how can you tell what's going on in their minds?'' asked Remo.

"Our satellites have photographed the new missile bases, so we know they exist. But we haven't picked up any trace of a response mechanism. That's a system that has several layers of checks and counterchecks built into it, so that the missiles are fired only after certain preconditions are met, including a determination that the country has been attacked. It's fairly easy to read from outer space. All we have to do is pick up the electronic signals created by the response mechanism. But this new command doesn't have any of that. They have one phone line and a backup. It's what we call a raw button.''

"A what?''

"The only thing you can do with those damned missiles is launch them. There is no waiting for confirmation, no protection against incoming missiles, no launch codes. Nothing. They are already aimed and await the press of a single button. All they need to start World War III is one phone call, and dammit, the way their phones work, a thunderstorm could set off that call.''

"We burn either slow from the sun or fast from the Russians,'' said Remo.

"Exactly,'' said Smith.

"So what do we do? Where do you want us to go?''

"You wait. Both of you. The entire world is watching

the skies for those crazies to try streaming fluorocarbons again. If they do, we'll get a fix on them, and then you two move in. No holds barred. Don't wait for anything. There aren't two people I would rather have between the human race and extinction than you. The President feels the same way. I just hope another incident won't set the Russians off. I never have understood them, and I understand them even less now."

"Of course," said Chiun. He always understood the calculated moves of the Russians, but could never remotely fathom Smith and his democracy.

"I do. You know," Remo said slowly, "sometimes I think what we do doesn't matter. Not as much as I'd like it to matter. But this does. You know, it makes me glad to be alive to do this. It's saving the world, I guess."

"Don't guess," said Smith. "It is."

"And it shall be recorded that the great Emperor Harold Smith did perform the wondrous act of saving the world through a trainee of the House of Sinanju."

"I am glad you feel that way, Master of Sinanju," said Smith. "By the way, there was a small problem with your gold tribute. But we will reship it."

"What? What problem?" asked Chiun. His delicate head cocked so suddenly that the wisps of white hair at his ears and chin quivered.

"The submarine carrying your gold surfaced five miles off Sinanju, in the West Korean Bay, as always. On the same day and at the appointed hour, as always. In agreement with the North Korean government, as always."

"Yes, yes," said Chiun eagerly.

"Would you like some water, Smitty?" asked Remo. He looked as though he could use some. The tribute to Sinanju would only pile up in that house above the village, so it was not of great importance to Remo that there was a delay of sorts. Smith did look especially worried by this, but they would be able to reship, of course.

"Shhh, fool." Chiun to Remo.

Smith said he didn't need the water.

"The gold. The gold," said Chiun.

"We have tea," suggested Remo.

"The gold."

"Well, it's nothing serious," said Smith. "Usually someone from your village rows out to meet the sub and collect our yearly tribute to the House of Sinanju which pays for your services as Remo's trainer. This time no one came."

"They must," cried Chiun. "They have always done it."

"This time, they didn't. But we will reship."

"Reship? My loyal villagers did not appear to claim the tribute that has sustained Sinanju for centuries, and you will reship?"

"What's the big deal, Chiun?" said Remo. "You've got so much tribute in that place that one year's gold isn't going to make much difference."

"The village starves without the tributes earned by the Master of Sinanju. The babies will have to be sent home to the sea by their weeping mothers, as it was done in the days before the Masters of Sinanju hired themselves out as assassins to prevent that very thing."

"That hasn't happened since the House worked for the Ming Dynasty in China. They can live off that treasure alone for a thousand years."

"We'll reship a double payment," said Smith in an uncharacteristic gesture of generosity. That told Remo more than anything else that Smith really feared for the survival of the planet.

Chiun rose in a single smooth movement, entering the bedroom like the wind.

"What happened? What's gotten into him?" asked Smith.

"I think he may be upset. That treasure is kinda important to him," Remo said. "I've seen it. Some of it is priceless. Mint coins from Alexander the Great. Rubies. Emeralds. Ivory. Gorgeous stuff. And a lot of it's junk, too. Things they used to think of as precious that aren't anymore. Like aluminum, when it first came out, centuries ago before it could be manufactured. They have gobs of aluminum. I've seen it right there beside a case of diamonds. Really. The diamonds are off to the side."

"It's all right that we're going to double the shipment, isn't it? I mean, how could he object?" asked Smith.

Remo shrugged. "Some things even I don't understand yet."

But when Chiun reappeared in a dark gray flecked robe, his face grave as a statue, hands folded within his sleeves and thick-soled sandals on his feet, Remo Williams knew that the Master of Sinanju was leaving. This was his traveling robe. But his trunks were not packed.

"Little Father, you can't leave now," Remo said in Korean. "The world may go up."

"The world is always being destroyed. Look at Nineveh. Look at Pompeii. Look at the Great Flood. The world is always destroyed, but gold goes on forever. And the ancient treasure of the House of Sinanju, which has survived catastrophes without number, may well be in danger."

"I can't go with you, Chiun," said Remo. "I have to stay here."

"And betray your responsibility as the next Master of Sinanju? A Master must protect the treasure."

"If there is no world left, where are you going to spend it?"

"One can always spend gold," said Chiun. "I have taught you strokes, Remo. I have trained you to fulfill the potential of your mind and of your body. I have made you strong, and I have made you quick. Most of all I have made you an assassin, one of a long line of honorable assassins. I have taught you all these things when I should have taught you wisdom. I have bequeathed the power of Sinanju to a fool." This in Korean. This said with rage.

So angered was he that the Master of Sinanju left the suite without giving a formal bow to his emperor.

"Where did he go?" asked Smith, who did not understand Korean.

"Did you notice that he didn't give you a proper farewell?"

"Yes, I thought it seemed briefer than usual. Does that mean anything?"

"He just said good-bye," Remo said quietly. Without

thinking, he dropped to a lotus position on the floor, easily and smoothly with the legs joining like petals as he had been taught so many years before.

"I am sorry. I had hoped to use him, too, in this crisis. Well, we still have you and that's the important thing. When he comes back, we'll use him."

"I don't know if he is coming back," said Remo. "You just got a good-bye."

"And you? Did he say good-bye to you?"

"I hope not. I really want to believe not," said Remo. And with soft, cutting motions, he tore up pieces of the thick pile carpet, not even noticing what his hands were doing.

"I am sure Chiun will return," said Smith. "There is an emotional bond between you two. Like a father and son."

"That treasure is pretty important to him. I don't think it can be *that* important, because nobody ever spends it. But then again, I am white."

3

Champagne corks popped. Noisemakers shrilled. Balloons clustered against the soundproofed ceiling like frightened owls. A gigantic white cake with the blue Chemical Concepts logo was wheeled into the main lab room on Route 128 as some of the technicians passed around freshly rolled joints. Bubbling laughter shook the room, seeming to set the bright-colored balloons in motion.

Reemer Bolt jumped up on a lab stool and yelled for silence. He got it.

"We thought it was marketable," he howled. "But before we could sell it, we needed a final test. And you delivered! So here is a toast to the great technical staff of Chemical Concepts who made it possible and kept their mouths shut. I promise to make all of us rich. Very rich.''

Reemer Bolt shook up a jeroboam of Dom Perignon and let the sudsy foam spurt over the screaming crowd in the laboratory. This wonderful crew had taken the wild, improbable concept of the fluorocarbon beam and not only made it work, but made it as directional as an attack plane. On this very day they had proved that they could fire the beam and make it strike any point in the atmosphere. Any point. They had harnessed it. They could control it.

They had aimed the beam at Malden, a village eighty miles from London, England. Like a high-pressure jet of water through cigarette smoke, it poked a hole in the ozone above that town, showering it with the full force of the mighty sun. Their control was absolute. They had focused the beam across an entire ocean and hit an area no larger than forty feet by forty feet.

''I love you, Kathleen O'Donnell,'' Bolt screamed into the open transatlantic line.

On the other end, in a field in Malden, England, Dr. O'Donnell simply hung up. She had work to do. Forty-seven precise experiments were laid on the field that they had prepared in advance for the great test. This had to be done in secret, because if the British government learned that a United States chemical company was conducting scientific tests involving banned fluorocarbons on their royal soil, it could trigger an international incident. Worse, the British might sue Chemical Concepts of Massachusetts into bankruptcy. The British were touchy that way.

So Dr. O'Donnell had disguised the nature of the experiment. To help with that disguise she had hired a British testing firm, and simply misinformed them about a thing here and a thing there. All she needed them for was to calibrate and quantify what was happening there in the little village north of London.

She walked among the experiments, the dead grass crunching under her feet. The cages, beakers, and vials were receiving the attention of white-coated technicians. The major experiment, of course, was already a smashing success. They could not only direct the fluorocarbon stream thousands of miles, but they could control the size and duration of the window with a small tolerance.

As she went from table to table, Dr. Kathleen O'Donnell realized that she was walking among the gravy. The meat had already been cooked. Perhaps that was what made her feel this sort of light giddiness. Then again, there were so many sounds of pain among the dying animals.

A cluster of rosebushes caught her attention. Beautiful black roses. She looked at her small chart. They had been yellow before the experiment. A kiss of a breeze shattered a few petals, and the buds fell like ashes.

This was a natural field with a small brackish pond. A white film coated the pond with a rather thick layer of shriveled insects. She couldn't believe how many bugs the little pond had contained until she saw them dead. She heard one technician mutter that even the microbes in the pond were dead.

She wondered where the strange music was coming from and then realized it was the dying animals. There were rabbits with extra thick fur, fur that had not protected the skin at all. It had peeled and cracked, turning black like a seared hot dog, fur or not. Kathy had shaved half of them, just to make certain. Same for the puppies. Except they whined and cried, instead of sitting in their cases shivering with the fear of the unknown. Dr. O'Donnell looked at them more closely and made what she thought was an interesting discovery. The puppies were blind.

Some of the technicians, hardened by other animal experiments, turned away from the suffering.

Dr. O'Donnell felt only exciting tingles on her skin, as though she were being caressed in her soft parts.

Apparently, the puppies' more developed animal senses had caused them to look up into the sky, the source of the unfamiliar radiation. The unfiltered sunlight had burned out their retinas.

One of the technicians came up to her with an important question.

"Can we put the animals out of their misery now? We've logged our findings."

Dr. O'Donnell saw the pain in his face. More than that.

She felt it. Her tongue moistened her lips. She didn't answer him, but let him stand there with the pleading in his eyes. Her body was good and warm. The old thing was happening to her again, here in England, here at this experiment.

"The animals. They're in real pain," said the technician.

Kathleen scribbled some notes on her pad. She saw the technician squirm as though every moment of delay was intense pain for him. It was definitely happening again.

"Can we destroy them? . . . Please."

"Just wait a moment, won't you?" said Kathy. She wondered if her pants were moist yet.

Half an hour later, most of the animals had died painfully and the technicians were sullen. People often reacted to suffering that way. Kathy was used to this. She had seen a lot of it in puberty. In puberty she had begun to wonder why grown-ups and other children were so horrified by the suffering of other creatures. Her parents had sent her to several doctors to find out why she was so different. But even at age twelve, the brilliant little Kathleen O'Donnell knew she wasn't different. The world was different.

So as she became an adult she hid her special feelings because the world feared what was different. She drove fast cars. She fought for control of companies. She competed for honors. And she let her special feelings be secret, secret even to her own womanly body. Men were never that interesting. Success was only a factor to be achieved because it was better than failure.

But when so many little animals began screaming, her body awoke on its own, sending delicious, delicious feelings throughout all the good parts. They felt wonderful. When someone offered her a lift back to London, she said she would rather stay here and work in the field a bit longer.

She wanted to play. She wanted to play with the people who were now suffering because the animals were suffering. People were fun. They were more complicated and challenging than numbers.

Sometimes they were easy, though. Like Reemer Bolt

back at CCM. He was a sexual game, easily played. Bolt was the sort of man, like so many other men, who needed sex to vindicate his sense of self-worth. Give him sex and he felt good. Deny it, and he felt worthless. He would literally give you control over his life in return for a little leg at the right times, provided you pretended to be pleased. Bolt needed that and Kathleen always gave it to him. She was a good actress. She always had been. She even fooled the psychiatrists when she was a teenager. But all this suffering now couldn't fool her body, even after all these years.

She wondered what a person would look like kept in a cage under the fluorocarbon beam, even as she told an ashen-faced technician that this experiment was important because they were establishing controls to make it safe for all mankind.

A technician came over to her to beg permission to put a terrier out of its misery. She commented on vitreous solutions as she watched him bite his lip. There was no blood, she noticed.

"How can you do this to these animals?" he asked.

Kathy put a hand on his arm. "I'm sorry you had to see it, John," she said. She knew this seemed soothing.

"Jim," he corrected.

"Whatever," she said. "The tragedy, Jim, is that people as sensitive as you have to look at things like this."

"They didn't have to suffer," said the man. His eyes were filling with pain. She showed deep concern for him as a person while she reminded herself that his name was Jim. Like pin. See the letters J-i-m on the blackboard in your mind, Kathleen told herself. J-i-m, like Jungle gym. Jim.

"Jim . . . they had to suffer."

"Why, dammit, why?"

"So that children won't suffer in the future. We don't want the sun's power perverted like atomic energy. We don't want these horrible things happening to innocent children." Kathleen looked into the man's troubled eyes. She hoped hers registered the correct amount of sympathy.

"I am sorry, Jungle—" He looked puzzled.

"—Jim," said Kathy, kneading his arm softly. It always

helped to touch a man when you worked him. That was
what made doing it over the phone so challenging. You
had to work without your hands. "Jim, we are learning
things here that will protect our most precious resource,
the children. And, Jim, I don't know of a better way to do
it. Jim."

"Do we have to let the poor animals suffer like this?"

"I am afraid we do. Children won't have the luxury of
being put out of their misery. Can you bring yourself to
watch?"

Jim lowered his head, adding the shame of his weakness
to his pain. "I guess I have to," he said.

"Good man, Jim," Kathleen said. "If the power we
have harnessed here ever got out of control, the children
would suffer the most. They would lie in the streets,
moaning and crying, unable to understand what was happening to them, unable to know why their tender skins had
turned purplish-black and peeled off in great chunks,
unable to see what happened because they would be sightless. Sightless, Jim, sightless and afraid. And dying.
Would you, Jim, if you found a baby dying like that in the
gutter, would you be able to slit its throat to put it out of
its misery? Could you?"

"No, no, I couldn't do that," said Jim. His face paled,
his arms shuddered, and his legs seemed to find other
places to go than to stay beneath him. He tipped over and
landed like a bag of peat moss off a truck.

Kathleen O'Donnell wanted to tell him it was good for
her, too.

The Jodrell Bank radio telescope picked up strange read-
ings in the jet stream of atmosphere. Something that
caused their signals to bounce back crazily.

"Do you think this is it?" asked one of the scientists.

"Never saw anything like it," answered the other.
"Must be."

"Over Malden, I gather."

"Well, let's give the intelligence chaps a ring, eh?"

"Odd effect on radio signals, I say. So that's how a

fluorocarbon beam, or stream, behaves. Have you considered what it might do to the ozone?''

"Don't think so. It's supposed to be coming from America.''

"Can't tell for certain. The source appears to be west of Great Britain.''

"America is west of Great Britain.''

"Quite.''

The phone rang in Remo's suite.

"Remo?'' It was Smith.

"Yes?''

"They got a hit in Great Britain.''

"Is that thing there?''

"No. It struck there, but they believe the point of origin was west of England. Which we think also.''

"So where is it?''

"Somewhere in America, but we're not sure where. Probably still on the east coast. The British should have a better read than we do. That's the thinking here. But there is a problem in Great Britain. They are not sharing their data with us. For some crazy reason, their intelligence services are keeping everything to themselves.''

"Which means?''

"You get over to Britain and find out what they're hiding. They get back here and tear the hearts out of these lunatics before we're all killed,'' said Smith. Remo had never heard the rigidly controlled man use terms of violence when he ordered violence.

"And do it fast, because I don't know what's happening with the Russians. I never could figure them out. The only one who ever knew what they were doing was Chiun. And I can't figure him out, either?''

"What's happening with the Russians?'' Remo asked.

"I think they picked up something, too. They knew what to look for now. But how they'll react is anyone's guess. There will be an Air Force jet waiting for you in a special hangar at Kennedy Airport. It's the latest fighter. Cost a quarter of a billion dollars to build and can get you across the Atlantic in half the time of the Concorde. Performs wonders.''

One of the wonders of the new Z-83 retracting wing Stratofighter was its ability to track all radar signals in the hemisphere and translate them into a tactical reading so that a staff officer in the Pentagon could feed them into a computer. This brilliant idea would in theory enable the Air Force to monitor all air traffic around the world using just two jets.

The problem with the Z-83 was that it had so many "enhance functions"; the radar-tracking computer, the navigational computer, and the automatic target select and track unit, that most of the time the engines wouldn't start. The Z-83 sat like a metallic-winged shark on the runway when Remo arrived, and kept on sitting.

"Does this thing fly?"

"She's best aircraft in the world when we integrate her multimodes." This from an Air Force general who explained that it would be militarily premature to assign any on-line function to the system; one should look at it as a launching mode strategically, rather than tactically.

In brief, the general explained, it didn't fly, wouldn't fly soon, and had every likelihood of never flying. He advised taking Delta Airlines. They would be ready when he was.

When Field Marshal Alexei Zemyatin was informed that another beam had been fired, this time above England, he muttered over and over:

"I do not want a war. I do not want a war. Why are the fools giving me a war?"

It was the first time that the Great One had been heard to call an enemy a fool. He had always saved that for allies. An enemy, he had warned every Russian leader, was brilliant and perfect in every way until he showed you how he could be defeated. And, of course, he always did because no one was perfect.

"How do you know they are not attacking Great Britain?" demanded the Russian Premier. "Some in the Politburo think America might be using Great Britain as a target because it is a useless ally. Contempt, it is. How can you say war when they are firing that thing against an ally?''

Zemyatin sat in a black leather chair staring into a room filled with Russian generals and KGB officers. They did not look back because they did not see him. They were on the other side of a one-way mirror and they talked quietly among themselves in aimless conversation. It was aimless because the Premier had left the room. He had left because Zemyatin had buzzed.

Zemyatin shook his hairless head. The sadness of it all. This mindless pack was Russia's future. Still, the rest of the world was run by the likes of these. But even the likes of these across the Atlantic should not start a war for no reason.

"How do you know they plan war?'' the Premier asked again. Zemyatin nodded. He motioned the Premier to bend down because he did not wish to raise his voice. He wanted the other to listen hard.

"When our missile base was hit by this thing—whatever it is—I allowed myself to hope it was an accident. Granted, one does not run a country on hope. That would be disastrous.''

"Why did you think it was an accident?''

"I didn't think it was an accident,'' corrected Zemyatin. "I *hoped* it was an accident. I reacted as though it was a willful act, but I had to ask myself why America would do something so foolish. There is no reason for them to test an untried weapon on us first. You don't do that if you are starting a war.''

"Yes. Good thinking. Yes.''

"But it was such a device that I thought perhaps the Americans consider us fools and believe that we would not recognize their device as a controllable weapon. A foolish idea, because we suspect everything.''

"Yes, yes,'' said the Premier, struggling to follow the twists and turns of the Grèat One. Sometimes he was so clear, and other times he was like the summer mists of Siberia. Unknowable.

"There was still the possibility, a shred of hope, that this was an accident. However, we knew there was one thing they needed from us. And if one can be certain of anything, I am certain of that.''

Zemyatin paused. ''They know what it does to animals, according to our reports. They know what it does to microbes. But they still do not know what it does to our current defenses. In my belief, they do not know how to use it for war. Yet.''

The Premier thought that sounded good. He was hesitant. He did not want to be called a fool even in private. He was relieved when Zemyatin refrained from doing so.

''But I am also sadly sure, now more than before, that they will use it for war. And why? When they tested it against us, they made a mistake. They couldn't find out whether it worked or not. As a matter of fact, it was such a severe mistake, it left open the one small hope that perhaps it was an accident. Of course, they fell into our trap when they desperately sought to 'share' information in our so-called common struggle. So what do you do now that your first test has possibly alarmed your enemy?''

''You don't test again. But they have,'' said the Premier.

''Exactly. In friendly territory, pretending for all the world that they have only a scientific interest. Blatant. If they had shot this thing at soldiers, I would be less sure of their intentions for war, because then they would not be disguising a first strike.''

''Oh,'' said the Premier.

''Yes,'' said Zemyatin. ''And it was I who had for all these years said they did not seek a war, but control of resources.''

''Why now?''

''If we had such an advantage, would we ignore it?''

''Ah,'' said the Premier.

''Yes,'' said Zemyatin. ''Our one defense is that they do not yet know how effective it is against our missiles. When they do, of course, they will take us apart like an old clock.''

''You won't let that happen?'' asked the Premier.

''No. We will have to strike first. The fools leave us no

other choice but nuclear war." The old man shook his head. "So many things are changing. I used to say there was no greater enemy than a fool for an ally. Now I have to say the greater danger in the nuclear age is having a fool for an enemy."

But there were good things, he added:

"Fortunately, this second test was made on England, which to our KGB is like downtown Moscow," said Zemyatin. He did not have to remind the Premier how thoroughly penetrated British Intelligence was. The KGB practically ran Britain's spy service. There were several high-ranking KGB officers on the other side of the one-way mirror. Zemyatin had turned down the volume control on the microphones listening in on them. In his youth he never would have had to issue this order. But the KGB had become quite fat on its own successes around the world.

"I want their best effort in England. No games. No politics. No cool British ladies for parties. Yes, I know about them. I want results. You tell them that. You tell them we demand that. Don't let them give you their fancy talk."

"Right," said the Premier, who had risen to his post by satisfying as many powers as possible, including the army and the KGB.

Zemyatin watched the Premier return to the other side of the mirror. He watched him make a show of being stern.

What Zemyatin would have preferred at this time was Stalin. Stalin would have had one general shot just to get everyone's attention. And with a comrade crumpled before a bullet-pocked wall, they would not be playing political games over the best course of action and the best man for the job. But this Premier was not made of the stuff of Josef Stalin. And Zemyatin knew the first rule of war was to fight with what you had. Only a fool hoped for more.

He watched the Premier through the one-way mirror. There was another discussion. He turned off the sound and pressed the buzzer again. Again the Premier left the generals and came into Zemyatin's room.

"Listen. If you let them have a discussion, you are going

to be run around. No discussions. No games. You go in there and tell them to break bones. No games. Blood. Get the sort of people into Britain who will not stop at the sight of blood. To hell with undercover. If this war comes, there will be no cover for any of us," said Zemyatin. He banged a hand on the armchair. If he were younger he might have literally strangled this man. Not out of anger, of course, but because this Premier was so susceptible to force. He had to make it strong and simple:

"Blood. Blood on the streets. Blood in the gutters. Find out what they know. There is no tomorrow. Now!"

An immaculately uniformed colonel met Remo at the airport, offering smiling pleasantries, expressing happiness over the opportunity to work with Remo, inquiring what department Remo reported to, and allowing that he was terribly impressed that the highest levels of the U.S. government had requested that all cooperation be extended to Remo. But.

But what? Remo wanted to know.

But unfortunately there was blessed little Colonel Aubrey Winstead-Jones could offer in the way of assistance. Her Majesty's government did not know what Remo was talking about. Really.

"Frankly, old boy, we would have told your State Department early on had you asked. No need to have you over here, what?"

Remo listened politely, and on the way from Heathrow Airport into London, with the gray industrial choke of Great Britain on either side of the chauffeured automobile, Colonel Winstead-Jones suddenly decided to tell Remo that he had been instructed to guide Remo around London, taking him nowhere in particular until Remo got tired and went home. Colonel Winstead-Jones was not to help Remo in any way. He was supposed to make sure Remo had all the wine, drugs, and women he wanted. He had been told this by the station chief of MI 12. When asked, he willingly gave Remo the address and cover used by MI 12, and a brief history of the ministry. Remo for his part was equally cooperative. He assisted Colonel Winstead-Jones back into his car, which had been dragging him along the British highway system. Joining the colonel to the native highway system had done wonders for openness in communication. The colonel might even regain the use of his legs in the near future, Remo assured him. At least those parts still attached.

The colonel told him exactly who had given him the orders to run Remo around.

"Thank you, old boy," said Remo.

Just off Piccadilly Circus, in an old Tudor building, stood the office of MI 12. It was inconspicuous in the extreme. Seemingly a tobacconist's shop on street level, a side door led up a single staircase to a second floor with dusty windows. Actually, they were ground opaque, impenetrable to eyesight or listening device, and looked remarkably like the windows in a quaint library. But inside, a crack team of British Special Service chaps lurked as a cunning trap for anyone daring to penetrate MI 12.

This was the building, the colonel said, that housed the station chief who gave him orders. Would Remo be so kind as to give him back the use of his legs?

"Later," said Remo. He got the same promise from the driver by running his hands down the spinal column and creating a small nerve block in a lower spinal vertebra.

"Be right back, old boy," said Remo.

Remo opened the door and saw the stairway leading up to the second floor. The place could have bottled the must and sold it. The wooden steps creaked. They were dry and old and brittle. They would have creaked under a mouse. But Remo did not like making noise when he moved. His system rebelled against it. He set his balance to ease the wood, to be part of the age of the wood, so that he now moved quietly upward. But he had made the first noise.

A door opened at the top of the stairs and an elderly man called down:

"Who is it? Can we be of service?"

"Absolutely," Remo said. "I've come to see the station chief of MI 12, whatever that is."

"This is the Royal Society of Heraldry Manuscripts. We are sort of a library," came back the voice.

"Good. I'll look at your manuscripts," said Remo.

"Well, can't be done, old boy."

"It's going to be done."

"Please be so kind as to stay where you are," said the elderly man.

"Not at all," said Remo.

"I am afraid we are going to have to give you your last warning."

"Good," said Remo. There wasn't going to be any surprise. He already heard the feet. They had the steady light movement of athletes: trained feet, trained bodies. Hard. They were getting into position upstairs. There were seven of them.

"All right, come on up if you wish," said the man.

By the time Remo got to the top of the stairs he could smell their lunches. The men had had beef and pork. The odor was about a half-hour strong in their bodies. They would move slower.

As Remo entered the room, two men came up behind him with what were supposed to be catlike movements. Remo ignored them.

"Suppose you tell us, young man, why you think this is MI 12?" said the elderly gentleman who had answered the door.

"Because I dragged a colonel two hundred yards along one of your lovely roads until he told me it was," said Remo. "But look, I don't have time for pleasantries. Take me to the station chief."

The cool muzzle of a small-caliber pistol came up to Remo's head.

"I am afraid you are going to have to make time for pleasantries," said a deep voice. At that point, the pistol nudged the back of Remo's head, presumably to make Remo more cooperative.

"Let me guess," said Remo. "This is where I'm supposed to spin around, see the gun, and turn to quivering jelly. Right?"

"Quite," said the elderly man.

Remo snapped back an elbow far enough to catch the

pistol and send it into the ancient ceiling like a rock into dried mud. The pistol went with its owner. A shower of old plaster and Spackle exploded over the room like a snow-storm.

A bulky commando type stepped out from a wall with a short stabbing dagger, angling for Remo's solar plexus. Remo sent him back into the wall with a side kick. The elderly man ducked, and from behind him appeared a lieu-tenant in full uniform, who began firing a submachine gun. The first burst came straight at Remo. There was no second burst because the bullets appeared to Remo like a line of softballs coming at him. Fast enough to hurt, but slow enough to dance around, even before they had left the barrel. His body allowed itself to sense the slow stream, and move through and then beyond it to its source.

The lieutenant, lacking such skill, found himself without gun and very much smashing backward into the steel door he had vowed with his life to defend.

The door shivered on its drop-forged pins and came down in the next room like a bridge over a moat.

Remo stepped over the unconscious officer into an office.

A man in a gray sports jacket looked up from his desk to see that his penetration-proof cover had been penetrated by a thick-wristed young man in dark slacks, T-shirt and loafers, using no other weapon, apparently, than a knowing smile.

"Hi," said Remo. "I'm from America. You're expect-ing me. I'm the one Colonel Winstead-Jones was supposed to dilly around London with wine, drugs, and women."

"Oh yes. Top-secret and all that. Well, welcome, Remo. What can we do for you?" asked the man, lighting a meerschaum pipe carved to resemble the head of some British queen. He had a long-nosed, gaunt-cheeked patrician face and a toothy smile. His sandy hair might have been combed by a lawn mower. He didn't rise. He didn't even look upset. He most certainly did not look like a man whose defenses had been turned to broken plaster.

"We have a problem with something that's poking holes

in the ozone layer, and the possibility that if we don't fry slow from the sun, we are going to fry fast from Russian nukes," said Remo.

"Would you kindly explain to me how this involves your barging in here and throwing our people around? I would ever so much like to know why."

The station chief took a puff of his pipe. He had spoken most pleasantly. Remo most pleasantly slapped the pipe out of his mouth, along with some frontal teeth that looked too long for anything from a human head outside of the British Isles.

Remo apologized for his American rudeness.

"I'm trying to head off World War III, so I'm in kind of a rush," said Remo.

"Well, that does put a bit of a different complexion on the matter," admitted the station chief, shaking his head. He did not shake too hard because blood was coming from his nose. He thought a brisk shake might loosen some of the brain matter above his nostrils. "Yes. Well, orders came from the Admiralty."

"Why the Admiralty?"

"You can kill me, old top, but I never will tell you," he said. But when Remo took a step toward him, he hastily added: "Because I don't know. Haven't the foggiest."

Remo took the station chief along. He took him by the waist, careful not to bloody things as he trundled him downstairs past his own dazed guards into the car. At the Admiralty, he found the officer identified by the station chief. He explained about the tradition of American-English cooperation.

The commander in charge of a special intelligence detail appreciated this long friendship. He also appreciated the use of his lungs which Remo promised to leave in his body. Considering that the way Remo was stretching his ribs, losing the lungs was a distinct possibility. The commander made every effort to figure out what Remo was talking about.

Since Remo was never good at explaining technical matters, this was not easy. It sounded like the sky was opening up for some reason. Then the commander, in great pain, recognized what Remo was looking for. The Jodrell Bank telescope fellows had tracked something.

Remo brought the naval officer along. It was becoming crowded in the back seat. In the entire crowd no one could tell him why they were not willingly cooperating with their best ally.

"Well, sir, if you didn't use violence we would be significantly more cooperative." This from Winstead-Jones, who had told the others about being dragged outside the car.

"I didn't use it till you weren't," said Remo. The car was very comfortable. The Jodrell Bank fellows, as they were called, were surprisingly cooperative. Strangely, they were the only ones not part of the British defense establishment.

Yes, they had tracked the beam. Somewhere west. Probably America. They were delighted to explain the details of the tracking. Basically one could tell precisely where the ozone shield was penetrated, and thus determine precisely where the unfiltered rays landed by the angle of the sun in relation to the earth.

Remo knew where they had landed in England early that morning. That was why he was here. The Jodrell Bank fellows knew a little more. The unfiltered rays had penetrated above the fishing village of Malden.

Remo returned to the car with the good news. No one was moving. Everyone knew someone should have left the car for help against the brutal American but the problem had been who. They had ordered the driver to do just that. The driver said his orders were to stay at the wheel, so the little piece of defense establishment was waiting for Remo.

"Hello. Good to see you back," said the colonel. The station chief stayed conscious as a way of greeting and the commander breathed.

"We're going to Malden," said Remo cheerfully.

"Oh, so you found it," said the colonel. "You won't need us then."

"You knew everything I was looking for. Why didn't you tell me?"

"Orders."

"From whom?"

"You know, those people who always give orders and then aren't there when the blood begins to flow, I would say."

"But we're allies," said Remo. "This thing threatens the whole world."

"Orders don't have to make sense. If they made sense anyone could obey them. The real test of a soldier is following orders no matter how unfounded they are in common sense."

On the way to Malden Remo tried to find out who had ordered them not to be cooperative. Did they know something he didn't know?

"It's intelligence, old man. No one trusts anyone else," said the station chief.

"I trust you," said Remo.

"Then who ordered you here?"

"You wouldn't understand," said Remo. "But take my word for it, the world is going to go up. Even with your separate departments."

Remo noticed a radio telephone near the driver's leg. He wondered if he could use it. The driver explained it was very simple. The problem was whether to talk over a very open line. If they didn't get that thing penetrating the ozone shield, there wouldn't be any reason for secrecy. He used the radiophone into which the whole world could listen.

"Open line, Smitty," said Remo when he heard Smith answer.

"Okay. Go ahead."

"Located source."

"Good."

"It's definitely the east coast."

"We already knew that. Could you be a bit more specific? The east coast is larger than most countries."

"That's what I have so far."

"Yes, well. Good. Thank you. I take it there will be more."

"Soonest."

"Good luck. Don't worry about open lines. Anything you get. Anything."

"Right," said Remo. It was the first time he had ever heard Smith's voice crack.

In Malden, everybody seemed to know everybody else's business. It was a small quaint village and yes, there was an experiment going on, some people thought by their own government.

In a small field, white-frocked technicians examined cages. Everyone but Remo looked at the field. Remo's training had given his instinct the full power others had stifled. And the main part of that power was a sense of danger. It was not the field he looked at.

It was the sky itself that seemed to say, "Man, your time has come." In the gray gloom of clouds choked with industrial char, a small, perfect sapphire-blue circle was closing. It was not the blue of sky, but closer to neon, yet without its harshness. It as as though a blue gem had been electrified by the sun, and then its light sprinkled into a small circle in the sky. Remo watched this circle close as the driver pointed to the field and said:

"That's it."

It was its beauty that alarmed Remo. He had seen great jewels and felt the fire that other men longed for, even though he had never longed for it. He remembered one of Chiun's early lessons. Like so many teachings then, he was not to understand it until much later. But Chiun had said that things in nature of great beauty were often the ones to watch most closely.

"The weak disguise themselves in dull colors of the ground. But the deadly flaunt themselves to attract victims."

"Yeah. What about a butterfly?" Remo had said.

"When you see the most beautiful butterfly in the world, stop. Do not touch. Touch nothing you are attracted to touch."

"Sounds like a dull life."

"Do you think I am talking about your entertainment?"

"Sure," Remo had said. "I don't know what you are talking about."

"Yes," Chiun had said. "You don't."

Years later, Remo had realized Chiun was teaching him how to think. Something was beautiful for a reason. Something was attractive for a reason. Often the most venomous things cloaked themselves in glory to attract their victims. Yet in the sky, what Remo saw was not something that intended its beauty as a lure, but the awesome indifference of the universe. It could end millions of lives without caring or even intending to, because in its basic atomic logic, life did not matter. Remo looked at the beautiful blue closing ring and thought of these things as the security officer kept repeating that the field he wanted was in front of him.

"Okay," said Remo to the car full of British security personnel. "Don't move."

"How can we?" said the Navy commander. His uniform had lost one of the fifteen medals he had earned by never going to sea. "I haven't felt my legs for an hour."

The field smelled of burning. This little patch of England was not green, but flecked with dead dried grass, pale white as though someone had left it in a desert for an afternoon. Several cages on metal tables held the blackened bodies of animals. Remo could smell the sweet sticky odor of burned flesh. Nothing moved in the cages. A few people in white coats stood around the tables, filling in forms. One of the white-coated workers gathered the dead grass. Another was packaging the earth into beakers and then sealing them in plastic. One of them banged his watch.

"It doesn't work," he said. He had a sharp British accent. It was a strange thing about that language that one could measure the class by the tones, as though on a calibrated scale of one to ten: the ten being royalty and the accent being muted; the one being cockney, its accent very strong like a sharp pepper sauce. The man complaining about his watch was a seven, his broad accent of the upper classes but with a trace of cockney whine.

"Hello," said Remo.

"Yes, what can I do for you?" said the man, shaking his watch. Several other technicians looked at their watches.

Two of them worked, three of them didn't. The man's face had the pale British look as though bleached of sunlight and joy. A face designed for drizzle and gloom, and possibly a shot of whiskey every so often to make it all bearable.

Even if he hadn't spoken with an accent, Remo would have known he was British. Americans would attend to a watch problem before dealing with any stranger.

"I am curious about this experiment. There might be some danger here, and I want to know what you're doing," said Remo.

"We have our licenses and permits, sir," said the technician.

"For what?" said Remo.

"For this experiment, sir."

"What exactly is it?"

"It is a limited, safe, controlled test of the effects of the sun without filtration by ozone. Now may I ask whom you are with?"

"Them," said Remo, nodding to the car filled with British security.

"Well, they certainly look impressive, but who are they?"

"Your security forces."

"Do they have identification of sorts? Sorry, but I must see identification."

Remo shrugged. He went back to the car and asked for everyone's identification. One of them, still groggy, handed up his wallet with money.

"This isn't a robbery," said Remo.

"I thought it was," said the dazed representative of the ultrasecret MI 12.

"No," said Remo, adding his clearance card to the other cards and plastic face-picture badges. He brought a handful of identifications back to the technician. The technician looked at the identifications and gasped at one of them.

"Gracious. You've got a staff officer in there."

"One of them," said Remo. "There is an intelligence guy there, too."

"Yes. Quite. So. I see," said the technician, giving back the identifications. Remo pocketed them in case he might need them again. "What would you like?" asked the technician.

"Who are you?"

"I am a technician from Pomfritt Laboratories of London," said the technician.

"What are you doing here? Precisely. What's going on?"

The man launched himself into a detailed explanation of fluorocarbon and the power of the sun, and the harnessing of the unfiltered rays of the sun and finding out in a "controlled"—he stressed "controlled"—atmosphere just what mankind could do with the sun's full power.

"Burn ourselves to cinders," said Remo, who understood perhaps half of what the technician was talking about. "Okay, what is doing it, and where is it?"

"A controlled fluorocarbon beam generator."

"Good," said Remo. "Where is that fluorocarbon . . . thing?"

"At its base."

"Right. Where?" said Remo.

"I'm not sure, but as you can see, this experiment is marvelously controlled," said the technician. He gave his wristwatch a little tap again to get it going. It didn't.

"Why aren't you sure?" asked Remo.

"Because it's not our product. We're just testing it."

"Good. For whom?"

The technician gave Remo a name and an address. It was in America. This confirmed some of the data he had gotten from the intelligence people in the car. He returned to the car and asked for the telephone.

The number rang. Remo held the black telephone attached to a unit in the front of the car. He stood outside the driver's window. When he heard the crisp "Yes" from Smith, Remo said:

"I am still on an open line."

"Go ahead," said Smith. "What do you have?"

"I found the source of that thing that opens up the ozone layer."

"Good. Where?"

Remo gave him the name and address of the firm in America. "Do you want me to return and close in on them? Or do you want to do it yourself? You're there in America."

"Hold on," said Smith.

Remo smiled at the group of men in the back of the car. The colonel glowered back. The intelligence officer stared ahead glumly. In the field, the lab technicians were comparing watches. Remo whistled as he waited for Smith.

"Okay," said Smith.

"Do you want to handle it there, or do we have enough time for me to fly back and do it right?"

"I want you to keep looking, Remo. Not only is there no such company as Sunorama of Buttesville, Arkansas, but there isn't even a Buttesville, Arkansas."

Remo returned to the laboratory technician and offered to fix the man's watch by running it through his ears and out through his nose if he didn't tell the truth.

"That's the name we have. We're participating in the experiment for Dr. O'Donnell. It's her company. That was the name she gave. Really."

Remo tended to believe the man. Most people told the truth when their dorsal root ganglion was compressed painfully into the sensory neuron along the spinal cord. Sometimes they would cry. Sometimes they would yell. But they always told the truth. This lab technician opened his mouth to yell when Remo allowed the pain to subside and thus enabled him to talk.

"Fine," said Remo. "Where is Dr. O'Donnell?"

"She left with a Russian-speaking guy," said the technician.

Remo noticed at that very moment that there were no British bobbies on the scene, no protection around this field that the intelligence personnel of America's ally had tried to keep hidden from America. Who was on whose side, and who was the Russian?

4

Harold W. Smith calculated, on a small old-fashioned piece of white paper, a line going up signaling reports of new missile sites in the Soviet Union. Also going up was the possibility of a rupture in the ozone shield that might not be closed.

It was a race as to which would destroy them all first. And Smith could only handle one line at a time. He had Remo.

If he had Chiun, he could launch the aged assassin into Russia, a good place for him. For some strange reason, Chiun seemed to be able to predict the Russians quite well. Chiun also seemed to be able to communicate with anyone, perhaps a necessity for a member of a house of assassins that had been around for thousands of years.

Under a secret agreement, Smith was not only allowed to send in gold by submarine, but he was able to contact Pyongyang when Chiun returned. Yet even that had changed.

Smith briefly wondered if the change had something to do with the Russian response. Even though the North Koreans were their closest ally in the world, the Russians did not trust them. They looked upon them as some poor cousins, an international embarrassment they were forced to endure. It was not even much of a secret. Almost every intelligence agency in the world had monitored the pleas of North Korea seeking Russian respect.

Few people knew it at the time, least of all Smith in his Folcroft headquarters on Long Island Sound, monitoring the approaching destruction of the world, but the President for Life of North Korea had left the moment the Master of Sinanju landed. He had done it on the assurance that it would be best for him to be out of the country when the Master of Sinanju found out what had happened in his village.

The district colonel who followed a full twenty paces behind the Master of Sinanju did not know what his superiors planned, either. He was told only not to provoke the Master of Sinanju. No one was to address the Master unless spoken to.

The Master had landed and walked through the honor guard, as though they blocked his way in some line, right through to the waiting limousine. He was immediately driven to the village of Sinanju. The colonel, like all security officers, could not enter. This village, alone among all places in North Korea, was allowed to keep its old ways. It paid no taxes, and once a year an American submarine was permitted to land in Sinanju and off-load cargo. Of this irregularity, the colonel knew only that it was not a spy mission and that he was not to interfere. The business of Sinanju was the business of Sinanju, he had been told, and was not the concern of Pyongyang. The Master of Sinanju would look after his village. And now that fabled entity, this Master of Sinanju, had returned to Korea because of something worse than a disgrace. A tragedy.

The colonel had been ordered to grant this frail old man's every wish. His superior, General Toksa, told him to report those wishes to himself, and the colonel knew that the general was to report the same to Himself, President for Life, Kim Il Sung. The colonel shivered a moment at the thought of his responsibility.

Not everyone reacted that way. As they walked through the airport, youngsters laughed at the strange kimono worn by the Master of Sinanju. Even a state security officer burst out laughing.

The Master of Sinanju spoke for the first time, using a term outlawed for forty years:

"Japanese kissers," he spat. It was an epithet dating from the time of the Japanese occupation. Many secret tales survived about Koreans who had collaborated with the hated Japanese. When the colonel had taken over the northwest province, which included Sinanju, he had heard

that the Japanese never dared to enter Sinanju, and that
before, when China occupied Korea, the Chinese never
entered Sinanju. But it was whispered that in times past,
the throne of the White Chrysanthemum in Japan and all
the dynasties of China had sent tribute to the tiny village
on the West Korean Bay. Yet they had never entered it.
Neither had the colonel. But now, because of what had
happened, he would at last see what secrets that village
had. He had been ordered not to mention what had
happened at Sinanju, but to take very careful notes of the
Master of Sinanju's every reaction. Nothing this man said
was to go unrecorded. Nothing this man did was to go unnoticed. But the colonel was to do nothing but report.

So he listened in silence and with as much dignity as he
could muster to the many treasons now issuing forth from
the Master of Sinanju.

The new uniforms would better serve as dressing for
meat than for people, said Chiun. He said he could sense
that the soldiers of Himself, Kim Il Sung, had replaced
courage with viciousness, a sure sign that they had not
gotten over kissing Japanese backsides. He called the
Third World poster on the airport wall an admission that
Korea was still backward because everyone outside of
Korea knew that "Third World" was just another term for
inferior, backward, less. And Korea was never less. It was
better. The trouble was that Koreans themselves failed to
appreciate that.

"I am Korean," the Master of Sinanju told the colonel.
"You are Korean. Look at you. And look at me. I am glad
my son born in America is not here to behold you."

The colonel drew himself up against the implied insult.
"I am a superior officer. I am a colonel," he said proudly.

"In the pot you keep by the bed for the wastes of your
body, what do you see float to the top, colonel?" asked the
Master of Sinanju.

The crowds in the airport suddenly hushed. No one ever
talked to a colonel of state security in such a way, a district
colonel at that.

And thus did Chiun, reigning Master of Sinanju, return
to the land of Korea by airplane. Thus was he met by a

toady in uniform and taken many miles from Pyongyang, west to the fishing village of Sinanju, as the toady made notes of all he saw and all that was said by the Master of Sinanju.

The village was rich in pigs and grain. The colonel noticed that there were several very large old-fashioned storehouses, indicating the village people never suffered from want or famine. He noted, too, that when the elderly man named Chiun approached the village from a hilltop, there were cries from below and the people ran away in fear.

Chiun saw and heard them, and told the colonel to wait on the hilltop while he went into his village, or swift death would be his reward for disobedience. The colonel remained in his jeep and Chiun walked down into the village and the silence therein.

The rich smells of fish and pig meat filled the desolate village, for the food was still cooking. But no children laughed and played, and no elders appeared to give thanks for the beneficence of the House of Sinanju that had kept them fed through the centuries, even through times of famine, fed and healthy before the West was strong, before even the dynasties of China with their great armies marched where they willed. Only the waves crashed by way of greeting, cold and froth white against the dark rock shores of Sinanju.

There was silence for the first time as a Master of Sinanju returned, instead of proper songs of triumph, and joyous laudations. Chiun was grateful that Remo did not see this—Remo, whom Chiun had enough trouble convincing of the glory of this village and the place he was destined to take here, Remo, who Chiun hoped would one day take a bride from this village to produce a male child to carry on the way of Sinanju so that he would not have to stoop to take a foreigner, as Chiun had. This then was the small blessing of this tragic day.

Chiun accepted the insult. The villagers would return to their pig meat and fish and rice and sweet cakes. Their stomachs would bring them back. They ate almost as badly as Remo used to eat. But, for them, it did not matter. No emperor would call upon them for service. No glory would ever be theirs, no demand would ever be placed on their bodies that required them to eat so that those bodies functioned at their utmost. Chiun remembered how, as a youngster, he had asked his father if he could feast on the rich meats his friends enjoyed, the meats his father's own services abroad paid for.

"It is hardest for the young to realize this," his father, who was then the reigning Master of Sinanju, had said. "But you are getting a greater gift than meat. You are becoming something they are not. You are earning tomorrow. You will thank me and remember this when they bow to you and the world again sings glorious praises to the Masters of Sinanju, as they did in centuries past."

"But I want the meat now," young Chiun had said.

"But you will not want it then."

"But it is now, not then, not tomorrow."

"I told you it was hard for a young man, for the young do not know tomorrow. But you will know."

And he did, of course. Chiun thought back to the days of Remo's early training and the difficulty of overcoming the bad habits of almost thirty years and the handicap of being white. He had spoken the same words to Remo, and Remo answered:

"Blow it out your ears."

Then Remo had eaten a hamburger after years of training and almost died. At the time, Chiun had scolded Remo, neglecting to mention that he, too, had snuck a piece of meat and his father had forced him to vomit it out. As far as Remo knew, all Masters of Sinanju were obedient in the extreme, except for Remo, who was disobedient in the extreme. Chiun wondered how troublesome Remo would have been had he ever realized that one of the qualities that made great Masters was their independence. He would probably be uncontrollable now, Chiun decided.

And so the Master of Sinanju stood in the middle of his village waiting for his people to return, thinking of Remo and wondering what Remo was doing now, glad Remo was not seeing this shame, but also sad that he was not here.

A night passed. And during the night, Chiun heard the

villagers clumsily sneaking back into their homes to fill their bellies with dead burned pig. There was even a side of spitted beef steaming upwind. It smelled so much of meat that Chiun thought he might be back in America. In the morning, however, one came out to give the Master of Sinanju the traditional greeting:

"Hail, Master of Sinanju, who sustains the village and keeps the code faithfully, leader of the House of Sinanju. Our hearts cry a thousand greetings of love and adoration. Joyous are we upon the return of him who graciously throttles the universe."

Another came, and then another, and still more while the Master of Sinanju regarded them all with unmoving visage and steely eye. When the sun was full over the village and they were all assembled, Chiun spoke:

"Shame. Shame on you. What do you have to fear from a Master of Sinanju that you flee to the hills as though I were a Japanese warrior, or a Chinese. Have not the Masters of Sinanju proved a greater protection than any wall? Have not the Masters of Sinanju gone out from this village and kept it fed, lo, these many centuries? Did not the Masters of Sinanju keep Sinanju the only fishing village on the West Korea Bay that did not have to surrender its babies to the cold ocean for want of food? You do not fish well. You do not farm well. And yet you eat well. All because of the Master of Sinanju. And when I return, you run. O shame. O shame that I should keep burning in my bosom in silence."

And the villagers fell to their faces, begging mercy.

"We were afraid," they cried. "The treasure has been stolen. Centuries of tribute given to Sinanju are gone."

"Did you steal it?"

"No, great Master."

"Then why are you afraid?"

"Because we failed to guard the treasure."

"You never guarded anything, nor were you supposed to," explained the Master of Sinanju. "Our reputation has guarded the treasures of Sinanju. Your duty is to give homage to the great Masters of Sinanju, and report all that transpires while they are away."

Now an old man, who remembered Chiun in his youth, and the kindnesses shown by the Master, and feats of strength demonstrated for the amusement of the young, spoke up:

"I watched," said the wizened old man, his voice cracking. "I remember my duty, O young Chiun. There were many who came. And they came with guns, taking a full day to remove all the treasure from your house."

"Did you tell them they were stealing the treasure of Sinanju?" asked Chiun.

"Yes, yes," cried the crowd.

But the old man sadly shook his head.

"No. No one did. We were all afraid," the old man said, tears streaming from his slitted eyes which, like Chiun's, were hazel in color.

Chiun stretched out a long-nailed hand, as if in blessing, and said:

"Because of your honesty and loyalty, this village will be spared the consequences of its treason. Because of you, your single act of loyalty, the honor of Sinanju has been preserved. You alone will walk with me, ancient one, and be revered when I leave because of what you have dared to tell this day. You have done well."

And so, the old man at his side, Chiun walked to the house where the treasure of Sinanju had been stored. The house had been built by Egyptian architects sent by Tutankhamen as tribute to Sinanju. They built it on what was rare in Korea, a foundation of stone, not wood. But upon that stone, they raised a jewel of wood—the finest teaks, firs, and ebonies, lacquered and artfully painted. The Greek kings had provided glass of a clarity not seen again until the West learned to produce it as freely as the myriad wheat of the field.

There were rooms of ivory and alabaster. Scents from India, and Chinese silk. The drachma, rupee, dinar, shekel, boul, reel, and stoneweight of silver had all known a home here. It had been a place of plenty. But now, in utter shock, Chiun beheld bare floors in the house of the Master of Sinanju, floors which had not been bare since the first Roman legion marched from a little city on the

Tiber. Even the walls of the room used to store the gold of Cyrus the Great of Persia were shorn of their leaf.

On the bare walls, Chiun could read the ancient Persian inscriptions instructing the workmen who were to lay the leaf, with a note cautioning them that this was for the house of the powerful Wi. Gone and gone were the treasures of Sinanju, no matter where Chiun looked. Rooms of fresh dust and bleached squares where chests had rested for centuries filled the barren house.

The old man was weeping.

"Why do you weep?" asked Chiun gently.

"So much has been taken. Your father took me through this house when I was a child. It is all gone. The gold. The ivory. The jewels and the great statues carved in amber and jade. O, the jade alone, O great Master, was an emperor's treasure."

"That was not what was stolen, old man," said Chiun. "Of jade, there is plenty in the outside world. We can get more. And of gold, much more. There are always craftsmen to make statues. Woods and amber and diamonds abound in greater weights than could ever fill this house. They can all be replaced, or recovered, as I intend to do, beginning now. But that was not what was stolen," repeated Chiun, pausing as he felt the anger burning in the perfection that was his heart.

"What they stole was our dignity and strength. By daring to steal from this house, they have violated the House of Sinanju, violated its strength and reputation. This they have stolen, and for that they will pay. Mightily will they pay. Before the world they will pay."

And then Chiun confided to the old man that the one whom he had been training as the next Master of Sinanju had not come with him to avenge this dishonor.

"I saw him when he came before. He seemed most noble . . . for a white."

"He appears to the untrained eye to be white," said Chiun. "But only now has he acted white. Do not repeat this, ever."

"I will not," said the old man who respected Chiun so much.

"The one who was to take my place does not even respect the treasure of Sinanju. He has gone off to help whites save the world."

"No," said the old man, trying to imagine such ingratitude. He clutched his heart. This encouraged Chiun to confide further in a mere villager.

"He thinks the sky is falling," whispered Chiun, and then it was too sad to discuss any longer, even with one so worthy as the old man who had been true to those who fed him.

"Is he crazed?"

"I thought he had overcome his backward white habits after all these years. You can train and train. But some whiteness always remains," Chiun said sadly.

"Still white?" asked the old man, shocked.

"A little. Not very much. It will go eventually. He was raised among them. But for now I must labor alone."

In Pyongyang, the capital of North Korea, the Master of Sinanju's every step was noted. How he had debarked from the plane, how he had entered the village, and what he had done there.

These things were told in an office only a few knew of, and one those few approached with dread.

It had neither spacious windows nor carpeting. If it had had a window, the view would have been bedrock. It was eight stories beneath the street, built during the time of the imperialist invasion of the homeland, known to the west as the Korean War. It had been dug out of the rock with picks. Two thousand laborers had been worked to death to get this far down into the bedrock. At its base was the most expensive steel imported to North Korea since Japan had ruled the peninsula. Around that steel was lead, and for a finish was rough concrete.

It had been built by the glorious leader himself, Kim Il Sung, President for Life.

If there was one building that would survive an atomic attack by the Americans, it was going to be that building. From that room would spring a new Korea with the soul of a sword and a heart of a shark.

In the deepest room of that building came the word about the village on the West Korea Bay. The information came to Sayak Cang, whose name was never mentioned, because to speak his name was to die.

Typists who worked in the building were told never to enter that corridor, because typists were in demand. To walk in the corridor without a permit meant instant death without appeal.

Those few who knew Sayak Cang had never seen him smile. They had never heard him say either a positive or unnecessary word.

When they did—with passes—enter that room, they did so with moist palms, having rehearsed everything they had planned to say many times over.

Sayak Cang was the director of the People's Bureau of Revolutionary Struggle for the People's Democratic Republic of North Korea.

Sayak Cang, in brief, was the head of their intelligence.

This day Sayak Cang had given every detail of the rest of the world, including the never-ending penetration of South Korea, to his subordinates. He wanted to know everything that had happened or was happening in the village of Sinanju.

This day, too, Sayak Cang ordered that, for expediency, anyone arriving needed neither a pass nor clearance. The most important thing was every detail that happened in Sinanju.

Sayak Cang had a melon-round face with slits for eyes and a mouth that was a harsh line. His lips always looked dry, and his hands showed a scar above the thumb knuckles. That was, people said, from his heavy use of the whip when he had been a junior officer in charge of interrogation.

The Master of Sinanju had entered the village. The Master had found that the treasure was gone. The Master was seen talking to an old man. Did Sayak Cang wish to know what the Master was saying?

"If anyone puts an electronic device to detect what the Master of Sinanju says or hears, I will have that person crushed under rocks," said Sayak Cang, who did not believe that a Master of Sinanju could be overheard without the Master knowing it.

And he was not about to upset his Glorious Leader Kim Il Sung with the possibility that the Master of Sinanju suspected that the People's Republic was in any way spying on him. Sayak Cang had insisted his leader leave before the Master's plane was given flight clearance, and so Kim Il Sung had taken off for Yemen with his son. Unfortunately, with modern jets, Yemen was not all that far away, and after reviewing the industrial progress of that Marxist country on the Arabian Sea, the glorious leader had only consumed a half-day. He was bored with Yemen within five minutes.

"Once you have seen one hand cut off you have seen them all," said the President for Life of North Korea.

"I am sorry, but you must stay out of the country until it is safe."

"A well-dug sewage ditch had more industrial progress than Yemen."

"What about Ethiopia? That is a friendly country," said Cang.

"Are there any socialist countries that are interesting?"

"Only before they are liberated, sir."

"Well, hurry, Sayak Cang."

"You well know, sir, I would not dare hurry a Master of Sinanju. I would lay down my life now for our struggle. But I would not for all our sakes and for the dignity of our nation hurry the Master of Sinanju."

"You have always known what you were doing, Sayak Cang. What can I do in Ethiopia?"

"You can watch people starve, Your Excellency."

"Another country?"

"Tanzania."

"What can I do there?"

"Pretty much what they are doing in Ethiopia without the intensity. You can starve."

"How about a white country?"

"East Germany. You can watch people being shot trying to climb over the wall they have used to seal everyone in."

"No."

"Poland. Maybe they will murder another priest for you."

"Is there any place with some fun in it?"

"Not if you want to go to a country that has freed itself from the shackles of imperialist domination."

"Do what you must do as quickly as possible then, Sayak Cang," said the Premier.

Sayak Cang had no intention of hurrying. While the others feared Sinanju, or had talked about the humiliation by a single archaic pack of murderers who served reactionary monarchies throughout history, Sayak Cang had told them all that the House of Sinanju was the one glory in the history of a nation shamed among nations.

"We have been the footstools of the Chinese, the Russians, the Japanese, the Mongols. There is no one who has not put his heel on the Korean neck. But in all that time, there has been only one note of glory: the House of Sinanju. Only the Masters of Sinanju have earned this nation any respect during those shameful times. Glory to the House of Sinanju, to the Masters of Sinanju who refused to be whore worms to those who sat on foreign thrones."

Thus spoke Sayak Cang at a most important meeting of the generals and labor directors of North Korea. He spoke to silence and to many who thought that he would soon be executed for such insolence.

But in that silence at that most important meeting many years before, Sayak Cang had won respect, for into that silence came the sound of soft palms touching each other. It was a clap from Himself, Kim Il Sung.

And now Sayak Cang himself was prepared to tell a Master of Sinanju what he thought of him to his face.

"If he is still in the village, beg that he come here. If he does not wish to leave the village, ask that I be permitted to enter."

This was sent by radiophone to the officer who was waiting outside the village. He asked a child to go to the house to which the Master of Sinanju had returned and tell Chiun himself that there was a message waiting for him. The officer promised a coin if the child would do this.

He was quite careful, of course, not to enter himself.
The child returned, saying the Master of Sinanju did not
wish to speak to any Pyongyanger, and it was as though
the officer had heard his own death sentence.

With trembling hands, he picked up the radiophone
made in Russia, as was all North Korean equipment, and
phoned the number of Sayak Cang. He had seen men who
had displeased Cang. He had seen one tied to posts begging
to die while Sayak Cang exhorted the rest of the man's
company to laugh at his pitiful cries.

"The Master of Sinanju does not wish to come to
Pyongyang although he was begged by myself to do so.
Begged."

"Exactly what did he say?" asked Sayak Cang.

The officer felt the cold sea winds from the West Korea
Bay blow through his thin uniform, but he did not mind
the cold. He saw his own breath make puff clouds before
him, and he wondered how long his own body would be
warm.

"He said, comrade sir, that he did not wish to speak to a
Pyongyanger."

It must have been the faulty Russian equipment because
the officer could have sworn that he heard laughter from
Sayak Cang himself at the other end of the phone.

"Tell a child, any child from the village, to show the
Glorious Master a history book. Any history book. Then
beg the Master to go to a neighboring village and see any
history book that the children read."

"And then what, comrade sir?"

"Then tell him that Sayak Cang ordered these histories
written. Tell him where I am, and that I would gladly come
to him."

The officer sent the child back with a coin for himself
and the message for the Master of Sinanju. The child disappeared into the mud and filth of the fishing village.
Within moments Chiun's flowing gold kimono could be
seen coming up from the village, the winds blowing the
wisps of hair, the gold like a flag of conquest whipping in
triumph.

The Master of Sinanju held a schoolbook.

"Take me to another village," said Chiun.

Hurriedly, the officer made way in his car for the Master of Sinanju and drove five miles to a farming town. Unlike Sinanju, there were red flags everywhere and in every building was a picture of Kim Il Sung.

Here people came to attention and hurried at the officer's command. Here he did not need a coin for people to do his bidding.

The Master of Sinanju was brought one history book and then another. He wanted to see every grade's text.

Finally he said:

"Almost correct."

"The man who insisted they be written like that is in Pyongyang," said officer. "He will come to you, or if you wish, you may come to him."

"Pyongyang is an evil city of much corruption. But I will go because in all the darkness of this day, one light shines from Pyongyang," said Chiun. "Would that my own pupil had shown such understanding."

The officer bowed profusely. Chiun kept the books.

The building that covered the eight-story excavation into bedrock was a simple one-story government office. But the elevators were lavish by comparison, with full use of aluminum and chrome and the most expensive metals. The elevator descended to the lowest level and there, with his face oddly changed, was Sayak Cang.

The change was noticed by those who worked on this lowest level, those who knew him. Sayak Cang, with great pain to his facial muscles, was smiling.

"You caused this to be written?"

"I did, Glorious Master of Sinanju."

"It is almost correct," said Chiun. "I interrupted a grave situation to tell you that."

"A thousand thank-yous. A million blessings," said Sayak Cang.

Chiun opened the books he had with him. They told of the misery of Korea. They told of filthy foreigners with their hands at the pure maiden's throat. They told of strangulation and humiliation. And then there was a chapter called "Light."

It read:

"Amid the darkness shone pure and glorious the light of the Masters of Sinanju. They alone paid no homage to foreign lands, but received it. They alone like the sunlight shone eternal, invincible, magnificently glorious, keeping alive the true superiority of Koreans while the rest of their nation waited, humiliated in darkness, with only Sinanju to foretell the coming of the true destiny of the Korean people."

Sayak Cang nodded at every sentence.

"Basically you have got this right," said Chiun. "But instead of 'light,' wouldn't 'awesome light' be more correct? A light could be a little match."

"But in darkness a match is glorious."

"Are you talking about the glory of Sinanju or the darkness of the rest of you?"

"Most correct. Every book will be changed."

"Usually, young man, historians lie and shade the truth for their own convenience. But here in Korea we have a passage that can be called absolute truth."

Sayak Cang bowed. One of the secretaries on the floor almost gasped. No one even knew that his vertebrae moved, much less bowed.

"But you have thieves in this country," said Chiun. And then he told him of the treasures of Sinanju.

On the lowest floor of the most secure building in North Korea came a scream of horror. It came from the lips of Sayak Cang.

"This is a disgrace to the Korean people. This is an indignity. A shame that knows no bounds. Better our mothers and daughters sold into slavery to whore for the Japanese than this insult to our history. When they have robbed the House of Sinanju, they have robbed us of our past."

At that moment the entire intelligence network of North Korea was laid at the feet of the Master of Sinanju that his treasure should be recovered for all the people.

Of course there was a saying in Sinanju that light from a Pyongyanger was like darkness from an honest man. But who, after all, could argue with what Chiun had seen being taught to schoolchildren?

Then again, within not too long a time, a North Korean embassy discovered that one of the treasures of Sinanju was being sold. At an auction no less. In a white country.

Shortly before noon, the gruesome luck of the Western world seemed to change. Chiun was putting through a phone call to Folcroft.

Smith almost wanted to breathe a thank-you to the heavens. But he said:

"Look. We have something we need immediately. We promise to replace much if not all of your treasure. We need you now."

"The House of Sinanju is honored to exalt your glory," came Chiun's voice. "But first, are you in touch with Remo?"

"Yes," said Smith.

"Good. Take this down, and be very careful. Do you have ink?"

"I have a pencil and a computer," said Smith.

"Use the pencil," said Chiun. "Now, write down, 'The Glorious Struggle of Korean Peoples Under the Leadership of Kim Il Sung, grades one through five.' "

"I have it."

"Pages thirty-five and thirty-six," said Chiun.

"Good."

"Tell Remo he must read that now."

"All right. Will do. Now, we have . . ." said Smith, but he was unable to finish his sentence. Apparently an operator from the other side had cut them off after Chiun had hung up.

5

Alexei Zemyatin did not trust good news, especially from
the modern KGB. He remembered how they had been
under Felix Dzerzhinsky, their founder. Then, they were
frightened, angry, and ruthless. Many of their leaders were
in their teens then. They were all learning, those early state
police known as the Ogpu: trying to copy the late czar's
Cheka, afraid of making mistakes, yet also afraid not to
act.

If one of those ragamuffins had told him they had made
a major breakthrough in finding out the source of this
deadly, invisible new American weapon, he would have
felt reassured. But when the KGB general in his tailor-
made green uniform told him, plump with imported
chocolates and fruits and sporting a wristwatch from
Switzerland which would tell him the time to return to his
lush dacha in the quiet suburbs of Moscow, Alexei Zemyatin felt only suspicion.

The West might fear the KGB because of its successes.
But they did not realize how much effort and failed motion
went into each triumph. They did not realize that for every
operative there might be one hundred officers living the
good life, whose main concern was to keep that life. And
to keep that life they would create reports to make themselves look good. Therefore, when speaking to the KGB
about something they were responsible for, one also had to
calculate how they were protecting themselves. One did not
accept good news at face value under any circumstances.

Alexei Zemyatin put his hand on the soft green felt of
the lavish desk in the lavish office. On the other side of the
desk was a defender of Russia's security making a very
comfortable job of it all. This KGB general was young, in
his mid-fifties. He did not really know of the Revolution,

and was a child during the great patriotic war against Germany. Apparently he had never been interrupted by anyone for the last few years. He was director of the British desk of the KGB, the unit responsible for what was perhaps the most successful penetration of any nation by another since the British infiltrated the Germans in the thirties and forties. He had made, in his own boastful words, "all England like downtown Moscow."

"Excuse me," said Zemyatin. "Before I hear of your triumphs, indulge me in the little details of the matter. I want facts."

"Of course," said the young KGB general coolly. His office was as large as a ballroom, featuring a plush couch, art on the walls, and, of course, a picture of the chairman behind his desk. His desk had once been used by a czar and still enjoyed the gilt design. The room smelled of rich Cuban cigars and the best French brandy. The young officer took the interruption by the old man as he would by someone in the Politburo who, while having more authority, would in a very few minutes acknowledge the young general's technical superiority. These old men were like that. The young general had heard about this one from older officers but dismissed their kudos as nostalgia for the past. Therefore he was not surprised or offended when the relic in the typical worker's baggy suit interrupted him. In just a few moments the old man would be as grateful as the others for the general's brilliant technical presence on the British desk.

"We ascertained a strike in the British area of Malden, approximately eight A.M. their time. The target area was a field of approximately one hundred square meters. The launch site was verified by Jodrell Bank as west of Ireland, which of course is continental USA. I think we have gone over this before."

"Go on," said Zemyatin.

"We have the woman responsible for the weapons. We have her," said the young general, "in a British safe house and she is cooperating fully." The general waited for Zemyatin to ask why they were using a British safe house. Then he could boast that it was a unit within British intelligence that they controlled; that the Americans had sent someone, and that the KGB British desk had intercepted him. There was even more if this old man would allow the true technological brilliance of the younger generation to show itself. The old man had probably started by throwing gasoline in old vodka bottles at czarist police.

"How do you know this woman is connected with the weapon?"

"She is the one who hired Pomfritt Laboratories, the British firm, to conduct the test. Not only did she do this, but she gave an artificial company as the one hiring. CIA of course. It was a cover."

"We know she lied. Do you have any verification that she is from the CIA?"

"Not yet. But we will. We will have everything," said the young general. He offered more brandy. Zemyatin shook his head. He had not touched the first glass.

"Be so kind as to indulge me. But how do you know she will cooperate?"

"How do you know the sun will rise, sir?" said the general.

"I don't," said Zemyatin. "I only presume it will because it has done so all my life and according to all the historians of mankind it has risen in the past. But I don't."

"Well, I can't give you anything more assured than a sunrise, sir."

"Give me the facts. I will work out the confusion. On what do you base your flamboyant conclusions?"

"We have her psychological profile."

"That head business?" said Zemyatin, referring to the experiments in parapsychology and psychology that the KGB prided itself on. People who could read minds. Others who could bend objects without touching them. People who could do all manner of hocus-pocus Zemyatin had seen Gypsies do for coin when he was a boy. Now the entire government was financing this nonsense. Not only was it all still a form of charade, but America was ironically still sending the CIA agents to discover what Russia had found. It was a lovely little trap if anyone wanted to remove a few enemy operatives, but, like most ventures of this kind, was meaningless even there. It only paid to remove operatives when an opponent was short of them. America had operatives falling over operatives in more secret organizations than the KGB had yet discovered.

"Psychological profiles are valid, sir," said the general. "Our profile of Dr. Kathleen O'Donnell explains why she came with our agent."

"To you, yes. Excuse me, young man, if I want more facts. Why do you believe she came with you out of pure motives? Why do you believe she is telling the truth?"

"The psychological profile tells us we are dealing with a woman who is a form of sociopath. Somewhere in her early childhood, her development took a strange turn. She undoubtedly was a beautiful and somewhat spoiled child. But her normal love patterns were somehow thwarted, and her sexual drive linked itself strongly to violence and suffering."

"I am looking for a weapon, General," said Zemyatin.

"Yes. Yes. Of course. Please. These sorts of people can hide their aggressions and hostilities very well . . . and I might add they usually are quite successful in life . . . until one time when they actually see and feel intense suffering. Then they will do anything to satisfy their insatiable urge to see more violence and suffering. You see, they are basically a bomb ready to go off within themselves. Many people are like that. War brings it out in them."

"People are not bombs. They are human beings. These games—"

"More than games, sir. Dr. Kathleen O'Donnell will tell us more and give us more than if we used some old bodyguard of Lenin with a nightstick. This woman has been awakened."

Zemyatin was not insulted. A jackass could do nothing better than bray at a horse. He was despairing and did not conceal his sigh. "How do we know these things?"

Now the young general smiled.

"We knew that the experiment was to take place in Malden, England. We didn't know its source then, but we knew the leadership was looking for it."

"Yes, that was good," said Zemyatin. He did not

mention that, with the awesome amount of the Soviet treasury that was poured into the KGB operations, they not only should have found the site but the weapon itself and had it for him on his desk. Nevertheless, one fought battles with whom he had. Not with whom he wished. Zemyatin's Russia had the KGB. To replace this man now would take time. However, if he had time, Zemyatin knew he could find someone else. Or do something to shatter this man's self-satisfaction. That complacent face could get them all killed.

"While we were a bit rushed setting up the surveillance, we did manage to make sure there would be no local police or intelligence operations from the British near there. We created what we like to call an environment."

"An environment?" asked Zemyatin.

"Yes. We observed the experiment and the experimenters. We saw that Dr. O'Donnell was taking a great deal of unusual pleasure in the suffering of these animals. We . . ."

Zemyatin raised a hand.

"I want that weapon. Get it now. She knows where the weapon is. Twist her arm. It works. Use an injection. That works. Get the weapon."

"Field Marshal? Do you think it is a pistol we are looking for? Some new kind of cannon? Just for example, we could put twenty American weapons right here on this desk, sir, and we wouldn't have the remotest idea of how they work. Today it is computer technology. The weapon isn't the pieces of metal. The weapon, Field Marshal, is here . . ." said the general, pointing to his brain. "That's where the weapon is. The knowledge. Now, this effort was a maximum priority in time and effort, correct?"

Zemyatin nodded.

"We might be able to put that weapon in your lap tomorrow, but there are very good odds we wouldn't know how to work it for three years. Maybe never. I could boot up a computer now, and without the knowledge of how it works, it would be only a hunk of metal. The weapon is the knowledge, and knowledge is in the mind."

"Most people in the world will tell you everything on

their minds, sometimes for a kind word in a harsh environment, or if they think they are going to lose their lives," said Zemyatin.

"In a simple world or a simple time," said the general.

"How long will it take until we have her mind?" said Zemyatin.

"A day. Two days," said the younger man. "I appreciate your wisdom and what you have done for the motherland. We are good at what we do, even though you might have your doubts. Let me dispel those doubts, comrade."

"Young man," said Zemyatin. "You will never dispel my doubts, and the one thing I worry about for the future of the motherland is how few doubts you have. Only lunatics don't doubt."

"We act instead of worry."

"I want you to continue your search for the weapon. I do not want you to let up in any way on any front. You may think you know, but you don't."

"Certainly," said the younger general with a confident smile.

"No. No. You don't understand."

"You are right," said the general. "We would not mind being told why this weapon seems more important to you than their space lasers or new deliveries of atomic devices. We have found that the more we know, the better we can serve you."

Zemyatin did not answer. It was an old saw in Intelligence that five people could not keep a secret. Zemyatin suspected the real number had to be two. He did not care about the reports that said the Americans were disorganized and could not move quickly without committees and teams of men. There just might be someone in America who, knowing the effect of missile batteries, would have the wisdom to launch immediately and then dictate terms of surrender. He would do that. And the one way to let America find out how truly dominant she was at this time was to tell one more person who would tell another person that indeed the U.S. weapon could render all of Mother Russia's weapons useless.

Zemyatin knew his country had neither time nor leeway.

And here was one of the bright new stars of the KGB sitting complacently behind his luxurious desk as the world headed toward a showdown. A showdown Alexei Zemyatin was not about to lose, not after all the millions of lives that had gone up until now into defending his country.

"Tell me. What do you know of the agent the Americans sent?"

"He was 'run around,' so to speak."

"It didn't bother you that they sent one person?"

"It is possible, Field Marshal, that the Americans do not think this weapon is as important as you do."

"Americans don't send one of anything to do anything. Americans work in teams. They have teams, and now we see one man. It is a man, isn't it?"

"Yes."

"There is an old axiom, General. An enemy is perfect until he shows you how to destroy him."

"Yes, sir. That was quite popular in the First World War among pilots involved in dogfights. Those were old, slow prop-driven aircraft in which individual pilots shot at each other. There are electronic devices and formations now."

Zemyatin did not answer the general but rose slowly. There was a gold letter opener on the luxurious desk. Zemyatin picked it up and fondled it.

"It belonged to a princess, Field Marshal. Would you like it?" asked the general politely.

Alexei Zemyatin noticed how smooth and comfortable the face was. Its very complacency terrified him. Carefully he closed his fingers tight around the gilt leather pommel of the letter opener. He smiled. The general smiled back. Then Zemyatin leaned forward as though to hand the letter opener back to the general. But as the general reached forward to take it, Zemyatin, driving himself with his rear foot, pushed the point into a smooth fat cheek.

The general lurched backward, his eyes wide in shock, red drops splattering the perfect green uniform. His cheek spit blood.

"War is blood," said Zemyatin. "You should know

what the rest of us have felt. I hope you understand what it is about a bit more now."

The general understood that the one they called the Great One was too powerful to move against at this time, possibly anytime. He was a dinosaur, from an age long gone. And he had to be humored. The cut not only continued to bleed, but it needed stitches. It was the first time in the general's life he had ever been wounded. For some reason he could not explain, it made him slightly more unsettled than he thought he should be. He never once suspected that he was reacting precisely the way the old man had intended him to. The young general was not giving in to the old man's crude brutality when he ordered a trace and analysis thrown at the American agent who had arrived in Great Britain. He was just humoring the old man, he told himself. He also requested an immediate response on the woman. The answer back from the chief London unit of the KGB was that the general should stop worrying. Dr. O'Donnell was not only beginning to talk, but she was secure in the safest safe house in all England. After all, what was good enough for Henry VIII should be good enough for the KGB.

6

The first thing Remo did was get an exact description of Dr. Kathleen O'Donnell. She had red hair and was gorgeous. One of the technicians said she was "a knockout." Another one amplified on this:

"A real knockout."

The eyes were blue, the breasts were perfect, the smile was elegant, the face was exquisite.

No one could tell him more. Remo realized that beautiful women were never really described in detail but in the way people felt about them. Which did him no good.

In the car, he explained his problem to the British intelligence and military officers who were still conscious.

"I am looking for a redheaded knockout of a woman," said Remo.

"Aren't we all," said an officer.

"Try Soho. Got a brunette there last week. Woman did wonders with leather," said the unit chief.

"I am looking for the redhead who ran this test."

"Can't tell you that, old boy. This whole thing's hush-hush. If you hadn't been such a brute you wouldn't have even found out where this test was," said the station chief.

"Let's try something else. Who said this was hush-hush? Who said you should try to run an ally around the block?"

"Can't tell you that. That's even more hush-hush," said the unit chief. However, when he discovered that he could end the incredible pain in his legs, where the American seemed to be exerting just the slightest pressure, by telling what he knew, he decided it wasn't that much of a secret after all.

"It's an agency we have. Doesn't even have an MI code. Good people. Right sort of schools and such. Best we have, and they don't make much ado about normal intelligence labels. You do know what a label is, don't you?"

"No," said Remo. "I just do my job. Where are these guys?"

"These guys, as you call them, are known as the Source. You don't just jolly well drop in on them. They don't have some crude concrete building, with guards and snooping devices and people with guns. They are, in brief, the very best there is."

"Maybe you don't know it," said Remo, "but we are on the same side. We have been for the last century and I expect we always will be. So where is the Source?"

"You'll never get through to them. They're not some little station disguised off Piccadilly surrounded by plaster walls and a few gunmen. The Source is absolutely British and your newfangled hand tricks couldn't get you within a hundred yards of them."

"Newfangled? I didn't show you anything that wasn't thirteen centuries old when you people were painting yourself blue," said Remo.

The place Remo was not supposed to be able to penetrate was on the way from Malden to London, about twenty miles outside the city limits.

The inpregnable edifice sat on a small hillock surrounded by hundreds of yards of lawn. The lawn was not for decoration. Remo knew that centuries before, all the trees would have been felled by peasants or captives or slaves. The land was always cleared around castles so that the enemy would be vulnerable as it approached. This castle was massive stone, twenty feet thick, smoothed so that attackers could not climb its high walls. There was even a wide moat. And parapets. And slit holes no bigger than a fist for the famous English longbow.

"This? This is supposed to be impenetrable?" asked Remo.

"Yes. Just try your newfangled techniques on that, old chap!"

"That," said Remo, "is your typical Norman castle, perfectly devised to stop Anglo-Saxon rebels, and other Norman lords. It's got a moat, a drawbridge, access to the outer walls from inner ramps to roll up vats of boiling oil. It also has the mandatory escape tunnel that runs under the moat for use if all of the aforesaid shouldn't work."

Remo reeled off this information quickly like a child reciting, which was the way he had learned it. He never thought it would come in handy. It was one of those early lessons in tradition. There was the Norman castle, the Roman stockade, the Japanese palace, the French fortress, and all those old defenses he thought were ridiculous to learn about because they weren't used anymore.

Remo had the car stop two hundred yards from the drawbridge.

"Giving up?" said the intelligence chief.

"No. You don't enter a Norman castle from a drawbridge. You can do the walls, but why bother? I like to surprise people."

Remo smiled and left the car. He would find what he was looking for between two hundred and one hundred and fifty yards from the moat. By now it would be well overgrown, but even when in use, it was disguised by rocks. Usually it was placed west of the castle so that the rising sun would be behind it. They liked to use the passages in daylight, because at night attackers would respond to sound. It was the escape tunnel, its location known only to the reigning Lord. The Japanese had long before abandoned that sort of escape route because of the danger of assassins using it. The British had never had that problem and had left the tunnels.

The beautiful aspect of these tunnels was that they always came from the lord's bedroom, always the safest place, and the point an assassin would invariably have to attack. The lord of the castle would deliver a stirring speech about holding out to the last man, then in the privacy of his sleeping room, don the clothes of his enemies, and with his immediate family make his way into or behind enemy lines. It was a perfect escape from any Saxons or Normans against whom they might be fighting a losing battle.

Remo could have gotten into this castle within the first month of his breath training. He felt the earth under his feet and tried to sense some different stone formation beneath. He stayed very quiet, smelling the fresh grass and sensing the odor of the oak and new life all around him. His steps became smooth glides, his arms like divining rods which seemed to rise so that his fingertips and the ground they hovered over rested on the air between them. A bird chirped in nearby trees away from the castle. Behind him the heavy gasoline chug of the car spit heavy fumes into the pure air.

Remo kept his pace, shutting his eyes because he could not find this place with his eyes. Time had made them useless.

Inside the car, the remaining conscious Britons discussed the peculiar American.

"What's he doing?"

"Damned well waltzing for all I know."

"He's not doing anything. Just gliding around there. His eyes are closed."

"Strange one."

"Bit brutal, yes?"

"I don't know. We're supposed to be his allies, after all. Why are we hiding these things from him?"

"We're not hiding anything."

"We're not exactly giving information freely."

"Well, we're not hiding anything."

"Don't think we should have at the beginning, if you ask me. The Americans are our friends. Who are we really protecting?" asked the military officer.

"You worry too much. Ask too many questions. People won't like you after a while if you behave like that," said the intelligence-unit chief.

"There. He's stopped. Over there. Now what's he doing?"

"By Jove, look at that."

The thin American with the thick wrists paused, quivering, then slowly, as though on some invisible quicksand, slipped down into the earth and was no longer seen.

Remo had found the escape tunnel.

There were those who knew of Guy Philliston, some who even said they knew him personally, and then there were his dear, dear friends.

Guy Philliston's dear, dear friends ran England. Pretty much the way they had always run England since the Industrial Revolution. It was not some great diabolical consortium of vested interests plotting against the common man. Many of them liked to call themselves common men. Guy Philliston's dear, dear friends were those people who generally made things work to a degree. They lunched together, theatered together, sometimes transgressed with one another's wives, and if they were really close, introduced one another to their tailor. They got government posts in whatever government happened to be elected, and generally, when there was a post to fill, filled it with one of their own. Governments might change, the Queen might die, but the dear, dear friends of Guy Philliston went on forever, in empire and in dissolution, in conquest and in defeat.

Thus it was that when Her Majesty's Secret Service found itself riddled with Russian agents, one section chief after another turning up in Moscow with the most sensitive of British secrets, this group turned to one of its own.

It occurred at the races in the right box. The men wore gray gloves and gray top hats and impeccable race attire. The Queen had entered. They rose out of respect.

"Guy," said his friend to Lord Philliston, "bit of a muck-up at MI 5."

"Rather," said Guy Philliston. He had heard at lunch the day before that Russia had not only gotten away with a master list of every British agent in the Middle East, but because the list was so incredibly sensitive, no one had dared make a duplicate. Now only Russia knew who Britain had under the sun where the West's oil energy lay buried.

"Got to do something, you know. Can't go on like this. Be nice if we, not they, knew who we had."

"Quite," said Guy. "Did you try the salmon mousse?" A silver tray of hors d'oeuvres rested on a mahogany stand next to a chilled magnum of champagne of a modest year. Nothing rude, of course, but nothing to make one stop and notice.

His friend thought about the salmon mousse awhile. Then he said:

"Do you want to grab hold of those boys and shake them up a bit, Guy?"

"Don't think it would work."

"What would you do?"

"I would use our misfortune, old boy," said Guy.

"The one thing I want to do with a disaster is forget it."

"Not in this case," said Lord Philliston. He was devastatingly handsome with fine strong features befitting a British lord. Indeed, more than one movie producer had asked him to take a screen test. He had always refused. Acting was too much like work.

"If we have a deuced mess, and we try to rearrange things, one chap here, one chap there, one chap somewhere else, then we may still be moving around people who might be loyal to Ivan. In which case we are only rearranging our problem, not solving it."

"Go on. Please do."

"Let's not close down the section. Matter of fact, let's keep it going. Strong."

"But we don't even know who we have there! The Russians know who we have there. They have the only list for our Middle East section."

"Which shows how stupid they are. Taking the only list was a mistake. They should have made a duplicate and let us go on thinking we had somewhat secure agents out there."

"I think it was a snatch and grab. No great internal mole. Some clerk slipped a few quid, snatched a list here or there, and it happened to be an important one."

It was then that Lord Philliston showed his true brilliance. The plan was to let the Russians know that MI 5 believed they had only carelessly misplaced the list. MI 5 would start a search for it and allow the Russians to do their job right by smuggling back the entire original list to some intelligence department.

"Then what?"

"Then we continue to rely on the useless people."

"Wouldn't that be a bit purposeless?"

"Not at all, because in our disaster is their comfort. We should stop at nothing to let the Russians and the rest of the world believe that we have become the worst, most riddled intelligence system in the world."

"I beg your pardon, Lord Philliston."

"Try the mousse, will you?"

"I beg your pardon. What is this insanity?"

"Because we will, starting today, start a new intelligence system, protected by the Russians' certainty that they own pieces, if not all, of ours."

"From scratch you mean? From the bloody start you mean?"

"Absolutely," said Lord Philliston. The trumpets were announcing the first race. "Our real intelligence system will be one no one has ever heard of."

"Brilliant. We will show the Americans we can still hack it."

"We will show them nothing. The Americans are addicted to talk. A major American secret is one that is reported by only a single television network."

"An excellent idea. I knew you were the right fellow for this thing, Lord Philliston. I suppose we will have to give you your MI code. Would you like MI 9?"

"No label. No codes."

"We have to call you something."

"Pick a word then," said Lord Philliston.

"Doesn't seem quite right to launch an intelligence operation without an MI code."

"Call the bloody thing 'Source.' "

"Why 'Source'?"

"Why not 'Source'?" said Lord Guy Philliston.

And thus the Source was born that afternoon at Epsom Downs. No one quite knew how Lord Philliston managed it, and he was not one to tell. Information that the Americans could not gather was immediately placed at the disposal of every British prime minister. News of major Russian decisions and the reasons for them began appearing on plain typed paper. More often than not it was too late to do anything about these major Russian moves, but the reports were always accurate, if not brilliant. Guy Philliston performed with a tenth of the personnel allocated to the public intelligence system. And never once did he seek promotion or fame.

His success only confirmed what all of the good friends knew in the first place: one of theirs knew how to run things best. Always had, always would.

One never went wrong trusting someone who used the right tailor. And the best thing about Lord Philliston's Source was that it never made public noise, never embarrassed anyone. A legend grew up among those who ran things that if it were brilliant and impossible to figure out, it had to be Source.

One reason Lord Philliston's Source could use so few men was that he didn't have to waste years and manpower penetrating the inner circles of the Kremlin.

He merely had lunch at the right club. There in his private mail, which no one would dare open, were the reports in English, neatly typed, of what was going on in the world. There was also a very handy summary of what they referred to, so that Lord Guy Philliston could get through a month's work in less than five minutes. One minute, if he chose to speed-read the summary.

The information about the Kremlin was accurate because it came from the Kremlin. And the original list of British agents had been returned.

In fact, everything Lord Philliston had told his friends at Epsom Downs that day had been worked out for him by his KGB contact, who was also his lover, and who knew that what Lord Philliston liked best in the world was generally to be left alone. The one thing he hated in the world was the Philliston duty of serving Queen and country.

Running the Source allowed Lord Philliston the utmost respect of his family and friends with the least amount of work or danger. Russia certainly wasn't going to endanger her absolutely prime position with him in charge of Britain's secret security unit. Daddy wouldn't press him to join the Coldstream Guards, and Mummy wouldn't demand he escort one properly bred sow after another if he could claim that his time was fully taken up by Her Majesty's Service. Being a traitor to Queen and country had been an asbolute blessing to a lazy lord who preferred the love of men to that of the women his entire family wanted him to breed with.

There was occasional elements of risk in this job. Like the day he was told by the Russian contact to retire to his safe room because an American was about, mucking things up.

He did not like Philliston Hall. Even the parapets where one could survey the Philliston countryside were gloomy. And the safe room, once the master bedroom of the lords of this fortress, was gloomier still. Not even a slit for air. Fifteen feet of rock on every side and not an inch of it provided insulation. Stone never did.

No one had even bothered to put in a proper toilet. Rather, one relieved oneself in a little niche with a narrow hole to accept one's discharge. It had taken workmen three months to cut in the narrow holes for the security lines. One of them went to Whitehall, another went to Scotland Yard, another went to Number 10 Downing Street, and the one that had the really impenetrable scramble system went to the cultural-affairs department of the Russian embassy. Guy, of course, had direct access to the chief KGB officer there.

"This is ridiculous," said Guy. He was wearing a scratchy cashmere sweater pulled on over a cotton shirt that had too much starch. The brandy was adequate, but it kept chilling. The only way to heat anything in the room was to start a fire, but fires made smoke and the air was already deucedly unbreathable.

"Stay right where you are," warned the Russian. "Do not leave the room. The American is near you."

"One American is forcing me to hide in this stone-cold chamber?"

"He has run through some of your best staff and right now he is parked less than two hundred yards west of Philliston Hall."

"Who told you that?"

"Your guards. Stay where you are. You are too precious for us to risk. This man may be dangerous."

"Well then, let's give him what he wants and get rid of him. Then let me get back to London. This place is worthless. Useless."

"Stay where you are."

" 'Stay where you are,' " said Guy Philliston, imitating the soupy Russian accent before he hung up with force. He hated the Russian accent. Always sounded like they had something they wanted to cough up. Israelis sounded like they were about to spit something out, and Arabs hissed. Americans sounded like their tongues couldn't handle vowels, and Australians sounded—rightfully—as though they had all just been let out of Old Newgate Prison. Why, Lord Philliston asked himself, couldn't Britain fight the French? The French would make lovely enemies. They were cultured. The only real flaw of their race was that the men liked women too much.

Into this dreary cold life came the most beautiful

surprise. Virtually out of a wall came the most handsome
man Lord Philliston had ever seen. He had magnificent
dark eyes, high cheekbones, and was in perfect trim. His
body movements made Guy Philliston quiver with excitement. He was carrying something white, which he let drop
to the stone floor with a clatter. They were bones. Human
bones.

"Is that your specialty?" asked Lord Philliston. "I've
never done anything with bones but it sounds absolutely
delicious. Smashing."

"They're your bones," said Remo. "I found them at the
end of the tunnel where your ancestors left him. Him and
about three more."

"My ancestors?"

"If you're Lord Philliston, and if you are in this room
you would have to be."

"Why would they leave bones at the end of a tunnel?"

"Because they were like the Egyptians, and others,"
said Remo. "When they constructed a secret entrance to a
pyramid or castle, they killed the workmen. Secrets are
always best buried underground."

"Oh, isn't that delightful. You found the secret passage
Daddy promised to tell me about someday. That is, if he
could ever get me to this place. Which he couldn't." Guy
Philliston looked at the opening in the wall. It was low and
concealed by only one stone. He wondered if saving his life
was worth getting so soiled by crawling through a tunnel
like that. This man in his dark T-shirt and light trousers
could apparently move through things and not get a
smudge. The very thought of it made the head of Source
tingle.

"Look, sweetheart," said the American in his magnificent rough voice, totally American-city-butch, "I am looking for a woman. You are supposed to know things. You
are the one who runs Source."

"Are you sure you want a woman? How about a really
attractive boy?"

"I am looking for a knockout of a redhead. Her name is
Dr. Kathleen O'Donnell."

"Oh, that little matter," said Lord Philliston, clutching

his chest in relief. "I thought you wanted her as a bed partner. You mean it's business-related?"

Remo nodded.

"Well, of course you can have her. She is staying in one of my personal safe houses. You can have anything you want."

"Where is she?"

"Well, you've got to give me what I want first."

Remo grabbed the smooth throat and pressured the jugular vein until the handsome features of Lord Philliston became red, then painfully blue. Then he released.

"You'll need me to get in."

"I don't need anyone to get in anywhere."

"I can help you. Just do me one favor. Do that thing with your hands again. You know the spot."

Remo let Lord Philliston down on the stone and wiped his hands on the Britisher's cashmere sweater. He snared a bunch of it for a handle and dragged Lord Philliston with him back through the tunnel. Remo had questions to ask. Why were the British obstructing him? Didn't they know that the entire world was in jeopardy? What was going on? It was not difficult to ask these questions while moving quickly through the underground escape tunnel. The problem was in getting answers. Lord Philliston tended to bang against the rough rock walls as they moved. He was gashed. He was cut. He was brutalized. By the time they surfaced to where Remo had discovered the entrance, Lord Guy Philliston was battered and quivering.

He was also in love.

"Do that again. Once more. Please," said the head of the super-secret special British security agency. The car was still waiting for the American. The survivors packed into the back seat had decided that he had done his worst, and if they didn't move, would do no more.

They saw the American appear from the exact spot he had descended into. Behind him was the man they had all learned to respect and trust.

The British colonel thought he might try a desperate lunge toward the American. His body wouldn't move. The intelligence chief wondered what Sir Guy was doing.

"Is he following him or being dragged?" he asked.

"Don't know for sure. Lord Philliston is biting his hand, I think."

"No. Not biting. Look."

"I don't believe it."

As the American opened the car door, they all saw the undeniable pressing of their chief's lips to the American's hand. The head of the unit to which they had devoted their lives was kissing the hand that dragged him.

"Sir," snapped the colonel.

"Oh, bugger off," said Philliston. He knew what they were thinking.

"A bit improper, what?" said the colonel.

The unit chief, who had been assigned an MI code but who had secretly worked for Source, gave Lord Philliston a big wink. He was sure this was some sort of maneuver of his, something so cunning that only a master of intelligence could think of it. He vowed to be ready to move against the American when the time came. The head of Source saw the wink, and returned it. Strangely he added another sign. It was his palm on the inside of the station chief's hand.

"Driver, to the Tower of London," said Philliston. He moved from the rear seat to the little pull-up seat just behind the driver facing the back. There was blood on a few of the men crushed there. One of them still pretended not to recognize him, as was the order with any secret personnel like himself. A bit silly, Philliston thought. The American seemed to sit without a chair. As the car lurched over the roads, everyone else seemed to bounce but the American.

"She's in the Tower of London?"

"Of course. Excellent safe house. Has been since 1066," said Lord Philliston.

"That's a tourist attraction, isn't it?" asked Remo.

"Whole bloody island is a tourist attraction," said Lord Philliston. "If we weren't using Philliston Hall as headquarters, we'd be bloody well selling tickets to it."

"Why are you holding back information from your allies?" said Remo.

"Everybody holds back information from everybody

else," said Lord Philliston. "Don't take it personally, please. Personally I would give you anything." He ran a tongue along his lower lip.

Brilliant portrayal of a flaming fag, thought the station chief. And the American just may be suckered in. But why is he giving away the location of safe house eleven?

"Are you aware that we all may be burning up in the sun's unfiltered rays if we don't go by nuclear holocaust first? Did you know that? Does it mean anything to you guys?"

"You are taking things personally," said Lord Philliston.

"I always take the end of the world personally," said Remo. "I am personally in it. So is everything I love personally in it. Also some things I don't like."

"What's this about filtered sun? Unfiltered?" asked the colonel.

"Ozone. Without that ozone shield no one could survive. I am trying to trace the source of a weapon that threatens it. I would appreciate your cooperation. Dr. O'Donnell was running the test on this side of the Atlantic. Now, why are you people withholding information from us?"

"Ozone? How are they doing that?" said the station chief.

Remo tried to remember whether it was fluorocarbons or fluorides, or spray cans, or what.

"We'll find out when we get there, all right?" he said.

All the way to London, his men listened to Lord Guy Philliston portray a flaming fag in love with a brute. It was shameful and disgraceful, but every one of them knew he was doing it for England. Everyone except the station chief, who sat on Lord Philliston's other side and continuously had to protect the zipper on his fly.

7

The message was clear, but brief. The American had not been misled in Great Britain. According to the fragments of information received in Moscow, the American was at this very moment outside the gates of the Tower of London, the perfect safe house he was not supposed to find. How he'd gotten there was not explained. Whether he realized the woman was being held at he Tower was not mentioned. Only the short notification of danger came through to British desk, KGB Moscow.

It came with a message equally brief, this from the psychological officer. The American woman was about to tell them everything.

The time had come to wrap all this up. KGB British desk Moscow immediately sent back a message regarding the American: "Put him down."

He was to be killed, despite all the ranting and raving from that old revolutionary leader Zemyatin, who seemed strangely concerned with the danger of one man. The KGB had more and better killers at its disposal today.

Very shortly, the American nuisance would be removed and the woman would lead them to everything they needed.

Kathy O'Donnell knew nothing of the messages going across the Atlantic or that someone was coming to rescue her. She didn't want to be rescued.

Until this day, she realized, she had not known real happiness. She was in a room whose floors and walls were stone, on a rough bed, with a man who really excited her. How he did it, she was not sure, but she didn't care. The excitement had started during the experiment at Malden and just hadn't stopped. It was wonderful, and she would do practically anything to keep it going.

Even as the rough hands pinched the soft parts of her body and the cruel mouth laughed, she remembered what had happened at the Malden site, where she met this Russian fellow. Perhaps he was the first real man she had ever known.

One of her hired technicians had passed out. The animals were weeping in delicious pain. And she, of course, was coolly pretending that nothing was the matter as the ozone shield began closing itself above the burned field.

There were looks of horror on all the technicians' faces. Some punk rockers with purple hair and yellow-painted faces even threw up. But one man standing nearby was watching her and the animals closely.

He alone showed only mild interest. His face stood out like a white mask in a black night. Here was everyone else squinting, and turning their heads away, and there he stood as though watching a curious animal in a zoo.

"Doesn't this bother you?" asked Dr. O'Donnell.

He looked puzzled. "What is to bother?" he responded in a thick Russian accent. He had a face like steel with slits of Slavic eyes. Even through his thick black facial hair, a sure loss for a razor, she could see scars. People had wounded this man. But what, she wondered, had he done to others? He had that sort of face. He was just under six feet tall and carried the massive presence of a tank.

"It doesn't bother you to see animals suffer?"

"People make more noise," he said.

"Really? Have you ever seen one burned like that puppy over there?"

"Yes. I have seen them cloaked in oil and burning. I have seen them with their bellies on the ground and their heads rolling along gangways as their bodies quivered uselessly above. I have seen it all."

There was a bit of confusion. First someone told the man that this was not his post. Then someone else said to leave him alone. They were getting results. Kathy O'Donnell didn't care. She had a question she absolutely had to have answered. Where had he seen them like that?

"All over," he answered. And she knew without his saying a word that he had been the one who had done those things. She asked him what he was doing here in Malden. He didn't answer. She asked if he would like to go somewhere with her. She saw his eyes undress her. She knew the answer was yes, even though he said he would have to ask someone. She saw him in a little conference with some men. She didn't care. He might be a policeman. He might be anything. The excitement boiled within her, and she felt that for the first time since childhood she did not have to disguise anything. She did not have to say how sorry she was when someone had an accident. She did not have to cluck her tongue at disaster. She could have what she really enjoyed with this man.

She did not know, of course, that the man was a minor functionary in a larger plan, that he was just there for muscle if it were needed. She did not know that he was being ordered to attend to her, and take her somewhere. She knew that whatever came, she could deal with it. Men were never a problem. Anything involving men was something she could handle, especially this man, and the way his eyes had played first on her breasts and then lowered.

"Come. Let us go," he said when he returned. "We will have romantic date, yes?"

"I think so," she said. And then to the technicians she had hired:

"Be back in a while."

And she was off with the Russian. He drove a car rather clumsily, perhaps because his eyes were only occasionally on the road.

"Tell me," she said, "about the first man you ever killed."

Dimitri said it was not a big thing. He said it while churning down a British country road, one of those narrow strips meant for horses or race-car drivers.

"You are doing experiment there, yes?"

"Yes. What was it like? How did it feel to know you had actually killed someone?"

"I felt nothing."

"Was it with a gun?" asked Kathy.

"Yes," said Dimitri.

"A big gun? With a big bullet?" she asked.

"Rifle."

"Far away?"

"No. Close."

"Did you see him bleed?" she asked. Her voice was a soft sexy breath.

"He bled."

"How? Where?"

"In the stomach. Why does beautiful woman like you care about something like that?" Dimitri did not add that he was chosen for his job precisely because these things meant nothing to him. His was not considered an important job. It did not require brains. The men with brains went on to become thinkers behind desks. He was a foot soldier in the intelligence war. With this beautiful American woman he had lucked out. He might even have a chance at the fun of things instead of breaking arms or shooting off heads. He wanted to get her to a bedroom. He wanted to talk of love, and if not of love then at least unclothed bodies. Still he had been ordered to switch plans and escort her to the safe house instead of providing backup muscle, as it was called.

He was told that if he could, he should ask questions about the experiment, but not press the matter. There were others who knew the intelligent questions to ask.

"When the victim bled—was it a lot? Like all over the floor?" asked the woman.

"No. It was outside. He fell down."

"And then?"

"And then he was put down."

"With a bullet?"

"Yes."

"In the head? In the mouth? Did you do it in the mouth?"

"No. The head."

"Would you kill for me?" she asked. He could feel her breath on his ear. He thought that if he were to feel her tongue, he might discharge at the wheel.

"What is crazy question like that?"

"Would you?"

"You are beautiful woman. Why do you ask crazy things? Let us talk about what you do back in Malden."

"I do lots of things. What do you do?"

"I drive," said the man called Dimitri.

All the way into London he could get nothing from her, so he did not press. She wanted to know details of his killings. Since he did not mention names or places, he assumed the details she wanted would be all right. They were not anything another intelligence agency would want to know, nothing to do with where, or why. She wanted the intimate details of groans and sizes of wounds and how long something took. Was it big? Was it small? Was it hard?

In London, he bought tickets to the Tower of London, like any tourist. It was not a tower. It had been a royal castle at one time, and later became the premier prison where the British liked to behead their old enemies of the state, or the crown as they called it.

Dimitri was not privileged to know exactly how his commanders had done this, but they had taken over crucial points in the many battlements and individual towers of the castle. He was to enter by the Lion Tower, cross the soil-filled moat once deep with water from the Thames, pass the Byward Tower and turn left at Traitor's Gate.

At the Bloody Tower he was to wait until he got a signal from a window. It could be a hand. It could be a handkerchief. Then he was to walk toward the large Tudor building called the Queen's House. He entered with other tourists and the woman. But where everyone else followed the Beefeater Guards to the right, he went toward an unmarked door to the left, where there was a descending stone staircase.

Kathy O'Donnell saw all of this. She knew they wanted something from her. But she wanted more from them. The experiment could wait. Life was too delicious at the moment. She did not care about planning. She only cared about this very moment.

She was left in a stone room with a large bed and a bear

rug. It had to be at least fifteen degrees colder in here than it had been outside. Dimitri returned in a bathrobe with a bottle of brandy.

Immediately she realized that his questions were really a psychological test. He didn't know it but she did. His other questions had to do with the experiment. On the psychological test she told the truth. She wondered if people were watching. She wondered if they would watch her make love. She wondered if she would make them want her, if they would suffer for not having her. She made up stories about the test, leading this Russian fellow on. And the gist of her response was that if he wanted more information, he had better entertain her. He took off his pants. She laughed. That was not what she wanted.

"What do you want, beautiful lady?"

"What you do best," she said. It was night. They had been there a long time. She was sure now that people were hidden somewhere in the walls.

"Kill one of them," she said, nodding to the walls. "If you want me."

At that point Dimitri might have killed the head of the KGB for this woman. But there was still that discipline wrought by years of living in a regime that depended on fear. He did not know that outside the very walls at this moment was Remo—the answer to everyone's fondest wishes. Remo did not care that the Tower of London was closed for the night or that it had been closed at this time for the last four centuries.

"I'm coming in," said Remo. His carload of British security and military people was parked just behind him. Lord Philliston was clearly blowing kisses. His words were heard as distinctly as he was seen by a command center. A console copied from American football games showed screens to video cameras set all around this old Norman structure. The American was on screen seven, set above an old Plantagenet standard of gold-and-crimson cloth, lion rampant. Lord Philliston was on screen one.

"Our orders are to put him down now," said someone standing behind the men at the monitors. He had just gotten word back from KGB Moscow. He wore a headset.

He also got other orders, these from the room where Anne Boleyn had awaited Henry VIII's royal divorce, which separated king from mate, queen from head.

"We'll have Dimitri kill him, giving the sociopath her bloodshed, and then we'll get our information," came the voice through the headset to the man behind the monitors.

"Let him find her in the Queen's House. And get Lord Philliston the hell out of there. It would take us years to replace him."

"He doesn't seem to want to leave the American," said the man on the monitor.

"I don't care. He'll leave when the American is sausage. The American goes down now," said the KGB security chief to the man on the monitor.

Outside the gate, with precise British rectitude, an employee of Her Majesty informed Remo that his presence would be perfectly acceptable inside the Tower at this late hour.

"I've got friends," said Remo, glancing back at the car. "Can they come too?"

"I'm sorry," said the woman ticket seller. "I'm afraid they can't."

"That's all right," said Remo just as pleasantly, "they are."

"I am terribly sorry, but they will have to stay." The woman smiled. She was polite. She politely asked the yeoman warders in red tunics with Her Majesty's seal upon their breasts to escort Remo inside the Tower of London. They wore squarish black hats and were called Beefeaters. Remo didn't quite know why these men in particular got that name because everyone on this island seemed to smell of beef-eating.

"And I am even sorrier," said Remo, "but I've got to keep one of these guys." He looked back at Lord Philliston. Britain's top secret agent blew him a kiss.

"Well, sir, I am terribly, terribly sorry but you can't keep anyone. Not in the Tower. These are special instructions I have received from the administration to allow in only you." Remo liked the way the British were always incredibly, cheerfully polite.

Unfortunately, he pointed out that he had found Lord Philliston and that he was his, and he wasn't going to the Tower complex without him, and he certainly was going in the Tower complex.

Lord Philliston rolled down his window.

"I love it when you talk so butch," said Britain's prime intelligence defense. Remo nodded him out of the car and Lord Philliston swished from the rear of the limousine, right to Remo's side.

"Not so close," said Remo.

For the first time in three hundred years, the Beefeaters, yeoman warders of the Tower of London, were called into action. Their orders: Keep the American from bringing the Briton inside. In brief, rescue the Briton, who apparently did not want to be rescued.

The yeoman warders advanced with pike, pick, ax, and bare hand in square formation. Afterward they would all swear the American was a mirage. He had to be. He not only moved through them as though they were air, but dragged the man they were supposed to rescue with him.

Remo had Lord Philliston by the sleeve. Lord Philliston was giggling and laughing and trying to skip. Remo did not feel comfortable with Lord Philliston skipping, so he kept him off balance.

Lord Philliston pointed out each turn. Dark ravens as large as eagles cawed menacingly. A few lights of the keepers shone soft and yellow, little dots of warmth in a cold stone fortress.

Remo sensed that they were in someone's sights. It could have been a spear or a rifle. The sensation was the same. It was not alarm. Alarm was a function of fear, and that tightened the muscles. It was a quietness about the place. Anyone could feel it, but few would listen to it. Often people would remember how sudden and surprising an attack was, when in reality it should never have been that surprising. Humans were equipped to know these things, unless they were trained to respect their senses, they would never perceive them.

Now, entering the Tudor-style Queen's House, Remo felt that quietness close in on him.

Guy Philliston showed Remo the door that led to the absolute safest safe house in all England. The special dungeon of Henry VIII.

A broadsword came down first, clanging into rock at Remo's side. But he was soon beneath it and beyond it, smoothly, even while he wondered why the large man was using a sword instead of a gun. A second man dropped from a concealed loft just above Remo's head. He dropped, kicking with steel-tipped shoes and stabbing with a sharp dirk, a nasty little dagger good for infighting in tavern and alley.

Lord Philliston stepped back. He was hoping this wasn't going to be messy. Someone behind him was trying to drag him away. When he saw one of the attackers lose an arm in a gusher of blood, he realized that this was going to make a rather untidy mess. He scampered into a stone doorway adjacent to the passage as another four men came hurtling down into the attactive American.

Lord Philliston's contact was motioning for him. Quickly, he stepped inside, and closed the door quietly behind him as the battle went on down the steps toward the room where they had the American woman.

"You almost got killed, Lord Philliston," said a short dark man, squat as a bale of hay. "We wouldn't want anything to happen to you."

"I suppose it would be useless to ask you to let him live."

"I am afraid we cannot do that," said the contact. "You must get out of here quickly and let us take care of this."

"You really are becoming quite British. Do whatever you want and then say you're sorry about that."

"A thousand apologies, my lord."

"He was beautiful."

"There are many beautiful men in your country."

"He was special," said Lord Philliston with a sigh. The Cold War was hell.

Remo knew Lord Philliston was gone and did not bother to stop him. He did not stop him because he heard a woman groan just around the curving stone staircase. And he wasn't sure what it was. It was not pain. And it was not fear. It certainly was not joy.

What he did not realize was that it was practiced. Kathy O'Donnell had been practicing this groan since her freshman year at college. Her roommates had told her how. You made sure you started the groan while the man was working toward his climax. Often, if you groaned properly, that would precipitate his release. And then it would be over sooner. Kathy O'Donnell gave Dimitri this groan as his face contracted and his body tensed, and then he was done. Tragically, he had been no better than the others after all.

"Wonderful, darling," whispered Kathy to the man who had shown so much potential, and because of that been such a failure.

She heard a commotion heading toward the room. A man came hurtling in against the stone wall with a knife still in his hand. He hit like old china in a burlap bag. You could feel his bones break. Blood shot out of his mouth in one spurt and nothing moved.

Now Kathy's body began to tingle the way it had at Malden. Dimitri moved off her, steadying himself, reaching for a lamp. Another body came into the room, head-first. The body followed an eighth of a second later. She felt her thighs become hot, sticky hot. Her nipples tightened. Two hard slaps against stone, unmistakably people being crushed. An impossibly tantalizing caress seized her, and drove her beyond control as she lay there alone on the bed.

A somewhat thin man emerged from the passageway. Dimitri's thick muscled body had him by at least fifty pounds. Dimitri squatted, waving the heavy brass lamp, then he charged, a nude man coming in for the kill. She could see Dimitri's muscles perfectly drive the heavy mace-like lamp into the thin man, but then, catching all his force, the thin man flipped Dimitri like a frisbee into a wall. The crack made his back into a rubber band and he fell without a twitch. He was dead.

And then the man spoke to her.

"Dr. O'Donnell," said Remo.

The answer was a groan. Not like the ones before. Kathy O'Donnell, on hearing Remo's voice at that moment, suddenly found out what all her friends were taking about. She had just enjoyed her first orgasm.

Finally with her body glowing in completed ecstasy, Kathy said, with the most girlish of smiles: "Yes."

"We've got to get out of here. Are you all right?" said Remo.

All right? She was magnificent. She was delirious. She was exalted, thrilled, triumphant, ecstatic.

"Yes," said Kathy weakly. "I think so."

"What were they doing to you?"

"I don't know."

"Can you walk? I'll carry you, if you're having trouble. I've got to get you out of here."

"I think so," she said. She reached out weakly and thought she was pretending to be unable to stand. But the man said:

"You're all right. Get dressed. Let's go."

So he knew her body, she realized.

"Yes. I am all right."

She noticed that his movements appeared slow but he got things done quickly. She thought he might be aroused by her nude body, but she sensed he was only as interested as one might be if a platter of hors d'oeuvres was served to someone nibbling all day. He might take her, but he wasn't thrilled. He said his name was Remo. He said he had come to rescue her. He said terrible things were happening because of an experiment in which she was involved.

"No," said Kathy. She covered her mouth as though shocked. She knew how to pretend innocence because she had had a lifetime of practice.

A noise came down the passageway. And then she saw what this man could do. It was no accident of ferocity that had gotten him through all those armed men.

With a slow breathing balance he seemed to run his hand along a five-foot-high stone that must have weighed three to four tons. Then he simply cocked a knee into it, and it seemed to come out of the wall on him, resting on his knee. But the strange thing about it was that it seemed so abso-

lutely un-strange. It seemed so incredibly normal the way
the stone rested on the vertical thrust of his body. He
simply plugged the passageway.

Only when the stone went in did she realize the massive
force Remo had exerted. Several stone stairs splintered
into dust.

"That was the only way out," said Kathy.

"Shh. It'll work," said the man.

"What will work? You've plugged our only escape,"
whispered Kathy.

"C'mon. Shh," said Remo.

"We can't get out of here," she whispered. What a fool.
Was this Remo like all the others after all?

"I want to get you out of here. I could go up those steps
and make it out in one piece, but you couldn't. So shut
up."

"I don't know what you're doing," said Kathy. Beyond
the heavy stone she heard noises. Men were beginning to
heave at the stone.

"Do you want to know?" said the man. He guided her
to a side of the stone, not even bothering to look at her,
but concentrating on the blocked passageway.

"Yes," she said.

Remo gave it to her exactly as he had learned it.

"What language is that?" she said angrily.

"Korean."

"Would you mind translating it?"

"Sure, but it loses something in the translation. It means
'the strong flower never grows to its food but lets its food
come to it.' "

"That makes absolutely no sense," said Kathy, putting
on her blouse and smoothing her skirt.

"I told you it lost something in translation," said
Remo.

He moved her against the wall, and then when the bodies
started to drop, she realized what he had been talking
about. To move the stone, several men in the passageway
had to put their shoulders into it. And when the stone came
rumbling out, she saw that the men had guns. Those guns
might have killed her. When she observed the smooth

speed of Remo's execution of the guards, she realized he might have easily escaped the gunfire. What he had done was let the danger to her mass itself outside the stone and come in with a rush, clearing the tunnel of danger to her. He took her quickly up the passage where only a single last guard stood at the upper level. It was a yeoman warder who did not know who was who, apparently, but who did see a stranger and, in stout British tradition, attacked same stranger. Also in tradition, he gave his life for Queen and country.

Outside, after they had run through the squares and tunnels, Remo found the car was gone. Eluding several bobbies, they finally came to rest in a charming Italian restaurant off Leicester Square. There, Kathy asked Remo how he knew his plan would work.

He seemed puzzled by that question.

"They were . . ." He didn't quite have an English word for it, but the closest ones were: "too anxious. Too bunched up. They were set on going in. I guess when the tunnel was blocked they had to surmise they couldn't get in and forced it."

"Yes. But how did you know they were going to do that?"

"I don't know. I just knew. Look, grab a bite. And let's get to the source of your experiment. Do you know the whole world may be wiped out?"

I already have been, thought Kathy, looking at this magnificent dark-eyed man who killed so well and easily and smoothly.

"No," she said. "That's awful."

Then she heard how their fluorocarbon stream had somehow panicked another country, and was believed by some American agency to be threatening to destroy the world by removing the entire ozone shield. She could have told him that that danger was past. She could have told him they had solved that problem with the short duration of the shield opening. The blue light that bothered this man was really the shield closing again.

Rather, she told him that all she knew about the experiment was that it came from a company in America. She gave him the phony cover address she had given to the British.

"No good," said Remo. "That's a phony."

"Oh, my lord. These people are evil," said Kathy O'Donnell. But there was not much tension in her voice. She was as warm and content as a milk-full kitten by a warm winter stove.

Chemical Concepts might as well be on the moon, she thought. "Do you remember anything about the people who hired you?" he asked. He didn't eat the food. Kathy sucked contentedly on a breadstick.

"I remember a bit. You look married."

"Not married. What were they like?"

"Never been married?"

"No. Were they Americans? What did they tell you about themselves? What didn't they tell you about themselves?"

She picked a name at random. Someone far away, someone who it might take some time getting to. She also picked one of the deadliest men in the world. He was in a jungle somewhere in South America.

"Do you like jungles, Remo? I hate jungles."

"Which jungle? Lots of jungles in the world."

"It was a jungle. You know, if you don't like Italian food we can leave. What do you eat?" she asked.

"I eat rice and sometimes duck entrails and sometimes certain fish eyes."

"What does it taste like?"

"Tastes like shit. What do you think it tastes like?" said Remo. She identified the jungle. She identified the man positively.

"He promised me it would be for the good of mankind," said Kathy O'Donnell. She said she could lead Remo to him. She did not know what they would do when they got there. But at least she would have Remo for a flight across the Atlantic.

A sign of hope. Remo had phoned in and not only gotten the person in charge of the experiment in Maldon, but had found the whereabouts of at least one machine.

It was not the most secure rope to hold a world together, but it was a rope. And there was no one better to put an end to that machine than the man who was on his way to South America. If only someone could get into Russia and somehow find out why they were linking a first strike buildup to that machine, Smith would feel that both fronts were being covered. But in Russia, America was limited so far to normal means. Normal means could get all manner of technical information, such as missile counts and the kinds of missiles being deployed. This was the stuff of wiring and electrodes. But the why of things, the human factor of things, was as mysterious to the CIA as the farthest side of the dark universe.

Only Chiun's Oriental formula, that Smith had never quite understood, explained in equally unexplainable terms why Russia did things. But Chiun was even more unreachable now than Remo. In desperation, Smith again attempted to work the formula translated into numbers, and then back into English. Often, when all else failed, this strange combination of mysticism and mathematics worked.

And sometimes it didn't. The translation came out "the bear hides in the cave." Was Russia afraid? Was fear prompting those new irresponsible missiles? But why were the Russians so incredibly afraid of America when the ozone shield was something that protected everyone?

And then Chiun got through again. The phone connect to Pyongyang had been reactivated.

"Chiun, we have a problem about the bear and the cave . . ."

"They shall breathe their blood in their vile throats that have dared profane thy magnificence," said Chiun. "But first a humble matter. You of course, forwarded my message to Remo."

"I did give it to him when he made contact."

"Good. Then he will understand. I can be reached through the North Korean embassy in France."

"Are you working for them now?"

"Only for the greater glory of your throne, Emperor Smith. This is a personal matter."

"We can increase shipments. The future of the world . . ."

"Is the past, O Graciousness. I am defending the past. What did Remo say when you told him about the passage? Did he read it? Did he say anything?"

"I secured the book. It was a school textbook for North Korea. I read it to him."

"In English?"

"I had to. I had it translated. I don't know Korean."

"And he said?"

"He said, 'Anything else?' "

"That was all? Just 'Anything else?' "

"Yes."

"It loses everything in the translation."

"Look, whatever anyone is paying you, we will pay you more."

"Can you give me yesterday?"

"I don't understand," said Smith.

"Can you give me Alexander the Great making his Greek phalanx stand in salute? Can you give me the dipped banners of the moguls, or the homage of the shogun? Can you give me the Roman legions stopping in Syria because an emperor was told that his foot soldiers could take not one more step east? Can you give me knights giving way in a court, and king and emperor saying in tongues, some now unspoken by human lips: 'You Sinanju have found the triumph of man'?"

"Chiun, we can give what we can give. And it will be anything you ask."

"Get the original text to Remo."

"And then you will perform this service for us?"

"As surely as the lotus petal kisses the dark smooth waters of night."

"That is yes, then?" said Smith.

And Chiun had to wearily explain that rarely had a stronger yes been expressed anywhere. It was a yes worthy of such a great one as Emperor Harold W. Smith.

"Well, good then. Thank you. I suppose," said Smith.

This one, thought Chiun, is especially slow in understanding. If he had time, Chiun would have tried to fathom what was behind the white's plan to "save tomorrow for the world," as he called it. Was it finally the secret maneuverings of a genius like Charlemagne of the Franks, playing one nation against the other until his desire for world conquest manifested itself? Or was Smith just crazed with his talk of secrecy and saving the world? If he had no intention of conquering it, why did he want to save all of it? Chiun certainly would not care if Bayonne, New Jersey, disappeared from the face of the earth. Why should Smith care about Sinanju or Pyongyang?

Only briefly did Chiun, Master of Sinanju, contemplate such puzzles. For he was in Paris of the old Frankish nation now called France, civilized to these many years since the Romans had called it Gaul, and trod their crude nailed sandals upon its dusty roads.

Chiun was about to give this land its first great history. Paris would be known forever as the city where Chiun, the Great Chiun hopefully, had recovered the treasure of Sinanju.

8

It was the rarest auction ever held by the House of Arnaud. And since it was the rarest auction in the House of Arnaud, it was the rarest in Paris. And if it were the rarest in Paris, then most naturally it was the rarest in the world.

Only the most select bidders had been invited to the great marble building on Rue de Seine, District Seven.

On either side, the posh art galleries had closed their doors in respect for what was going to happen this day.

One hundred gold Alexanders were for sale. The gold alone would have been worth a half-million strong American dollars. But these coins, 2,500 years old, were as shiny as if minted yesterday. And rarer yet, no other coin ever saved from antiquity bore such markings.

On one side was the unmistakable strong head of Alexander, seen so often in brass, gold, and silver; the flowing locks, the proud nose, the sensuous lips. Alexander the Great, Conqueror of the World.

But on the other side, instead of the sign of the city, such as Athens' owl, was a phalanx of Greek foot soldiers, their spears raised in salute. And Greek lettering for a word unknown in the Greek tongue. The sound could be translated roughly as:

"Sinadu."

The first thought of some was that it was a forgery. Yet scholars identified the tooth-edged die markings as typically Greek. The head of Alexander was also typical. So was the lettering of the strange word.

And then, of course, there was the history itself. The hundred-gold-coin tribute minted by Alexander as he approached India. What the tribute was for, what god of the East he was honoring, history did not tell. But he had minted the coins, and there were one hundred and no more with the saying in Greek. Here was the hundred.

Ordinarily the House of Arnaud would announce a major auction of which even the most famous of treasures were only one object. But such was the magnificence of this collection of one hundred coins that they were given the unique privilege of being the only item on the agenda for the day. Not even the *Mona Lisa* had had that honor.

The auction was scheduled for three in the afternoon. An invitation to this event quickly became the most-sought-after social item in Paris and much of Western Europe.

Even more intriguing was the fact that the owner was listed simply as anonymous. Of course, this famous anonymous was Valery, Comte de Lyon. The joke was that he was the most famous anonymous in all France.

The Count of Lyon was head of SDEC, Service de Documentation Extérieure et de Contre. While most of the rest of the world had heard of the famous Deuxième, it was the SDEC that ran the most formidable opposition to Russia in the world of espionage. The count had beaten them time and again, and lived on their death list, everyone knew.

It was said among the knowledgeable that to remove the

count would be more valuable to an enemy of France than seizing Paris.

Therefore no one, of course, expected him to show up at the auction. And he didn't, for his whereabouts were always secret. The questions abounded. Were these coins in his family for centuries? Where had he gotten them? Could they have been some bribe?

These questions were not entertained long, however, among the fashionable elite entering the marble floors of the House of Arnaud.

For one, any financial dealings of a man in such a delicate position were always secretly investigated by the government. And many in this audience knew what the investigation had found because they ran the government.

First, the package had been mailed from a Paris post office to the postal drop used by the SDEC. It carried a fraudulent French return address. Since there had been several attempts at destroying the SDEC, all packages were opened by robotic arms in a bombproof room.

Then the logical question posed to the investigators was, had the Count of Lyon accepted a bribe and had it mailed to himself?

Possibly. Except every paper and package he handled was counterinvestigated, because the French, like the Russians, had enough experience in the affairs of men to understand that they were not dealing with a reliable species.

The count had probably not sent the package to himself.

Third, had he accepted a bribe and used this as a cover? Maybe. But why a bribe of this nature? Why a bribe of such rare and perfect coins as to become a major item of Paris gossip?

The conclusion was that the coins, as the accompanying note had said, were a gift from someone for the Count's service to France. The paper and ink were French. The handwriting—printing—was somewhat shaky, as if done by someone not used to French script.

The count immediately had the package shipped to Arnaud for auction.

"I have no time to waste men guarding one hundred coins," he had said.

Now, under a glass case, the gold Alexanders sat on one hundred small velvet pillows. Each bidder was allowed to pass by the case twice. Some lingered.

"It is strange. I have the feeling they were just paid out this morning. They're so real. So modern," said one woman. Her bosom was raised in the modern fashion by her white silk gown. Diamonds of inordinate brilliance graced her neck. When she looked down the rows of Alexanders, each on its own velvet pillow, she would have traded all her jewels and all her wealth, including the gown and what was in it, to own them.

"It is like owning eternity," said one French official.

The bidding floor was ten million dollars. It was established by an Arab whose main contribution to the economy of the world was having been born over a lot of oil and then having figured out how to gouge the rest of the world for it.

The figure was topped immediately by a million. This from a man who had figured out how to transfer thoughts more quickly from one computer chip to another.

And that was topped, with applause from the audience, of course, by a Frenchman whose family had owned most of a province since Charlemagne forced illiterate bandit kings into a grand nation of Franks.

At twenty-two million American dollars the coins were sold, bid final. A Texas financier, who felt something that fine ought to be his, had made the winning bid. He was planning to make the "little fellers," as he called them, into cufflinks.

"Give 'em out to fifty friends, but shoot, I don't have no fifty friends. Ain't fifty people in the world I know who are worth a set of them little fellers."

Applause echoed through the great hall of the House of Arnaud. Even the auctioneer applauded. The guards stood at attention. They too knew they were part of something important. It was history.

And then amid the applause came the high squeaky voice in a French so ancient that it resembled Latin tinged with Gallic.

"Woe be to you, Franks whose fathers were of the

Gaulish race. Heed now a warning. These coins are not yours, but meager tribute to ones who deserved them. Do not traffic in stolen goods but save your lives if you do not have the decency to save your honor.''

Guards ran into closets looking for the voice. Detection devices searched out hidden microphones. The best of France in that marble bidding hall looked for the voice and found nothing.

Later the Texan, ashen-faced, would say he happily gave the coins back to the real owner, but would not describe the owner. He would repeat over and over again:

''What ain't mine, ain't mine, and I was durned glad to give it back.''

But the Master of Sinanju that day of infamy in Paris did not care who had bought the coin tribute to Sinanju, did not care which thief passed goods to which.

The goods were Sinanju. They would be reclaimed.

What the Master sought that day among the Franks was he who had dared defile the House of Sinanju. And the answer to that was not in the coin. The answer came later that night when the proceeds were tallied.

The chief accountant prepared the check for the director of the House of Arnaud. Since the Count of Lyons' whereabouts were always a secret, the director would not even have the joy of mailing such a huge sum. It was to be given in a plain white envelope to a squad of SDEC. The plan was, of course, after such a public display involving the director of the SDEC, to move the check itself through a warren of what were called street baffles.

In simpler terms, if anyone wished to follow that check, he had better be prepared to lose a multitude of agents because each baffle was designed to strip anyone following the squad.

It was a brilliant maneuver, which at best would act as a magnet for any enemy agents operating in France. At worst, the check would be delivered unharmed and untraced to the Comte de Lyon, director of the SDEC.

What they did not know was that this maneuver was as new as the King of Crete, the Ojab of Odab, the Emperor Theodosius. In fact, it was more traditional than deceptive, and the Master of Sinanju easily kept pace with the check through the darkened streets of the French capital.

For this night, he had chosen a black velvet kimono with darkened purple lines to smother the light. His shoes were sandals of soft wood, cut round and smooth for the perfection of friction. Because, too, this was Paris, Chiun had swept his hair back, but under a dark night cap, it was raised like a cone.

It was an ensemble to bring the French to their knees.

The squad passed through three baffles and saw no one. A younger member mentioned that he felt a frightening presence, but he was ignored, and told if he mentioned such immature fears again he would be put on report.

When they were sure no one was following, they delivered the envelope to another squad which took it to the director himself.

"Monsieur le Comte, we are here," said the leader of the second squad. All of them had every right to feel secure. This old mansion on Rue St. Jean was a gigantic electronic trap put together with the brilliance that had made the SDEC the only real counterweight in all of Europe to the Russians.

How many agents had died in the streets of Paris looking to eliminate the director? How many times had the SDEC stymied the triumphant legions of the KGB? If any enemy did find this house, he would only find his death.

"The returns from your gift, director," said the leader of the squad. Already rumors throughout Paris had told of the millions paid for the coins, even before the envelope had made its way through the city streets.

The leader and the squad waited for their commander to open the sealed letter. As a treat for his "boys," as he liked to call the most dangerous men in France, de Lyon opened the letter to show the size of the check.

It was a fortune, but such was the inner calm of this French aristocrat that he had to force a happy surprise. He did not care. If it weren't for minor inconveniences, he would not have minded being penniless.

Valery, Comte de Lyon, was one of those rare persons to walk upon the face of the earth who was always successful.

He had overthrown governments, performed eliminations around the world for France, and whenever it was in the interest of France, Valery de Lyon stopped the Russians every time.

It was not, of course, in the interest of France to see Russia stopped all the time. That was America's problem.

The SDEC was inordinately successful and de Lyon was happy for that same reason. Alone in this world, de Lyon loved his work. He knew many of the KGB by name, not because it was his job but because, like boys would admire soccer stars, de Lyon admired the perfect coup, the successful assassination, the theft of state documents done in such a way that the other country did not even know they were missing.

Every time de Lyon sent France up against another power, he imbued his men with respect for the enemy's deeds. He followed details of secret missions in a way a father might inquire about his son's first job. He did not take work home, because it was not work. Parties were work. His stables on the estate in the southern province were work. His wife was work. Even an occasional affair was work.

Fun was observing hand-to-hand fighting by his selected operatives in the sand pits outside of Marseilles, where any blood spilled would be soaked up instantly.

Fun was watching a good Danish counterintelligence operation wither in Eastern Europe because it lacked support. The joy was picking the month it would founder.

De Lyon came by this love of his work not by some quirk but by blood. His ancestors had been the most ferocious of Frankish knights, the first royalty to side with Napoleon. They had been warriors not by greed of conquest, but by love of the fight.

Thus did de Lyon that dark night have to pretend joy before his men at the fortune coming his way. To this trim, arrogant noble, all the fortune meant was that he wouldn't have to worry about money for his lifetime, which was something he wouldn't worry about anyhow. But the men always liked the show.

"Twenty-two million American dollars. Hah, it will pay

for a liter of wine or two, or a woman or two. Or if it is the right woman, one woman on a shopping spree for an afternoon.''

The men laughed. De Lyon was about to order drinks for them to salute their good fortune, a ten-minute act of grace before he could get back to an interesting African situation on his desk. Then he saw it.

At first he was not sure he saw anything. It was a darkness in the hallway, moving beyond the open door. Since he did not hear it, he assumed it was a fleeting aberration of his eye. Certainly nothing could move in this house without his own men knowing and reporting it.

But the wine did not come. He sent one of his men out to hurry along the steward. The man did not return. De Lyon checked his buzzer system. It worked, but no one answered it.

"Come, there is something strange going on," said de Lyon. The two operatives unholstered their machine pistols. They made a sandwich of their commander as they left the room, looking for any possible trouble.

It was in a hallway that de Lyon finally saw the darkness. The darkness was a robe, and the count's men fell like pitiful stalks of wheat to movements he could not even see. He only knew they had to have happened when the heads rolled on the hallway floor.

"You," said the apparition in a French so ancient that de Lyon had to translate from the older Latin. "Where is my treasure?"

De Lyon noticed the trunk of a nearby body twitch as the heart pumped out the last blood from the open neck. The head looked dumbly at the ceiling farther down the hall.

The apparition had the face of an Oriental. Its voice was high-pitched.

"I have stolen nothing," said de Lyon. Where were the guards? Where were the safety devices?

If he had not smelled his own fear on his breath, he would have thought he was dreaming. But could a person hear a language he did not understand in a dream?

"Franks steal everything. Where is the treasure?"

"I cannot help you," said de Lyon. He noticed that the

strokes this man had delivered were apparently so fast that the nerves in the dead man's hands, still on the machine pistol, had not been activated. A useless hand on a useless body on a useless gun. He stole a short look behind him. The trailing man had also been taken care of. Head gone.

De Lyon sensed that if he could reach that gun, he could put many bullets into the darkness before him. His sense of the fight was overcoming his initial fear. A de Lyon had been confronted. And de Lyons never lost.

He would have to get the gun in such a way as not to look as though he was attacking. There was a small derringer tucked inside his evening robe, but he chose to ignore that. He would use it for another purpose.

"One should not steal like a tawdry thief, Frank," said the man. De Lyon saw the face was old.

"How did you get in here?"

"A thief's home is always a hovel. You may tell me where the treasure is now."

"I would love to," said de Lyon. "May I give you my personal gun as a sign of surrender? It is quite valuable and a treasure itself."

"You have sold my coins. Where is the rest of my treasure?" said Chiun. He would use this man to carry it back to his village. The House of Sinanju had not taken slaves for over three thousand years, but this Frank would be enslaved before being given over to someone else for the lowly task of execution. The House of Sinanju were assassins, not executioners.

"Ah, the rest. Of course. Please take this," said de Lyon. He handed over his derringer with one hand as he seemed to bow toward the darkness which now was clearly an old man in a black kimono. He would shoot off the stranger's knees, and then begin his own questioning.

The old man, for all his awesome talents, made a foolish move. He took the gun, exposing his midsection and allowing de Lyon to get the machine pistol with the other hand. In a motion so smooth as to be the envy of swordsmen from generations past, de Lyon put the machine pistol to the kimono and began firing.

It was a silent firing. The gun was broken. He started to

throw it to the floor, but the machine pistol would not throw. De Lyon had lost control of his hand. It was his hand, not the pistol, that was broken.

And then the pain began, a pain that knew his body better than he did. Pain that came when he lied, and left when he told the truth, and then pain that would not stop even when he told the truth.

"The coins were a gift. A gift. I do not know where they came from. Yes, millions of dollars' worth and yet a gift. We did not find out who sent them."

The man, of course, was telling the truth. That was the sadness of it. It was a thing to ponder. They were tribute coins from Alexander. Not enough to make up for all the good markets he ruined by removing his kings of the West to his control, the reason the young Greekling Alexander did have to die.

As, of course, did the Frankish lord who spoke the good French so badly.

He had dealt in stolen goods. And with his good hand, the Count of Lyon wrote out a promise that he regretted having dealt in the treasures of Sinanju. Then he was allowed to join his ancestors.

When the body was found, secrecy was immediately installed around the whole episode. SDEC's sister intelligence factions, the Deuxième, most noticeably investigated every aspect of the killings in the house. The fact that the check was not stolen. The strange manner of death of both de Lyon and his men.

They were sure, in their final report to the President, that there was a link between the sale of the coins and the death of the director of the SDEC, strange because so many in the international scene had tried to kill him, and now a peculiar personal matter had done him in.

They were sure it was the personal matter of the coins because the same strange word appeared both in the note and on the ancient coins themselves. The word was:

"Sinadu."

In the note, a Latin inscription. On the coin of Alexander, a Greek one.

* * *

Having recovered the coins, Chiun accepted the services of the North Korean government that flew him back to Pyongyang. At the airport was an honor guard led by Sayak Cang, the Pyongyanger who knew the true history of Korea.

There had been no calls, he reported, from the man called Remo, but the number established for the House of Sinanju had indeed been transferred to the man called Smith.

"And was there any other word? Did the man called Remo read your wonderful little truth?"

"The man called Smith gave no information about anything."

"He is white, you know," said Chiun. He said nothing else as he silently brought the coins by car to the village on the West Korea Bay. There in silence he returned the coins to the great house of many woods, the house that had held the tribute of centuries. And there he placed the coins in their corner, alone, a few pitiful coins in a very big house.

This house had been given to Chiun when his father knew that his time to pass the body into the earth had come. Chiun had spent all his life preparing to receive this house, preparing to pass it on properly. Even during the darkest times, when it looked as though there would be no one to pass the house on to, he had not despaired like this.

For he, Chiun, had lost all that had been gained; all the references in the scrolls of Sinanju to this treasure and the other were now cast in doubt because coin and ingot, gem and bullion, had vanished into the world.

Still and all, the reference to the Greekling with blond hair who ventured too close to the House of Sinanju could be proved again with the tribute coin.

But he who would one day have all of this was squandering his time and Sinanju-taught talents on unworthy causes. Chiun had lost both the treasure to pass on and the one who would value receiving it.

The House of Sinanju, if it was not dying, wished it was dying on that day of dark gloom on the chill shores of the West Korea Bay.

Chiun could feel tremors and then heard far-off explosions. Eventually even the villagers heard them, and with great fear they came to him, saying, "Protect us, O Master."

And Chiun turned them away, saying, "We have always protected you, but what have you done to protect the treasures we left in your care?"

He did not tell them it was just another war going on. Wars never came to Sinanju because generals were taught that they would not survive a battle, no matter who won.

The ground continued to shake and many planes roared overhead, dropping bombs on soldiers in gun emplacements. The battle went on until the morning when the guns on shore were silenced. And then the villagers came again up the path to the house where the Master was and they said:

"Master, Master, two submarines have come with your tribute. They are heavy-laden, and they seek thy presence."

"What color are the bearers?"

"White, the color of those who used to bring tribute."

"Is there a thin white man there with thick wrists?" said Chiun. He did not know how many could recognize Remo. Long noses and round eyes all tended to look alike to these good simple people.

"There are many whites."

Remo has come, thought Chiun. And while the house was empty still, there would now be two chasing the treasure. They had the coins, he and Remo would get the rest, would make the world respect the property of Sinanju. Who knew what all this public retribution might earn? Governments might bring back the golden age of assassinry, disbanding large expensive armies for the more civilized hand in the night.

Chiun moved quickly into the village and to the loading docks as the people parted for him. He looked on the two submarines. Remo was not there. Gold bullion was being off-loaded onto the dock that groaned under the weight. The white captain wanted to speak to him.

"What happened to the agreement with your government? We had to fight our way in here. We had to bring the fleet and bomb the shore batteries. What happened to our deal?"

"That is a minor diplomatic matter. I will fix it. Tell Remo I do not wish to speak to him. Tell him he cannot make up to me his desertion in an hour of need."

"Who?"

"Remo," said Chiun. "Tell him he cannot leave one day and expect to find me waiting for him with joy. I am coming down for my gold."

"Look, you have ten times the amount of gold ever delivered before, and one message. Contact someone called Smith. You know the number."

"I am going to take my gold and return to the house he should have loved from the very beginning. Tell Remo he is not welcome in Sinanju anymore. One must serve Sinanju to be welcome here."

"We don't have any Remo," said the white captain of the submarine. "Do you want us to drop the gold here on the wharf or carry it up to that warehouse you people keep?"

"Remo is not with you?" asked Chiun.

"No. No Remo. What do you want done with the gold?"

"Oh, whatever. Whatever."

"You will make the phone call to the Smith person?"

"Certainly," said Chiun, but his voice was as dreary as the bay. He walked slowly back through the village to the house.

He had lost the treasure of Sinanju, but more important, he had lost the person who should have cared about it. He had lost tomorrow as well as yesterday.

A child came to the door with a message. A great battle had taken place and Korea had lost. Still, there was a man who wished entrance to Sinanju, for the greater battle might yet be won. The man was Sayak Cang, and he entered the village bowing.

Chiun sat in the empty treasure house, his legs crossed, his eyes vacant as Cang talked. They had thought the extra submarine signaled an invasion, but now that they had seen it was tribute, they would allow future submarines in as before.

"For the tribute to Sinanju is a tribute to everything

proud in our great race." Thus spoke Sayak Cang before he gave the important information.

His intelligence network had found yet another who dared to sell the treasure of Sinanju. This time it was the modern form of the old Roman office, Pontifex Maximus.

The modern people called him pope.

"A Christian holy man," said Chiun.

"Yes. It is disgusting how their shamans add to material treasure already so great."

"Yes, holy men are sometimes not holy," said Chiun, who now knew who had really stolen the treasure. It explained why the Frankish knight had told the truth, and why people could move so freely into the village of Sinanju.

"The pope must die," said Sayak Cang, the Pyongyanger.

9

For the last fifty miles the roads were ice and rock and a vague outline that some other vehicle had been there before. That was called a road. Up ahead on the map, where Colonel Semyon Petrovich was leading the command, were no roads.

Behind him were enough hydrogen warheads to incinerate the entire Yakut region of Siberia and irradiate Mongolia as well. What absolutely terrified this missile officer leading the eighty-seven-truck convoy for the four-missile battery were the missiles themselves. He had never been near missiles like these, and had been assured that Russia would never build them, for "the safety of mankind." The problem with these "burning hells," as he made every one of his men call them, was they could go off right here, right behind him, right in the middle of Siberia, leaving a crater the size of two Leningrads. The road, what there was of it, was colossally bumpy, and the warhead had come out of the factory armed, a lunacy never before heard of in atomic weapons. Even the Americans with the first atomic bomb did not arm it until the airplane carrying it was near the target. You did not arm the weapon until just before firing. Everyone knew that. And now all Russia had gone mad.

This madness, this strange new missile he and every officer had once been promised Russia would never build, was all over Russia. It would be mass murder, not war. He would murder millions without even the flimsiest excuse. There could be no excuse fo the madness he was now so carefully trying to guide to its new base in Siberia.

It had started just a few days before. In his apartment at Saratov, a central farming city southwest of Moscow, Petrovich had received the first strange word. He had just finished waiting in line for a fresh batch of writing paper for his grandchild. He had retired the year before, and getting fresh paper had always been difficult when he no longer had access to military supplies. His wife was waiting in the apartment with a block leader of the party who had not even taken off his coat, but stood with his hat tapping his side and his feet tapping the floor.

"His telephone has been ringing all day," said the retired colonel's wife, a round, sweet-faced woman.

"Your command has called using my telephone," said the block leader.

"They could not phone me, of course," said Petrovich, who had applied for a telephone in 1958.

"There are other phones they could have used, but this is an emergency. You are to report to Evenki immediately. You have top priority on any aircraft in the area, any car to get you to the aircraft, any telephone line at your service."

"Are you sure, me? What would they want an old man for?"

"They want you. Now."

"Is there a war? Where is there a war?"

"I don't know. I don't even know who is running

Mother Russia anymore. That they would rudely instruct a party member to act as a messenger is obscene. I could see it if there were a war. But nothing is happening."

"Maybe something is wrong. Maybe something has failed. Maybe an entire missile army has blown itself up somewhere."

"We would have heard," said the party member.

"No. You would not have heard. Although there may have been a rebellion somewhere, and people have to be replaced."

"Is that possible?" asked the party member.

"No," said the retired colonel, shrugging. "It is not. Everyone who attends a missile is reliable to the extreme. They are all like me. We do what we are told, when we are told, and if we are lucky we get a telephone. If we are not, we settle for fresh writing paper. I take it the car to the airport is to be provided by you."

The party member gave a short nod. The retired colonel hugged his sweet-faced wife and tried in his kiss to tell her how much he loved her, how good a wife she had been, in that remote case he did not come home again. The communication was perfect, and when she cried, no denial on his part would convince her it was only some silly bureaucratic mistake that had called him to Western Missile Command in Evenki.

The party member carefully laid out plastic strips on the front seat of his black ZIL limousine, warning the retired colonel not to sit too heavily because the material underneath the plastic could wear. Petrovich felt like flinging the strips in the party member's face. But his wife might be vulnerable to this man's reprisals, so he only nodded dumbly. He even offered an apology to the self-important pip with the Communist party card and automobile and telephone and all the things that Communism had come to mean in the land where it was practiced longest.

It was a very small airport, but the runways, like those of all commercial airports in Russia, were built to handle the newest, most powerful jets. They were not only long enough for anything that flew at that time, but for anything that might be flying in fifty years.

The terminal building was virtually a shack. It was there that the nightmare began in earnest. There were young boys who had not yet shaved and old men from the original nuclear bomber commands. All of them had been called up like Petrovich.

Every thirty seconds a loudspeaker above warned everyone to keep silent. When they boarded the plane for Evenki and Western Missile Command headquarters, they received another warning. This time in person, from an officer of an elite KGB unit with special patches on their especially expensive green uniforms. No unbuttoned shirts in that unit.

"Soldiers of Mother Russia," the officer said, reading from a piece of paper as he stood in front of the airplane. "You are called in a dire time in the history of your people and in the history of your motherland. As much as it may be tempting to discuss what is happening with another soldier of the motherland, we must forbid it. Because of this emergency, violators will be dealt with in the severest manner."

The airplane was quiet. No one spoke. The jets hummed, the KGB officer left the compartment, and then everyone spoke.

"It's war," said an old bombardier. "Got to be."

"You are jumping to conclusions," said a young man whose face was smoother than the colonel's wife's.

"No," said the old bombardier. "If it is not a war, we hear about the wonders of the Communist party and what it is doing for the people of Russia. But when they want the people to fight, they never mention the party. I remember the great patriotic war against the Nazis. It started with defending communism against fascism, and very quickly became Mother Russia against the Hun. When they want you to die, it's the motherland. When they want you to wait in line for some goods, it's the party."

"Is he jumping to conclusions?" the young man asked the colonel.

"If there is a war, he is not. If there is not, he is," said Petrovich with very Russian fatalism. "But look around. I think it is more important who is not here than who is here.

I have not seen one active officer of a missile command."

"In an emergency why would they call up all those who are less qualified?" said the old bombardier.

Their question was answered with the nightmare. One did not need expertise in missile technology to use what they were all shown at Evenki.

They drove through columns upon columns of trucks whose cargo was covered with tarpaulins. Guards stood by each truck. A missile-command officer entered each transport bus to insist that no one turn on anything. Some of the older retired officers' hearing aids were snatched away and smashed, leaving them helpless.

They were herded into a shell of a building. A strange crude missile sat on a gun carriage on a stage. Ordinarily, to show how safe the missile was before arming, an instructor would stand on it. This time, he very gingerly walked up to the stage and stood on its very edge. He did not move.

"Here she is," he said. He did not use a loudspeaker, and he spoke without yelling. Everyone leaned forward. Those whose hearing aids had been removed waited to be told later what was being said. They just looked at each other.

"She has been designed so that you need exactly thirty seconds of additional training."

There was a buzz in the room.

"Please. Quiet. Most of your training with nuclear weapons—and she is nuclear, comrades, nuclear as hell— has been in the areas of safety and guidance. We will be using the old guidance systems which are not that accurate. We are making up for this with a warhead that had previously been discontinued. A dirty warhead. The big blasters. That's what she has got in her nose."

And then, just before he got down from the stage, he added:

"She's primed and loaded and ready to go."

For a moment there was the silence of a blank universe and then even the youngest of cadets understood. Eleven months out of every training year had to do with all the safeguards to prevent an accidental nuclear war. The reason they needed no more training was that there were no safety devices.

This new ugly weapon was the first nuclear weapon produced in any country without safeguards. The nickname being bandied about for it was the "raw button."

You pressed the button and the missile went. It was like the trigger of a gun. So that was the reason active missile-command officers were not chosen. Any fool could use a first-strike weapon. There were only two choices. War or no war. And to produce something like this meant someone was sure of war, because moving these things was a nightmare.

The weapons had no electronics whatsoever, and they wouldn't need much more aiming than an old cannon. They might hit anywhere, and the warhead was so big that it didn't matter. One warhead could take out an entire quarter-country. All the sender had to hit was North America. Mass murder.

If Petrovich hadn't been so concerned about his wife he would have stepped down. But he had not. For a week now he had been driving incredibly slowly along the bad roads; now there were no roads. He faced bumpy hills, and slowed everything down to less than a mile an hour.

His chart was equally crude. He would establish a new base, one that America could not have identified before because it would not exist until he created it. Then he would take rough aim, and according to his instructions, unless otherwise heard from, he would fire the missile at a specific time two weeks hence. He had been given an old Swiss winding watch so that he would not mistake the time. He was going to start World War III unless he was told not to.

His movements did not go unnoticed by the CIA. It was not the missile itself that was detected from outer space, because it could have been one of the thousands of dummies the Russians had scattered over Siberia. Rather, it was the telephone communication from the retired colonel informing home base he was primed and ready.

From the frequency and the analysis of the code, the

Central Intelligence Agency concluded that another of the raw-button batteries had been activated.

Harold W. Smith had privileged access to this information. And more. While the Russians were getting edgier, the President had received a protest from England about the violence attributed to one American agent. He passed it on to Smith, who provided a routine denial used in such instances. The first part was official, bemoaning any violence and offering to help the country in which multiple killings had occurred track down the perpetrator. Informally, the President added a little joke he used when Remo and Chiun were operating outside of the United States:

"If you get their names, we'd like to hire them." The insinuation was that the protesting party had been misinformed, that people really couldn't do those sorts of things. It struck Smith at that time that his country's denial of a weapon threatening the ozone layer was quite similar to the normal cover used for Remo and Chiun. In other words, a lie. Russia had every good reason not to trust America. The truth sounded so much like the normal lie.

He could almost understand Chiun's formula:

"They see evil in their own evil."

Of course, the House of Sinanju did not consider the bloodiest Russian czar, Ivan the Terrible, evil. That was because he paid them well. So what Chiun meant by evil and what the West might mean by evil were different things. Smith did not know what Chiun meant by evil, and that made Chiun's formula difficult to use.

The red phone rang again. Smith answered it, glancing out through the one-way windows of Folcroft, that sanitarium in Rye, New York, that covered for the organization. It faced Long Island Sound, gray and bleak this autumn day. Normally the President's line rang three, perhaps four times in a year. This was the third time this day.

"Here," said Smith.

"I think the British believed us. But do you know what your operative did? He went around England collecting security personnel like baggage and then killed I don't know how many men in the Tower of London itself.''

"He's located the weapon."

"Where?"

"In the Chitibango province of San Gauta."

"Another Central American problem. Damn. Maybe we should just bomb that province."

"Wouldn't work, Mr. President."

"Why not? In this instance you have to get the weapon and the people behind it. Just destroying one device won't do. It would be like trying to end an atomic threat by destroying one atomic bomb.

"There is no good news out of Russia," said the President.

"Are they close to launch? How much time do we have?" asked Smith.

"They could launch now, with those damn raw buttons. They might have enough to do us in. But they're still building."

"So we do have time," said Smith.

"Until they get frightened enough."

"When is that?"

"Can you read a Russian mind?" said the President. "By the way, we also had to answer to the French on the head of the SDEC. What do the French have to do with this?"

"Are you sure it's our people?" said Smith. "Word I've heard is that he was on some Russian hit list for something. Has been for years."

"They'd like to get rid of him, we know. That's been established. The Russians sent in the Bulgarians some years ago, and then a Rumanian team for hire. Then they gave up. The way he was killed smells of your people."

"What do you mean?" said Smith.

"They're not looking for the person who killed him, but the machine. Some of his bones were fused."

"Maybe one of ours," said Smith. He wondered if it were Chiun. Remo could do many things, but being in two places at the same time was not one of them.

"These are dark days, Smith. I am glad we have you and

your people," said the President. He did not know that neither of Smith's personnel was heading anywhere near the fluorocarbon gun.

The generator was sitting in the Chemical Concepts of Massachusetts, Inc. complex off Route 128 outside of Boston, being prepared for another shot.

The news was not good from any front. The Premier had asked Zemyatin to his dacha beyond the city to reassure select members of the Politburo that everything was in control, that Alexei, the Great One, was making the right moves.

Zemyatin was brief and to the point.

"We are not in control of events. We are still struggling to survive them."

"Is it better or worse than it was at the beginning? I've got to have something to give my Politburo."

"Do you mean when should you all go to your shelters?"

"No. Good news. I want good news."

"Then read Pravda. You will see that capitalism is falling on all fronts and we are gaining ground through the will of the masses."

Zemyatin looked at the faces of the other old men. If he had time for pity he would have shown more of it. But he had no time. The old men looked as though they were staring into their own graves. Despite all the talk of being ready for war, none of them were. Despite all the talk of continuous war for the socialist revolution, they were comfortable old men in their dotage who were suddenly at war.

No one spoke. There weren't even any questions. Zemyatin saw the chairman of all armed forces, an accountant by training, lift a trembling glass of vodka to his lips.

Zemyatin turned and walked out. There were scars on his body and they did not make moving easy.

What he had now was what he'd feared. A system so confident of its superiority that it had become useless. At almost every level there were ones like those old men, especially now when they could least afford it.

The Premier and the rest of the Politburo would have been even more frightened if they had known that their vaunted KGB, the biggest, most efficient, most feared intelligence structure in the world, was underneath it all even worse than the other useless men in the Premier's dacha. A thin man with large wrists had beaten his way through all of them and taken back the one lead they had to the American weapon. This had happened quite naturally in the one other country where they felt most secure. This Zemyatin found out from his own men within the KGB, even before they tried to cover for themselves.

Zemyatin knew that if his Russia were going to survive, he would have to make all those comfortable KGB boys much less comfortable. The world was not a fine desk from which you ordered someone killed. It was blood. And pain. And treachery. And very, very dangerous.

Even as he entered 2 Dzerzhinsky Square, the massive concrete building in Moscow that was KGB headquarters, he felt the tiredness of combat. But this time there was a sense that events could not be turned. Zemyatin brought with him two old combat soldiers he could rely on to put a bullet in someone's head without arguing. Nothing fancy. Stick the gun in their faces and pull the trigger. He could reasonably expect everyone to follow his orders, but he was too tired now to work with people who might ask him questions.

He went right to the British desk of the KGB and ordered the heads of other desks to be in the room. He ordered the general who had seen what had happened at the missile base to be there also.

Assembled in this one office were forty-two generals. Zemyatin told no one why they had been called. The young general in charge of the British desk tried to restrain his tension. He had phoned the field marshal just an hour earlier to report the minor difficulty encountered in England. The field marshal had hung up on the general after telling him he would be over soon. Stay there, had been the only order. All of them had been kept there for half a day. Good. Now the room buzzed with the upper echelon of the KGB. Some looked to Zemyatin, who sat in a chair with his two old friends behind him. Zemyatin said nothing, gathering his strength by drinking a glass of water.

The conversation among the generals drifted to personal things. Zemyatin did nothing. He let their talk wander to all the things they thought were important: watches, dachas, special Western goods, the price of a woman in Yemen. Several were embarrassed to be standing near him, because no one took it upon himself to ask why they had been called. They all wanted someone else to do it.

Finally Zemyatin nodded to one of the two old soldiers he had brought with him.

"Anyone but this one," he said, pointing to the young general of the British desk. "I'll need him for a while."

He said it so casually that no one seemed to notice. They continued talking. The shot rattled every eardrum in the room. It shivered the gilt on the chairs. The old soldier had taken a big-caliber pistol, still smoking acrid gunpowder now, and shot the brains out of the KGB officer closest to him, the one who had smiled when the old soldier approached.

For just one moment there was incredible silence in the room. Everyone was stunned, everyone but Zemyatin and his old Russian infantrymen.

"Hello," he said. "I am Alexei Zemyatin. I am sure most of you have heard of me in one way or another."

The Great One had just gotten their attention.

"We are engaged in a battle of survival of the motherland. This man has failed," he said, pointing to the young general sitting behind the desk. Little beads of perspiration now formed under the young general's immaculately combed hair, slick with Italian lotion. The young general gulped. Zemyatin wondered if he had ever seen a dead body before. The others were all wondering, of course, why the British desk officer had not been shot if the British desk had failed.

"I want you to listen. We had been assured that we had a fancy psychological profile coming in on a woman who could lead us to a weapon we deem vital. Correct?"

The young general nodded. He tried not to look at the body. So did the other superior officers of the strongest intelligence network the world had ever seen.

"I wanted information. I wanted what was simple. We had been assured that an American operating alone was no danger, even though Americans do not operate alone. It takes three of them to go to the bathroom. But America had sent one man looking for this woman. And what were we told?"

The young general's voice barely got out the words:

"We said he had been taken care of."

The other officers in the room were sure the general was going to be shot. Some of the older ones had not seen an execution in an office since the days of Stalin. They wondered if the bad old days were coming back.

"He'd been around the block or something like that. London was downtown Moscow, you said. You were so sure, weren't you?"

The general nodded.

"Louder," said Zemyatin.

"I was sure," said the young general. He wiped his forehead with the perfectly tailored sleeve.

"I said here, as I said fifty, sixty years ago, that your enemy is perfect until he shows you how to kill him. No tricks. No games. Blood. Think. Blood. Think. Think."

No one answered.

"There is no gadget so exotic and useless that you will not copy it from the Americans. Well, we don't have time for that. Your motherland faces destruction. Your motherland faces a threat far more powerful and odious than anything we have seen before. Your motherland needs your brains, your blood, and your strength. Now, boychik. Tell us all about this American."

"He penetrated our most secure London system, and got the woman who knows about this weapon that . . . concerns you, a weapon I am not sure about . . ."

"Anything else?" asked Zemyatin.

"I guess I failed," said the young general. He adjusted his gold Rolex. He had thought he might be killed someday in some foreign land, but not here at KGB headquarters in his own office.

"You don't even know how you failed. That is the danger. You don't even know how you failed."

"I lost the woman. I underestimated the American."

"Anyone can lose a battle. Do you hear me? Do you all hear me? We have lost many battles," boomed Zemyatin, and then he was quiet to let it all sink in. "We are going to lose more battles."

And he was quiet again.

"But," he said finally, raising himself from his chair and purposely stepping on the dead body of the man he had ordered shot at random, "we need not lose any war. The failure of our young boychik here has probably escaped every one of you."

Zemyatin paused for only a moment. He knew he wasn't going to get an answer. They were all too shaken. Which was exactly as he had to have them.

"The failure is something this young man did not do. He did not find out the methods by which this American operated. Today we know little more than we did before we lost that battle. We did not find out how to kill him. Now, from this day forth, I want the entire world network to look for this American and the woman. And I personally will prepare the team to go after them. Who is in charge of execution squads?"

There was an embarrassed mumble in the rear of the room.

Finally someone said:

"You're stepping on him, sir."

"Doesn't matter. Give me his number-two man. As for the rest of you, there is nothing more important in your lives right now than finding the whereabouts of that American and the woman. We do have her picture and identifying material, don't we? Or are we just dealing with her psychological profile?"

"No. We have her picture," said the young general.

The man in charge of Russia's execution efforts was simply named Ivan. His last name was Ivanovich. He was really a staff officer and explained at the outset that he had never actually killed anyone. Perhaps, suggested Colonel Ivan Ivanovich, Field Marshal Zemyatin would prefer one more skilled in the art of killing. The young paper shuffler had a face clean as a washtub, and lips like rosebuds.

What were they making policemen of nowadays? wondered Zemyatin. Still, he had to have some intelligence to have risen so far.

"No, no," said Zemyatin. "You're all the same. What we are going to do, Ivan, is let this American show us how to kill him. Until then, he is perfect."

This time there was no reference to old theories being outmoded. The first random shot into the crowd had settled that. It had unsettled the most settled bureaucracy in the Kremlin. Now he might be able to get some work out of these incompetents.

There had been no reports of weapons testing in the last two days. This lull had given Russia time to build more raw-button missiles. Meanwhile, a man and a woman had to be found somewhere in the world, and if the KGB did one thing well, it was keeping track of the world. There was more useless information coming into Moscow than even the computers stolen from the Americans could handle. But on this day, the entire network shifted to searching for three things. A man. A woman. And a weapon.

Alexei Zemyatin felt the tingle of war come just a touch closer that cold night. The Americans had sent their best to protect the woman in charge of the experiment. Therefore, there wasn't even the slightest doubt that they were behind this weapon as a weapon.

If they had been honest, a fact Zemyatin would never have believed too readily, why steal the woman back? And why use a heretofore secret force? One only exposed a secret to protect a geater one. It meant war. And yet, the millions who would die in this one made Alexei Zemyatin push the waiting time to the limit. They would look for things. Watch America closely. Maybe the experiments would stop. Maybe there was a flaw in the weapon. Maybe it did not work in certain situations.

Russia would continue to build its raw-button missiles.

The day of war would remain the same. He had designated it to make America prove to him that they were not preparing their own final solution to communism. And the only way it could be proven now was for his security system to find the three things he had requested of them.

Zemyatin walked with just a single bodyguard that night through the streets of Moscow, hearing drunks sing sad songs and watching an occasional dark car head busily out of the city toward the better apartments. He breathed deeply. The air was good. He even wondered, if they did get a good first launch, how much—if any—of this would be left.

He also wondered what the Americans thought they would win by such a conquest. Stupidity in an enemy bothered Zemyatin. There was still time for him to stop the crude nuclear assault system which continued to add more sites. Still time. He did not know that even now an American was going to erode the very mildest hope of peace, because he had something more important to think about than the survival of the human race. His career was in jeopardy.

10

Reemer Bolt hadn't heard from Kathy since immediately after the test. It did not matter. The system had cost CC of Massachusetts more than the magic fifty million dollars. The figure was magic because now the corporation could not, under any circumstances, fail to push forward without being destroyed. In a way this financial disaster had put Reemer Bolt in the driver's seat, and he realized there was only one last bug to work out. One little obstacle that had nothing to do with the machine itself.

"Praise the Lord," said the chairman of the board. "It does work, then?"

The board was meeting in the director's room, a comfortable spacious room with wood floors, open windows, and a sense of an exiting tomorrow in it. It was used for board meetings and for presenting possible customers CC's solutions to their chemical problems.

"We can direct the ozone opening across an entire ocean for a controlled period," said Bolt. "Gentlemen, we have put a window into the ozone and we control the sash cords. What we can deliver is no less than the most powerful force in our universe."

Bolt stood up when he said this. He paused. There were smiles on the faces of the board of directors. Reemer Bolt had dreamed of a day like this. And now it was happening. Men with the money giving him approval. Actually, if he had told them that everything was still not a disaster, they would have been pleased. But this had replaced their fear with greed. He smiled back.

There was applause. Light at first, then hearty. Reemer Bolt knew how to work an audience.

"And we have the patent."

More applause.

"And we submitted this patent in such a way that no one will know exactly what we have until we make our announcement."

More applause.

"Gentlemen. You have gambled and you have won."

Applause.

"You have bet on tomorrow, and that was yesterday. You own today. The sunlight and all."

There were a few technical questions which Bolt delayed answering "until Dr. O'Donnell returns."

"This is CC of M's most important project," said one of the directors. "This is the whole story now, so to speak. Why isn't Dr. O'Donnell here?"

"She has phoned and told us she is taking what I believe is a well-deserved rest."

More applause. Even for this. Reemer Bolt owned these men. The phone call was not so much a request for a vacation as a hurried message from a phone booth, saying she would get back to him soon and not to do anything without her. And then: "He's coming back now. I have to hang up."

"Him? Who's him? A he?"

"Not like you, darling," Kathy had said, blowing a kiss through the phone and hanging up. So his orders had been to do nothing. But he knew what that was about. She wanted to take the big share of the credit for the device's success. If there was one thing Reemer Bolt prided himself on, it was his knowledge of women. After all, he had been married many times.

So he told the board that Dr. O'Donnell had done well within her limited area, and that her presence was not necessary for pushing on the success of CC of M's sun-access device.

"I don't know if I like the name 'sun access,' " said one of the directors. "Everybody has access to the sun. We've got to sell something exclusive."

"Good point, sir. 'Sun access' is just a working name," said Bolt.

"I think 'Mildred' might not be a bad working name," said the director. He was a stuffy sort, quite erect, who smoked long cigarettes neatly and then tortured the cinder into submission.

"Why 'Mildred'?" asked another director.

"My mother's name," he said.

"Perhaps something more sellable," said the other director.

"Just a working name. I like it."

"Why don't we let Mr. Bolt continue? He's brought us this far."

More applause. Reemer Bolt had dreamed of a day like this.

"Where to now, Reemer?" said the chairman of the board. He did not smoke. He did not drink the water set in front of him, and his applause was the weakest. He had a face with all the human warmth of cold cooking fat.

"Toward making you all the richest men in the world."

Applause.

"Good. What's your direction?"

"Multifaced, yet with a strong directional thrust, only

when we devise the maximum benefit avenue for us to drive down. In other words, we have so many damned streets to take, we want to make sure we have the best one."

"Sounds good, Mr. Bolt. Which streets are you considdering?"

"I don't want to lock us in right now. I think the worst thing we can do is go running off in a direction just to run. I don't want to look back at these days and think we had the power of the unfiltered sun in our hands and then we let it get away because we didn't think."

"I am not asking you not to think. What direction?"

"Well, let's look at what we have. We have controlled access to unfiltered sun, the power rays, so to speak. They are ours. And they are ours safely. You know that in any experiment like this there was a danger we could rip the ozone shield and turn the earth into a cinder. Then none of our ideas would have been any good." Bolt looked everyone in the face and paused. There was no applause.

"So," said Bolt. "We now move into the applications phase with a fantastic advantage."

"Yes?" said the chairman of the board. "What are we going to do with this thing to get our fifty million dollars back and make money? Who are we going to sell this to? What are we going to use it for? I have read your secret reports, and so far all we can do is ruin lawns and kill animals painfully. You think there is a market for that?"

"Of course not. Those were just experiments to define what we have."

"We know what we have. What are we going to use it for?"

The chairman of the board had hit the last little bug.

"I don't want to rush this. I want Marketing to come up with a good range and a direction I can stand behind," said Bolt.

"Bolt, that fifty million dollars costs us one hundred and thirty-five thousand dollars a week in interest. Please don't take your time in coming up with an application we can sell."

"Right," said Reemer Bolt. And he got out of that

boardroom as quickly as he could because he didn't want anyone asking him about ideas for commercial use.

The problem with something that cost fifty million dollars to develop was that you couldn't use it for something small. You had to have something big. Big. Big.

That was what Reemer Bolt was yelling at his staff the following morning.

"Big industry. Big ideas. Big. Big."

"What about as a weapon? It would make a great weapon. And fifty million dollars would be pennies for something that might end all life on earth if used improperly."

"Not fast enough. The money's there, but the government takes forever. A weapon is the last resort. There has got to be something we can do with this thing. Something big. Big industry. It's got to revolutionize something."

Then a lower-level employee had a magnificent idea. It didn't have to do with animals. And it didn't have to do with lawns. But it did have to do with a baking effect.

None of them knew as they were congratulating themselves that even to a lower-level Russian general, the experiment they were planning could only be a prelude to ground action all across the European front.

Even if Bolt had known, he might not have dwelt on that. Here was an idea that would not only get CC of M out of the hole, but possibly revolutionize a major industry. And even better yet, a lower-level employee had thought it up. He would have no trouble taking full credit for it.

"Are you sure this is the right jungle?" said Remo.

"Sure," said Kathy. She was still suffering from jet lag and the atrocious landing at Chitibango airport in San Gauta. The runway was built for smuggling out cocaine and bringing in tourists who liked to discover new vacation spots unspoiled by other tourists. San Gauta was always being discovered for the first time. It was the sort of place that photographed magnificently.

What did not appear in the photographs were the bugs and the room service. In all Gauta there were only four people who could tell time. And they were all in the

Cabinet. The rest of the people thought that the only time one had to respect in this little tropical paradise was bedtime and dinnertime. Bedtime was determined by the sun and dinnertime by one's stomach.

Only crazy foreigners and the Maximum Leader for Life had to tell time. The Maximum Leader needed the time device to know when to meet airplanes, start parades, and most of all to declare when time was running out.

In the 1950's Generalissimo Francisco Eckman-Ramirez declared time was running out against atheistic communism. During the sixties it was imperialism. During the seventies it became, on alternate days of the week, either Cuba or America. Now, the new time running out was for population control.

The Generalissimo was not exactly sure how it worked, but somehow the Western World, especially America, was to blame for the incredible promiscuity of the San Gauta maiden and the magnificent sex drive of every San Gauta male. Ordinarily bad sanitation, disease, and the starvation that had afflicted this area for aeons kept an almost mathematical balance of people.

But because of all the warnings that time was running out, Western agencies began shipping food, cleaning up sewers, and teaching new methods of living longer. They sent down doctors and nurses. There was medicine. The shame of so few babies living to maturity had been conquered. Which led to more grown-ups. Which led to more grown-ups making more babies. The whole place was like a giant guppy tank run amok. And now time was truly running out on San Gauta for Generalissimo Eckman-Ramirez. With all the people crowded together, pollution was getting worse. Starvation was getting worse and then came the worst assault of all. It was a combination of liberal Protestants, Jewish intellectuals, and an order of nuns. Between them they came up with a massive social program to eradicate all evils.

They presented it in such a way that anyone who allowed the current state to persist appeared to be some form of devil. Therefore, anyone fighting that person was on the side of good. Willing to fight the Generalissimo were the usual hill bandits who had specialized for generations, even before the arrival of the Spaniards, in pillage, rape, and the murder of innocents: women, children, unarmed farmers in the field.

But now they put a little star on a red flag, called the pillage and rape "guerrilla warfare," and announced their goal as liberation. What they wanted to liberate was what they had always wanted to liberate: everything the towns-folk couldn't protect.

They were immediately armed by the Cubans, which left the Generalissimo reaching out for the Americans to help him counter their new and better weapons. Whereas before, a village or two might suffer an attack by the hill bandits once a year, now the attacks came weekly. Whereas before, the national army might respond once or twice a year by shooting some cannon into the hillsides, now there were daily fusillades.

The death count became enormous, especially as the nuns returned with stories of atrocities to America, where they called upon their countrymen to donate money to fight barbarism. This was not altogether a lie. The Generalissimo was indeed barbaric. But so were the liberating forces whom the nuns in their innocence now declared as saviors. The one thing the nuns never seemed to entertain was the possibility that they themselves were indeed innocents and didn't know what was going on. But they were always good for a story of suffering.

There seemed to be no end to the blood running daily through the streets of Chitibango, because not quite enough people were killed to balance out the new advances in medicine and agriculture. This was a problem typical of a Central American country.

And thus did San Gauta receive journalists who detailed the atrocities of the Generalissimo. And thus did Kathy O'Donnell, like anyone else who followed the news, hear of Eckman-Ramirez the butcher, the man whose estates were guarded by fire and steel and barbarous henchmen.

It was this time that came first to Kathy's mind when this magnificent specimen with the thick wrists entered her life. She wanted to see the butcher of Chitibango pulped.

She could have chosen someone else. This wonderful man she was with could destroy anyone. But she wanted someone far away from Boston and the fluorocarbon generator. She wanted someone who would be a challenge for her brutal stranger. The Russians apparently weren't. And so, in that one instant, she fondly chose the butcher of South America. She thought of the nice fight his notorious guards would put up. If this man called Remo lost, she could always buy her way out, but if he won, well, she would be there for the magnificent thrill of it.

Even more important, now she didn't care what happened. She just wanted more of Remo.

"Yes. I am sure of it. This does look like the right jungle. He had a magnificent hacienda."

"All these dictators down here have one," said Remo.

"He had a high peaked hat."

"That's standard, too."

"He had a nose that didn't look like a balloon," said Kathy. "And hair that didn't look like it was manufactured in a Bayonne plastics factory."

"Might be Eckman-Ramirez," said Remo. He had seen his picture once in a magazine.

"He said he would pay well for my conducting the test. I didn't know there would be all that suffering. Those poor animals."

"Did you see the weapon?"

"He said he had it. He had it hidden. I should have known."

"Why?" said Remo. He noticed she was having difficulty moving along the path. The natives had looked at his wrists and trusted him immediately. Why, he wasn't sure. But he was sure that they were looking at his wrists when they told him not only where the Generalissimo lived, but that he was there now.

"All the news articles. I didn't believe them. I didn't believe they were telling the truth, and now you tell me this device can do harm to people."

"You didn't see the animals there?" said Remo.

"I saw them. I saw them suffer. Yes," said Kathy. She allowed her blouse to open, revealing a rising bosom glistening with San Gauta warmth. Ordinarily Kathy could allow her blouse to open with such artistry that she could play with almost any man's eyes, getting him to lean over a table, keep his head cocked at an awkward angle, and usually not think about what he was supposed to be thinking about. It was a lovely business tool. A properly opened blouse was as useful to her as a desktop computer.

But this man didn't seem to dwell on her body. He seemed to be involved with everything around them, knowing where the path went when of course he couldn't have known. He told her he felt it.

"Your blouse is open," said Remo.

Kathy let her chest rise and looked at him coyly.

"Is it really?" she said, letting him get the full magnificence of what was pressing up out of her bra.

"Yeah. Now, why didn't you believe you would be doing any harm?"

"I trust too much," she said. She felt the whole jungle slither with things she couldn't see. Things with hairy legs and little teeth that some television show had probably photographed laying eggs or eating some other thing with legs just as hairy and almost as many teeth.

The magazine article did not show the smells, or the fact that your feet sank into the jungle floor, into dark leafy substances that she was sure must have contained millions of those hairy-legged things.

"Are you married?" she said.

"I think I told you no. Don't walk so heavy," said Remo.

"I walk beautifully," said Kathy. Suddenly she didn't mind the jungle. She minded the insult.

"No you don't. Clunk clunk. Try not to crush the ground. Treat it like your friend. Walk with the ground. It'll be easier on you and the ground and we won't be announcing ourselves to whatever it is behind that hillock up ahead."

Kathy couldn't see anything beyond the dense green foliage. She couldn't even see the hillock.

"How do you know there's something there?"

"I know. C'mon. Walk with the ground, not on it."

Exasperated, Kathy tried walking with the ground to prove to herself it didn't work. But she found that by watching Remo walking and trying to think as he had instructed, she was not so much pressing forward, as gliding forward. She shut her eyes. And stumbled. She had to watch him to do it.

"Where did you learn this?"

"I learned it," said Remo.

"It's wonderful," she said.

"It's all right. What is Eckman-Ramirez like?"

"He is a sociopath. They are the best liars in the world. After all, he convinced me. I should have believed the magazine articles. I thought they were propaganda."

"No. They just don't know what they're doing. No one knows what he is doing. Nobody. These yo-yos are going to fry the earth with that thing."

"Some people know," said Kathy. "Whoever taught you to walk like this knows. He must know something. Or was it a she?"

"A he."

"Your father?"

"Shhh."

"Who?"

"Someone, that's all," said Remo. He thought of Chiun going off for some old dusty pieces of gold and wood, the collection of centuries of tribute. Some of the stuff was almost worthless now, as modern man had learned to manufacture some of those materials once considered valuable. But even so. What was a ruby worth if there was no one left on earth to say it was valuable? And still Chiun had gone.

"I don't miss him, you know," said Remo.

"The one who taught you?"

"Crazy. That's all. He's got his ways. And that's it. You can't reason with him."

"The one who taught you?"

"Never could. Never will. I don't know why I bother."

"The one who taught you?" asked Kathy again.

"Watch how you walk," said Remo.

"That is the first time I have seen you angry about something. You don't ever seem to get angry."

"Try walking where you're told," said Remo.

That was the second time. It was clear there was someone he loved. But what sort of a relationship was it? Was there a reason he was not attracted to her? Was it all women he wasn't attracted to?

"Watch how you're walking," he said.

He turned out to be more than right. There was a hill up ahead. And just over it, set like a white jewel topped with red ceramic tile, was a classic hacienda surrounded by unclassic machine-gun nests. There were fierce-looking guards at the gates and enough antennas set into the tile roof to direct an air attack on the rest of South America. The land around the hacienda was cleared to prevent any possible hiding place.

"Oh, wow," said Kathy. "We'll never get in there."

"No. Those defenses are for bandits. Where did he put that device?"

"He would know," said Kathy.

"If you're frightened, you can wait here, and I'll come back for you."

"No. That's all right. I owe it to mankind to try to make up for any harm I've done," she said. She certainly wasn't going to waste this filthy walk through the jungle to miss all the crunching of bones and breaking of bodies. If she wanted safety she would have stayed somewhere in London and sent this one off to Tibet or someplace.

"Stay with me."

"I'll never leave you."

The thing about Remo; the thing she noticed most, was that he used people's reactions to operate. Like walking pleasantly up the road right past the machine-gun nests. He waved. They waved back. She realized that perhaps his greatest deception was that he was unarmed. He presented no threat of danger. It was as hidden as it was magnificent. Kathy could feel the sense of danger vibrate into her body. She wondered if he was going to kill a guard for her.

"Hi," said Remo. "I'm looking for the Generalissimo. I've got good news for him."

The guard did not speak English. Remo spoke in Spanish but it was the strangest Spanish Kathy had ever heard, more Latin than Spanish and strangely sing-song, as though an Oriental had taught him.

"The Generalissimo does not see everyone," said the guard, noticing Remo's wrists. There was no wristwatch, therefore the gringo was not a gringo, but a citizen of the country. The guard asked why Remo was not out in the fields working or in the hills with the bandits or in the army of the Generalissimo. Also, what was he doing with the beautiful gringo woman? Did Remo want to sell her?

Remo said he didn't want to sell her. But he was here to give the Generalissimo the best deal he could ever make for himself. He might let the Maximum Leader live to see the sunset. The guard laughed.

Then Remo moved. His hand seemed to brush across the guard's arrogant face. It was not a fast move, but fast enough so that Kathy only noticed it leaving the face. The laughter on the guard's face disappeared. It was impossible to laugh without lips or teeth. The guard couldn't even do anything with his hands but try to stanch the flow of blood. He also quickly indicated the Generalissimo was in the top floor by pointing. There was another guard nearby. He pulled the trigger on a machine pistol. But the pistol didn't fire. The finger pulled again. The pistol did nothing but jerk with a little gush of red. The gush came from the hand. Even on the ground the finger was still pulling. Remo walked right on through with Kathy. The guards back at the machine-gun nests didn't even notice. She knew that because they were still looking at her and blowing kisses.

The guards back at the gate were trying to patch themselves as Kathy tugged at Remo's shirt.

"Aren't you going to finish them off?"

"No. I wouldn't even have touched them if I could have gotten in with a letter."

"But you started something with them. I mean, how can

you get something going and then not finish? You know.
Break a neck or something.''

"I didn't want to kill them unnecessarily."

"Why the hell did you get everyone so excited, and then
just leave? Wham, bam, not even a thank you ma'am."

"You want to finish them, lady, you finish them."

"I don't know how to kill," she said. "I hate that. I hate
that in men. You know, a touch here, a touch there, and
then nothing.''

"Shhh," said Remo.

"What?"

"I'm thinking."

"Well, don't strain."

"Where did he meet you when you came here?"

"Remo, everything was so strange. So reeking with . . .
the strangeness, I guess, that I couldn't tell. They may have
done this on purpose. I don't know.''

"Sometimes they do that. I am asking because if people
have something they really treasure, they don't go far from
it. Not really far.''

"Has that been your experience?"

"No," said Remo. "A lesson."

"From that man?"

"Will you lay off that subject?" snapped Remo. "Just
lay off. There must be something *you* don't want to talk
about." He looked around the palatial hallways with their
cool polished marble floors and tinted glass windows two
stories high. Rich wood polished to a warm luster. High-
backed chairs. Gold in the chandeliers.

He heard laughter on the second story, and headed
toward it.

"Does laughter tell you where the lord of this manor
is?" asked Kathy.

"Nah. Maybe. I hate places like this. You know. A bit
of Spanish, which means a bit of Arab because they were
the real architects of Spanish styles. A little Mayan. A little
Aztec and some California American. The place is a mess.
You can't get a read on where the owner is. I hate it when
they mix styles on you.''

He went up the stairs with Kathy running to keep pace.

Outside there was some noise from the guards. An alarm sounded somewhere. Remo seemed to ignore it all. And then he saw an officer running into a room, locking the door behind him. Remo followed, springing the lock like a stone from a slingshot. Panting, Kathy caught up with him. It was safe to stay behind him. Perhaps the only safe place. That is, if he knew it was you.

"It's me," she said.

"I know," said Remo.

"How did you know?"

"I know. C'mon. I'm working."

Work was disarming two bemedaled officers who were aiming pistols at them. When Remo disarmed, he did it at the shoulders. Again he did not finish them. He didn't even touch the two brutes who dropped their weapons when they saw the horror of the officers losing their arms. He was even pleasant as he walked into the next room, where an officer was excitedly telling Generalissimo Eckman-Ramirez about the dangers of a single man who had come here to threaten His Excellency.

Remo, Kathy realized, could be a tease. And she also realized that she needed him to finish one of these men, or she would go crazy with want.

"Get on with it," she said.

Remo nodded her way. The Generalissimo, it turned out, spoke English. He spoke English rather well, in fact, and quite rapidly when it was pointed out to him that the man who had gone through his guards like tissue paper was now standing there.

"What can my humble house offer you, friend?" asked the Generalissimo. He had fine features: a thin small nose, sort of blondish hair, and dark eyes. He also sported a glistening yellow tooth right up front. When one had gold, one apparently flaunted it in this country.

He kept looking at Remo's wrists.

"I want your fluorocarbon thing."

"But, sir, I have no such thing. But if I did, you, sir, would be the first to have it."

"Oh what a liar," gasped Kathy. "These butchers are such liars."

"Who is your beautiful friend who calls me a liar?"

"You mean to say you didn't stand right there and tell me to measure oxidation and liquid refraction of ultra-violet intensity on a transatlantic angle?"

"Señora?" said the Generalissimo helplessly.

"Malden. In Malden, you bastard," said Kathy.

"Malden. I don't know of a Malden."

"You don't know of little dead animals? You don't know of the ozone layer? What else don't you know?"

"I don't know what you are talking about, lady."

"He's the one," said Kathy.

What happened next posed an immediate problem for her. She had been planning on Remo's killing off the Generalissimo and leaving her free to her own devices.

Unfortunately Remo could do things with bodies that she hadn't even suspected. Like run just two fingers along a spinal cord, creating pain, turning the general's fierce eyes to watery tears, and his pallid face to red pain. What if the Generalissimo denied any knowledge of the machine to his death? Would Remo find out she had lied to him?

"They usually tell the truth under this," said Remo.

"Apparently he's more afraid of the person he works for than you. Look at his face. He's in pain."

"That's why they tell the truth. To stop the pain." Kathy saw the face flush red, ease, then flush red again; it was as though this man had gotten control of the General-issimo's entire nervous system.

"It was the North Vietnamese, wasn't it? You showed them it could work didn't you? That's how you used me, wasn't it? To develop a weapon for Hanoi," said Kathy. She felt her body alive with his pain.

The Generalissimo, who would have admitted to murdering Adam and Eve at that point, let out a resounding yes. Especially when the pain eased. So delicious was this lack of pain that with Kathy's help he embroidered on the sale to North Vietnam. He even confessed guilt and asked forgiveness.

"But Hanoi isn't west of Great Britain."

"It is if you go far enough," said Kathy.

"I did it. I did sell this horrible . . . thing?"

"Fluorocarbon generator," added Kathy helpfully.

"Yes, fluoro . . . thing. I did. I confess."

"Where in Hanoi?" said Remo.

"I don't know. They just came and put it in a car and drove off," said the Generalissimo.

Remo looked at Kathy. She was shaking her head.

"You're a scientist," said Remo. "Does that sound right to you?"

"Could be. Could be," she said. What they would do in Hanoi, she did not know. What she would do, she was not certain. But she needed a climax to all this excitement.

"Are you going to let him live? Maybe he'll warn the others."

"Sometimes it's a help," said Remo. "Then they all run to protect what they don't want you to have."

"I'd feel safer if you killed him. I can't go with you knowing this butcher and his officer would be phoning a warning ahead. It's been so hard on me, Remo. I couldn't."

And then she cried. She was good at tears. She had found out just how good she was at them when, at five, she had strangled her own hamster and had the house looking for the killer who had done that bad thing to Kathy's Poopsie Woo, her pet name for the little rodent who had squirmed his furry last in her hands.

"All right. All right," said Remo. "Stop the crying. Look, they're dead."

There were two very quiet bodies on the floor, the Generalissimo's sandy blond hair facing the ceiling, his nose pressed into the floor, the officer's arms out in the same hysterical motion he had used to warn his Maximum Leader that a horrible man and a beautiful woman had just breached his security like butter.

"I didn't see you do it. How did you do it?" said Kathy.

"Never mind," said Remo. "I did it."

"Well, don't be so fast. Why did you have to rush? Don't you have any consideration?"

Dr. Kathleen O'Donnell did not see the small swellings on the back of the necks of both men. But the general's physician did. It was unmistakable. Two spinal vertebrae had been cracked and fused as though with heat. An extraordinary feat, especially since the guards reported that no machinery had been brought into the Generalissimo's room. It was just one man and a redhead. The doctor very carefully got their descriptions. And then he phoned a large embassy in a nearby country.

"I think I have the answer to your problems," said the doctor.

"This had better be major for you to break cover," came back the voice.

"If it was major enough for you to warn me to look for, I assume it is major enough for me to get back to you."

"That was a general warning this morning."

"I think I found them."

"The man and the woman?"

"Yes. She had red hair and was beautiful."

"We've had ten reports like that this morning from all over South America. One of the beautiful redheads turned out to be an orangutan in the Rio de Janeiro zoo whose keeper was taking her to the veterinarian."

"This man killed two persons by fusing cervical vertebrae with what I have to assume were his bare hands."

"What did he look like?"

The doctor heard the tension in the man's voice. Every bit of anxiety would mean many dollars for him. He gave a description of the two, told where he thought they were, and then added an afterthought.

"He did not wear a wristwatch," said the doctor.

"What is that supposed to mean?"

"All foreigners and cabinet ministers wear wristwatches. They must have thought this man was one of their own. The peasants, I mean."

"You wear a wristwatch, doctor," came back the voice from the KGB control center.

"Yes," said the doctor. "But I am also Minister of Health for San Gauta."

The report was sent immediately by radio message—because it had maximum priority—to Moscow, which had been receiving similar messages all day. But this one was different. In all the others the man had either shot or stabbed someone, but this message indicated a person who, with his bare hands, could create enough pressure to fuse vertebrae as though they had been baked in an oven.

"That's him," said the KGB colonel Ivan Ivanovich, who now first had to report to Zemyatin and then, with the old one's help, prepare the way to kill him.

"Good," said the Great One. And then he found out the news was even better: the couple was still in San Gauta.

"We can dispatch a team before they leave the country," said the young colonel. He felt his hands begin to sweat just talking to the field marshal. Who knew whom he would kill and when?

"No," said Alexei Zemyatin. "This time we do everything right."

11

Reemer Bolt didn't know whether it was the heat or his excitement, but he was sweltering in his silver radiation suit. One of the experiments at Malden had proved that a radiation suit could protect a person under the sun's power rays for a maximum of twenty minutes. What else had been discovered was not quite certain because he had not heard from Kathy O'Donnell again. He missed her luscious body, her exhilarating smile, her quick mind, but most of all her body. When he really thought about it, he didn't miss her smile or her mind at all. In fact, without her here he would be the sole architect of the most amazing industrial advance of the twentieth century. Perhaps ever. The person who invented the wheel may have been forgotten, but Reemer Bolt would not be.

Credit would be given where credit was due. Reemer Bolt had worked out the last bug this bright autumn day. He had not only found a use for the device, but one in a major world industry. In one paltry year CC of M would be able to recoup their entire investment and they'd all be on their way to exotic wealth forever.

The cars and trucks had been arriving all morning, their bare metal skins glistening in the sun. Some were old, with deep, mud-red primer patches. Others were new, with rivets still visible. A small valley had been cleared of trees just north of Chester, New Hampshire. Into this valley came the cars and trucks all morning. Into this valley came the board of directors of Chemical Concepts of Massachusetts.

Into this valley came a crate of glistening radiation suits. Reemer Bolt had the board of directors put them on. The chairman of the board looked at the fifty cars and calculated a cost of more than two hundred thousand dollars and probably less than five hundred thousand dollars. He looked at the suits and figured that they had to go for a thousand apiece. There were fine brass fittings over the face plates, and soft padding under the silver skins of the suits. Reemer Bolt was talking in a hushed voice as though someone over his shoulder would hear him. The chairman of the board noticed it was quite effective. Other members were being caught up in this as though they were part of some great secret raid.

"Reemer," said the chairman of the board, beckoning Bolt with a finger. He spoke loud enough to break the spell. "Reemer, this experiment must have cost us at least a half-million dollars. At least."

"Two million," said Reemer almost with joy.

The other directors, most of whom still had the face masks of their suits in their hands, turned their heads.

"The cars here and things cost about a half-million. But the real money went for something even more vital," said Bolt. And then as though he had not baited this hook, he went about helping another board member don a radiation suit.

"Reemer," said the chairman of the board.

"Yes," said Bolt. "Your face mask goes over the shoulders, almost like a driver's suit, except we don't have to screw the helmet down into the shoulders."

"Reemer," said the chairman of the board. "What is the one-point-five-million-dollar 'even more vital'?"

"You don't think one-point-five-million-dollars is worth securing control over the entire auto industry? Trucks, cars, sports cars, off-the-road vehicles, tractors. Do you really think, sir, they are going to give up control like that?" Bolt snapped a finger and gave a knowing smile.

"One-point-five million dollars," repeated the chairman of the board. "How did you spend that additional money?"

"In providing you all with drivers who didn't know who they were working for. In setting up interlocking dummy corporations, each one providing a greater maze than the next. In buffering all of us, especially the name of our company, which I asked you not to mention today in case the ears of these people pick it up. It costs money to set up dummy corporations leading to the Bahamas. It costs money to hire people through these corporations. It costs money to weave a web that cannot be traced, because, gentlemen, when we leave here today we will leave a paltry two million dollars sitting in a field we bought but will not claim. Yes, gentlemen, we leave a few dollars, and we walk away with control of the entire auto industry."

Bolt grabbed his helmet tightly in both hands.

"We have something so valuable, something that will become so necessary that the auto industry will do everything to break our secret. And until we are ready to dictate our terms, we must keep what happens today to ourselves."

Bolt placed his clear face mask over his head and turned his back, knowing that there were still more questions. But these would be answered in a moment. He had wooden stands built for the board of directors, very much like those in a football stadium. He wondered if they would raise him to their shoulders and carry him off the field when the experiment was done.

Almost tripping on the padding over his shoes, Bolt waved an arm. A score of workmen advanced on the cars with spray nozzles. Pink and lavender clouds filled the air.

Then there was fire-engine red and living-room beige. Mushroom and melon. Daisy and chartreuse. The paint hissed onto the cars moist and glistening.

With a control radio, Reemer Bolt, who had purchased a new scrambler system, contacted a technician back at Chemical Concepts. He had purposely kept from this technician the exact nature of the experiment. He had disguised it as something financially meaningless, like saving the air for people to breathe.

The device was now secured under a small office. When the technician heard the signal, he lifted the red shield over the initiating button. The floor above the device opened. The roof of the building opened.

Sunlight poured in over the device—now reduced to the size of a desk—with a five-foot chrome nozzle pointing upward, much like a small cannon. Except this cannon had two storage drums, and an iron beam generator that acted like a sluice for the fluorocarbons, transferring them just short of the speed of light up to the ozone shield.

The roof closed, the floor above the device closed, and the machine had done its work. It was now down to less than five seconds in operating time. The directional problems had been overcome at the Malden experiment. The duration time, namely protecting the remaining parts of the thin globe-girdling shield, had been determined in the first Salem, New Hampshire, experiment. The technician knew by the almost upright angle of the generator that the experiment point had to be very close.

Up in the treeless valley near Chester, New Hampshire, a miraculous blue light opened up above. For five seconds it seemed to bubble and then it closed rapidly. The fifty cars and trucks did absolutely nothing. Wettish reds, pinks, blacks, browns, grays, and blues glistened from the cars.

Reemer Bolt took off his mask. He signaled the board of directors to do the same.

"Is it safe yet?" asked one.

"Safe," said Bolt. He glanced up at the sky. The ring was now down to a circle. The technicians had even gotten the ozone shield to close faster. The air smelled faintly of burned grass. Small plops like bags of candy could be heard hitting the field. Birds caught again.

Bolt's feet crushed dried dead grass. The ground itself felt brittle underneath.

"C'mon," he called out to the board of directors. "It's safe."

He signaled the workmen to stand off. In case they didn't move fast enough, one of his dummy corporations had hired guards. They moved the workmen away. With great ostentation he nodded to a man with a control box sitting to the right of the stands. With so many people in glistening silver shield uniforms, it looked as though Martians or other spacemen had landed in this little valley in Chester, New Hampshire, where the device had been used for the third time.

Despite careful instructions the workmen tended to mill about confused, and the man at the sound shield box looked the most confused.

"Turn it on," yelled Bolt. He had been assured that certain sound waves obliterated other waves. He had been assured that even the CIA was just getting this device. He was assured that a person could yell five feet from another person and not be heard if the sound shield was in effect.

The man at the box shrugged.

"I said turn on the damned sound shield," yelled Bolt.

The man mouthed the word:

"What?"

Reemer saw one of the delivery cars take away a batch of workers who would no longer be needed. He saw the cars cough out exhaust and move silently along the woodland road out of sight. The man at the sound shield box was turning red in the face mouthing the word "What?"

But he wasn't mouthing.

"Perfect," said Reemer with an extra big grin and an extra-obvious nod. "Perfect."

And then the men who had provided the money and his future:

"Nothing we say here must be heard by other ears."

"There is nothing about a bunch of paint-wet cars that

I care to keep secet," said the chairman of the board.

If he knew nothing else, Bolt knew drama. He took the hand of the chairman of the board and forced it down into the glistening pink of a sedan roof. The chairman yanked it back and was about to wipe it off when he realized it was dry. He rubbed the car again. Glistening and dry. He rubbed another car. The other directors rubbed metal that shone with a luster they had never seen in an auto show-room.

Now Reemer spoke, hushed and precise.

"We can take three hundred dollars off the price of any top-grade auto finish. We can transform the cheapest grades of paint into top quality. In brief, gentlemen, we can hold the entire auto industry hostage to our cheaper method of applying finish paint. In brief, gentlemen, to the robots of Japan, to the workers of Detroit, to the technicians of Wiesbaden, Germany, we say: your car-painting days are over. There is one finish worthy of the name, and only we can apply it."

The chairman of the board hugged Reemer Bolt like a son. He would have adopted him at that moment.

"Don't applaud. Don't carry me away from here. Very quietly, as though this was routine, walk to the cars I have rented for you and leave."

They nodded. A few gave Reemer Bolt a wink. One of them said the hardest thing in his life at that moment was not jumping for joy.

"And on your way out, tell that sound-shield guy to turn it off."

When wonderful was made in this world, Reemer, thy name was you, thought Bolt. On his face was the delicious glow of magnificent success. Reemer Bolt loved the world at that moment. And why shouldn't he? He planned to own much of it soon.

Suddenly he heard noise from the cars leaving and knew the sound shield was off. In a few moments he was alone. He waited, whistling. The next phase was about to begin.

Buses pulled up, chugging to a halt. Fifty people got out, some men, some women. Each with a ticket. They poured out onto the field, a few of them stumbling because they were reading their tickets.

The ones who had driven in the cars were gone before the paint went on. The ones who would drive them out would not know that they were freshly painted.

Bolt unpeeled his suit when he realized he was getting glances. He would go out with the last car, and then be dropped off at a nearby town two blocks from where another driver in a normal car would pick him up.

It was massive. It was brilliant. It was, thought Bolt, Boltian, expressing audacity, complexity, and most of all success. And then the little idiots just sat in their cars doing nothing.

"C'mon. Move along," he said. But they just sat there staring at their wheels, straining with something. Reemer went to the closest car and flung open the door. A young woman was at the wheel.

"Start it," he said.

"I can't," she said.

"Well, try turning the key," he said.

She showed him her fingers. They were red.

"I have been," she said.

"Move over," he said.

Outside of Kathy O'Donnell, all women were good for only one thing, he thought. He turned the key. There wasn't even a groan. He turned the key again. Not a flicker on the dashboard. The car was still.

"See," said the young woman.

"Proud of yourself, I bet," said Bolt, and he went to a man's car. Again nothing. Not in the Beige Buick or Caramel Chrysler. Not in the Peppermint Pontiac or Sun Shimmer Subaru. Not in the Tan Toyota, the Mauve Mustang. The Porsche, the Audi, the Citroën, Oldsmobile, Bronco, Fairlane, Thunderbird, Nissan, Datsun, or Alfa Romeo.

Even the Ferrari was dead. Dead. Reemer Bolt's fingertips were bleeding as he told everyone they would be paid, just get in the darn buses and go. Go, now. "You can do that, can't you?"

As the buses pulled off, he was left alone with a field full

of cars that would not start. Alone was the word for it.
Failure nestled sorely inside his belly.

He couldn't move the cars. He wouldn't know where to
begin. So he just left them and walked away. No one could
trace them, he thought. But two worldwide networks had
already zeroed in on the brief and dangerous puncture of
the ozone shield. And no one in Moscow or Washington
was calling it a window to prosperity.

The President had always known the world would end
like this, with his looking on as a helpless bystander. The
beam had been shot off; Russia had spotted it, too, and
would not, under any circumstances, according to the best
reports, accept the fact that America could not find a
weapon being activated in its own land. But it was true.

The FBI reported that its search for something that produced a fluorocarbon stream had been fruitless. No one
knew what to look for. Was it a gun? Was it a balloon?
Did it look like a tank? Did it look like a giant can of hair
spray?

But there was one good report as the world stumbled
blindly toward its death. This from that most secret of
organizations, the one he found out about on inauguration
day, when the former president had brought him into the
bedroom and showed him that red phone.

The President had used it more in the last week than all
his predecessors had during their terms of office. The man
on the other end was named Smith, and his voice was sharp
and lemony. It was a voice from which the President drew
reassurance.

"We tracked down the source to one place, but it had
been moved. It's in Hanoi."

"Are you sure?"

"We will only be sure when we get our hands on the
damned thing. But our man tracked it to San Gauta and
then that led to Hanoi."

"So the commies have it. Why are they being so mysterious?"

"I don't understand, sir."

"More than anything, I would like to get into the

Kremlin and find out what the hell is going on. Could you use the older one for that? The Oriental?"

"He's on sort of a sabbatical."

"Now?" screamed the President.

"You don't order this one around like some officer. They have traditions a lot older than our country, or even Europe for that matter, sir."

"Well, what about the end of the world? What about that? Did you make that clear?"

"I think he has heard that before also, sir."

"Wonderful. Do you have any suggestions?"

"If I were you?" said Smith.

"Yes."

"One of the problems, perhaps the main one, is that the Russians don't believe we are helpless about this fluorocarbon weapon, if it is a weapon."

"But if it's in Hanoi, they have it."

"Maybe they have it now and maybe they don't. If they do, I think they might step away from the brink. Let's hope they do. My man is only following the best lead we have, and frankly, Mr. President, I am glad we have that man doing it. There is no one better in the world we could have."

"I agree. I agree. Go on."

"I would suggest something I have been thinking about for a long time. Give them something to show that we want their trust in this matter. That we are just as interested in finding out about that fluorocarbon device as they are. We should give them some powerful secret of our own. That secret would be a proof of trust."

"Do you have one in mind?"

"Some device. We must have scores that they would be interested in. But make sure it is not one they think we think they already know about. The one thing we have to be in this matter is absolutely open. We have no choice, sir. I mean you'll have to open it all up."

"That is frightening, Smith."

"This is not a springtime of peace, sir."

"I wonder what my cabinet will think. What the Joint Chiefs will think."

"You don't have much of a choice, sir. You have to give orders."

"You know, Smith, the buck hasn't stopped here. The whole world has."

"Good luck, sir," said Smith.

"And good luck to you."

"Good luck to all of us, sir," said Smith.

The man chosen to bring the secret to Moscow was in his early sixties, a close friend of the President's, a billionaire, a fervent anticommunist, and the owner, of among other things, a technological corporation in the forefront of science.

When he saw what he was supposed to deliver, he almost accused the President of being a traitor. Laid out quite neatly, even to partial Russian translation, was the diagram of America's major missile defense system.

"I won't do it," said McDonald Pease, who possessed a crew cut, a Texas twang, and a doctorate in nuclear physics.

Then he heard about the new missile sites, and he softened a bit. Then he heard about a device that may have been the cause of the Russians' alarm, and he softened totally.

"Of course I'm going. We could all fry like biscuits in a desert. What sort of hound dog lunatic would play around with our little ozone shield? Sweet rib-snappin' muskrat. There won't even be a roach left on this planet. Give the Ruskies everything. Let's get this world back to being just generally dangerous. Holy cowdung. What is going on?"

"Your plane's waiting, Hal," said the President. That was McDonald Pease's nickname. With a first name like his, a nickname became mandatory.

With this one move the President was not only revealing a major American secret, but committing perhaps the shrewdest bargainer in the West. Pease would need it all, the President knew. What he did not know was that McDonald "Hal" Pease did not stand a chance, and was going to make matters even worse by being honest.

12

McDonald Pease arrived in Moscow aboard a specially chartered jet given clearance to land in a vacant airstrip by the Soviet government.

He wore a Stetson hat and a four-thousand-dollar London suit. The chill wind of the autumn snows almost ripped the skin off his face. He didn't care. He hated these people. The only thing they ever did was steal technology and put poison into the minds of people better left to their own devices.

But more than that. He felt they were the most consistent liars the world had ever seen—and that was going some, considering his business partners and worldwide diplomacy, which he knew was a polite term for fraud.

The reason the Ruskies and other Marxists excelled at the blatant lie, Pease calculated, was the way they treated the word. In the tradition of the monotheistic religions, the word was supposed to carry the truth. Not that Christians, Jews, and Muslims always told the truth. But they were supposed to.

In Marxist-Leninist ideology, words were just tools to exhort. Agitprop. It had been that way since the beginning of Marxist-Leninist ideology and it was that way now. So even though the world was at the brink of destruction, it still turned the stomach of McDonald "Hal" Pease to be bringing plans for an American defense to the Russians themselves in an effort toward mutual trust.

Trust? Who knew what they meant by trust? The word probably had a special meaning, like their meaning for "peace." Namely, that lull in fighting between wars that would ultimately lead to their conquest of the world.

A Russian offered his own coat so that Mr. Pease would not freeze.

"No," said Pease. He let the wind tear at his skin.

Besides, they had brought cars right to the airplane. He counted all his people entering the cars and counted them again when they left. He'd started with twelve, and twelve got out of the cars inside the Kremlin walls.

The Premier had that typical Russian face: something that looked squashed. He had thick stubby hands. He expressed cautious optimism that America was willing to share her secrets.

They were in a large room. Behind the Premier were twelve Russian officers in wicker chairs. There were two translators and a large mirror on one of the walls. The fluorescent lights wouldn't have passed muster, thought Pease, in a Mexican junk heap.

"I am here," said Hal Pease, his twangy voice almost cracking in pain, "because we face a common danger. I understand that you do not trust us, and I am here to convince you that we are on the same side in trying to save the world."

The Russian Premier nodded. These Russians had necks like barrels, thought Pease. They'd make good football players.

"We know that you are building great amounts of new nuclear weapons, weapons that we believe are lacking the usual safety devices. For the first time in the history of atomic warfare, a nation has not taken proper precautions."

Pease heard his words translated as he spoke. He saw the bull neck turn. The Russian Premier answered, and the translator began:

"We did not introduce atomic weapons into the world. We, like the rest of the nations, are victims of the atomic weapons which you introduced to this planet. Now you tell us we do not have the proper safety precautions. That is a lie. We are a peace-loving people, and have always been so. We would not endanger ourselves or the world with devices so heinous as you say."

"Get off it," said Pease. "We know you have 'em. You know you have 'em. Now, dammit, we're here to give you something to show you our good faith. You don't have to keep up that silly lie, fella."

The Premier and the translator exchanged a few words. Hal Pease didn't need the translation. He had been told to go to hell.

"All right. Here it is. We're going to give you our command defense structure. What we want is your understanding that we are not behind this irresponsible attempt to pierce the ozone shield. All we ask is that you pause in your march toward world destruction."

The translator began explaining the Russian love of peace, and Hal Pease told him he wasn't interested. It made him want to vomit when the Russian officers began poring over the layout of the American defenses. He saw several nods. They knew they were getting the real thing. One of the officers disappeared for about five minutes and then returned. He only nodded to the Premier. Then the Premier disappeared. The Premier was gone for a shorter time.

The translator was not even needed. Pease could tell by the way the Russian Premier folded his arms that he had been rejected.

The translator started on a denial of the new, more unreliable weapons, and Pease cut him off.

"Hey, buddy. Are you out of your mind? We just laid out our belly to you bastards. What do you want? You want a war? What are you going to win? Will you answer me that? Will you go to your boss and tell him he is crazy? You're starting something no one will win, and meanwhile, if we don't blow ourselves up, we're all sure as hell going to fry like a mess of chili beans."

He got the same blunt lie about Russia's peaceful intentions.

"Look, there is a thing going on with the ozone layer that scares us as much as it scares you. We wanted to prove it to you by showing you our defense plans. Now here they are and you're still stonewalling. We need your help in getting to the base of the fluorocarbon danger. Dammit, we know it hit your territory. We know you have to know about it. We want to work with you toward saving the whole damned world. What are you going to win if the world is a damned parched cinder?"

The Premier thought a moment, left, and then returned.

"If you want the truth," said the Premier through the translator, "we know for a fact that you Americans are the biggest liars on the face of the earth."

Hal Pease almost went right at his thick Russian throat, right there in the Kremlin. Trembling, he contained himself. He needn't have bothered. If he had punched out the eyes of the Russian Premier, he couldn't have done more damage than he already had.

Alexei Zemyatin watched behind the one-way mirror. He watched and heard the American claim that he knew there was someone else pulling the strings and that that person should realize that the end of the world was the end of the world for both Russia and America.

By the man's passion, Zemyatin was almost willing to trust. Except Alexei Zemyatin knew what the man was doing, and long ago he'd learned not to trust his emotions. Too many people depended on his decision for him to trust something so unreliable as instinct. Sometimes it could be correct, of course. But it never supplanted a fact.

And too many men had already been lost trying to find out facts for Zemyatin to indulge in that absolute essence of egotism: a hunch.

So he felt that the man was telling the truth. But that wasn't nearly as important as what he had known for the last half-hour.

Even as Mr. McDonald Pease's plane had taken off for Russia, the Americans were testing their weapon. And there was no question that it was the American government, not some renegade, some little business somewhere that didn't report to the government. Zemyatin could accept that businesses would run wild. He knew how healthy and uncontrollable the black market was in Russia, where there wasn't supposed to be a black market. No market at all except the state providing beautifully for everyone's needs.

But the price had already been paid for the truth. The report, compiled from many sources—some of them now in American prisons because their safety had ceased to be a factor—had ironically arrived the very moment Mr. Pease began his speech. Alexei had listened with only half an ear. What he read in the report froze his bones. It was like all the German troops massing just before their invasion of Russia. The trains, the armor, the munitions, the food. None of it could be missed. The Americans were far shrewder, shrewder even than he had previously thought.

The Americans had just determined the day before that they could make all Russian armor in Europe and Asia useless. They could leave Mother Russia with only infantry-men and tanks that could not move.

America was preparing to slaughter the armor-denuded Russian infantryman in numbers that would make the Nazis blush. There was going to be a land invasion of Russia itself. And it was going to work, even with the lesser forces of NATO. A push right into Russia's heart, and any resistance would be ruthlessly crushed. First the missiles, next the armor, then Russia's heart would be taken out and baked dry. Of course.

Even while the American technicians and Russian military technicians were poring over the large maps and the fields of detection, which were, as the Russians were determining, absolutely genuine, Zemyatin was demanding details. In the details lay the truth.

Officers were running in and out of the field marshal's private room with scraps of paper, reports, and sometimes the officer who had received the initial report.

The Americans had indeed done a test. It was picked up immediately because Russian monitors had been on the alert. Incidentally, he was told, the British had picked it up, too. Although badly damaged, the British system was still functioning.

"The Americans did not warn the British of our pene-tration. They had to know. From what I have been informed they had to know."

"They did know, sir, but there is no indication at this time, Comrade Field Marshal, that they have notified their supposed allies in any way."

"Didn't bother to notify," said Zemyatin. He felt he needed water on that one.

"Something bad, sir?"

"When you are in a fishing contest, and your opponent has caught a minnow, do you stop to take it away from him?"

"The Americans are after bigger fish?"

"The Americans are far shrewder than we ever imagined. At this point, if they believed I had a secure advantage, should they disabuse me of it? Go ahead."

"Shorter duration this time in firing. More precise."

"Weapons-grade accuracy," said Zemyatin.

"Apparently, sir."

"So that if they used it on, say, an entire front, it could be so brief as to not endanger the rest of the world."

Zemyatin, of course, had hit upon the key giveaway: the device was a weapon. There was a time that Russia itself had stacked so many heavy atomic weapons that to use them, their scientists determined, would ruin life for themselves. Ironically, when cleaner weapons, as they were called, were invented, that would be the signal not that the inventions were more humane, but that they were more likely to be used in a war.

The Americans had made the fluorocarbon device weapons-grade.

"I might add, sir," said the officer, "that we had networked the entire American continent to locate the source."

"It failed?"

"No, sir. We located the source, at great risk of manpower. I think the Americans must have caught about fifteen of our people. The priority was not safety but success."

"Yes. Good."

"We had cars alerted. Actually, people driving with dishes on their vehicles once the device was fired."

"That would attract attention."

"That is why we lost so many operatives. But it also enabled us to establish that the beam was generated just north of the American city of Boston, in an area of high military and industrial technology."

Zemyatin knew the area. It was a secondary atomic target in the Russian order of battle, war nuclear. The primaries were the missiles and then came the bases that created them. The armies, of course, could be ignored, considering the leadership.

But far from rejoicing, Zemyatin had warned the Russian generals not to rejoice in American incompetence. If one remembered the Second World War, the Americans had also been considered incompetent then, and they had won a war on two seas defeating armies that had had years of preparations.

In the Russian order of battle, American ground forces had been designated as a low priority. Now, with what he was seeing out of America, they were suddenly becoming a major priority if there was no great Russian armor to oppose them.

The test had consisted of fifty new cars, expensive cars, finer than the Russians could build.

"Within five seconds, Comrade Field Marshal, every one of those cars was inoperative. Not even the paint was damaged."

"How inoperative?"

"All the electronics had failed."

"Not another mark on them?"

"Not a scratch. But more important, the agent who got this information was picked up by the Americans. And they questioned him as to what he knew about it, as though he were the cause."

"Correct deception."

"But that is not all. As you know, America is a commercial country. We discovered who owned that land, who had bought the cars, and who had paid for people to attempt to start them."

"Yes."

"Not the military."

"Of course not," said Zemyatin.

"Dummy corporations. We have estimated that it cost them at least three times as much to disguise who ran the experiment as it did to conduct it."

"CIA," said Zemyatin.

"Of course," said the officer. "Dummy corporations, money without end. Our old friends."

Zemyatin let out a grunt as though he'd been punched. And then, with a sense of helplessness he had not felt since he was a boy, said to the young officer:

"See? I have said it a thousand times. Here it is. You are laughing again at the American officer corps. You thought their invasion of Grenada was a sloppy operation. You were so confident. Look at this. Look at what they have done."

"We still have our missiles, Field Marshal," said the young officer.

"Yes. Of course we still have them," Zemyatin said, dismissing him as the Premier left the table on the other side of the soundproof one-way mirror. If the young officer should find out about that missile battery made useless, he would probably have to be killed along with any of those who had told him.

The Premier entered.

"The officers say the American diagrams are genuine. Absolutely genuine. I guess we should share with them now what we know about this weapon. After all, Field Marshal, what is the point of any of us living in a world where we cannot live? It is a good point that the American millionaire made."

"If he came to you with a bow and arrow, would you take down your pants, bend over, and spread your cheeks, Premier?" said Zemyatin.

"I am still your Premier."

"They give you their defense arrangements because they don't need them. They will not matter in the next war. The only thing between us and an American tank outside these walls is their lack of knowledge of what they can do to our missiles. That's all."

And then he explained what the Americans had done with the cars.

"If they can make useless the advanced technology of Porsche, Cadillac, Citroën, and all the glossy Japanese junk, do you really think they will have problems with the crude electronics of a Russian tank? Is that what you think?"

"They lied to us," said the Premier.

"Did you think they were honest? Our tanks will be useless. Our infantry will be useless. They will only provide a bloody road on which the American armies can march to Moscow and take it. And Leningrad. And Siberia. This time there is no retreat. There is only one thing we want, and that is for them to give us that weapon. Admit they have it, and hand it over."

"They are liars. They are the biggest liars in the world."

"The other side of the one-way mirror, Premier," said Zemyatin, nodding to where the American was waiting. Both American and Russian staffs were still exhanging information in the friendliest manner engineers could manage, the neutrality of scientific fact. "That they gave us this information about their defenses is the final proof for me that they have the better one, the one that opens the skies and makes our missiles and tanks useless."

Zemyatin watched the Premier return to the American and tell him he was a liar. He saw that the American was outraged. It was the sort of act he would have believed, if he did not have proof that the Americans were lying.

Later, on the way back to America, Mr. McDonald Pease was told that the coin of cooperation was to be paid in the weapon he was still insisting America wanted help in tracking down.

He was told, in case America did not know, that it was north of Boston. Pease wired this information directly back to America.

America knew that, he was informed. They were still looking for the weapon.

Harold W. Smith heard from his President again and this time the trust was tinged with doubt.

"The weapon is not in Hanoi. It's here. Somewhere north of Boston," came the President's voice. "I have given the search for it over to our public agencies."

"Good," said Smith. He did not have the sort of ego that demanded that he stay in charge of a project to which he had been assigned. That was one of the requirements of his having gotten this job in the first place.

"Do you know what misleading damage might have been done if we had based everything on the belief that the weapon was in Hanoi? They don't believe us, and dammit, I wouldn't either, Smith. Now, get your people into the Boston area and we'll close in with them when and if or if and when we find it."

"Can't do that."

"Why not?"

"One's on the way to Hanoi."

"And the other?"

"I don't think he is speaking to us, sir."

"I want you to remember, Smith, that when the human race depended on you, you let it down."

"I know, sir."

"Get back to me as soon as you reach either of them. I can't believe it. *You*, America's last and best hope."

"Yessir," said Smith. When Remo checked in again, he was going to have him give more information on that woman. Was Remo somehow falling in love?

Harold W. Smith didn't know. He used to think it was Chiun he didn't understand.

In Moscow, the Russians were beginning to understand many things. The young colonel in charge of the assassination squads was getting the reports on the whereabouts of the lone American agent and the red-haired woman. They checked out in San Gauta. They checked out at the airport. He was headed for Hanoi.

"I think, sir, that Hanoi would be the right place to put him down," said Colonel Ivan Ivanovich. He had been trained in Russian schools. His father before him was KGB and had served with Zemyatin in the great patriotic war. Therefore, the young colonel had been precisely taught not to pray. It was at this time, speaking to the man who terrified him, that he was discovering ways to ask the Almighty for help.

"Yes," said Zemyatin. "But I will plan the details of the putting down."

"Sir, yes sir," said Colonel Ivan Ivanovich to the brute

who had so shocked his senses within Dzerzhinsky Square itself. The old wretch had purposely killed an innocent officer.

Without the terror in the young colonel's heart, there would have been a thousand reasons not to take certain actions and a thousand more memos.

But the strangest fact of all was that Zemyatin was not a cruel man. He had never been a cruel man. He had never killed another person without a reason. He was ruthless, but then he never really had much choice. Events had made him what he was. All Alexei Zemyatin had ever really wanted was to be a good butler.

And because Field Marshal Alexei Zemyatin, the Great One of the Russian Revolution, had once been a butler, nothing an American or anyone, even his superiors, could ever hope to say would stop his planned attack. He had been taught too bitterly and too well that there was no one in the universe who could be trusted.

13

"Alexei, Alexei," his mother called. "The count wants you now."

Alexei Zemyatin heard the calls while he was in the pantry supervising the silver, which had to be polished in the French manner. No matter that it lacked the sheen of fine Russian silver. The count, like so many Russians, wanted everything French. That was why he had taken young Alexei to France with him before the war. There was enough silver in the daily service to feed two hundred serfs for a year. At the time, young Alexei Zemyatin did not give this much thought.

The silver belonged to the count, and the most important thing about two hundred hungry serfs, thought Alexei, was that he was not one of them. And he would devote his life to keeping it that way.

In his youth, Alexei had had fine sharp features, not unlike the count himself, giving life to rumors that in his veins flowed noble blood. This he did nothing to discourage, although his mother told him his father was really a merchant who had passed a night on the estate, paid her a compliment, and left her with Alexei, whom she felt was the true joy of her life.

Alexei did not rush from the pantry when the count called. He made sure the silver tally was correct when he handed it to the older butler. He had discovered early that just because it was logical that people should be honest, it did not necessarily make them that way.

Alexei trusted none of them. The only person he trusted besides his mother was the count. He was the perfect man.

Count Gorbatov was the big father of the manor that stretched for over a hundred miles and contained forty to eighty thousand souls. No one knew the exact number. At that time, no one counted the tillers of the field, or those who were born and died in the cold darkness that was the peasant's hovel.

The peasants believed Count Gorbatov was above lying. In some way, like many of the peasants, Alexei had come to believe that if there were no master for the estate, the fields would no longer provide sustenance. It was the count and God who gave them life, many felt.

"Alexei, hurry," said his mother. She was a maid on one of the floors, and this was a very important thing. To be a maid in the manor house instead of a serf meant ten to twenty more years of life. It was that simple and that valuable.

"Hurry, hurry, he calls," said his mother. She was always afraid that Alexei would not respond quickly enough and be sent to the fields.

He smiled at her and knew that she was proud of him in his gilt uniform and powdered wig, looking ever so much like a royal servant from some ancient French royal court. Even his shoes cost the equivalent amount of a peasant's income for a year.

Alexei walked crisply to the morning sitting room where

the count sat in a silk-covered chair so plush that it threatened to envelop his frail old body.

"Your Excellency," said Alexei as he formally entered the vast well-carpeted room. He stood, his legs symmetrical, shoes touching at the heel, his hands rigid at the side, for a crisp bow. He could smell the sweet seasonings of the master's morning drink. Like every servant, he had learned early to control his hunger, among other things. These controls would prove to be of enormous value in his survival, and later the survival of an entire nation. For hunger, like panic, was only an emotion. If one could ignore the one, one could ignore the other. Young Alexei stood waiting for the old man to speak.

"Alexei, I am going to take you into my confidence, young man."

"Thank you, Your Excellency," said Alexei.

"There is a great war going on. Very great. We will not win it."

Alexei bowed, showing he had heard.

"You probably cannot understand military strategy. That is for people of different blood. But that is not your fault, nor is it your duty. Very soon many soldiers will be coming here."

"You wish us to make ready for the Germans, Your Excellency?"

"Not Germans. They will be Russian soldiers."

"You wish us to prepare to receive Russian soldiers?"

"No. There is nothing we can do about them but get out of the way. Alexei, our soldiers are retreating and disorganized. A disorganized army is a mob. They will loot. They will pillage and they will rape. We must remove the valuable things, but we cannot give alarm to the rest of the people on the estate. We must prepare things in secret. The silver and the gold and the good porcelains must be hidden in carts."

At the time Alexei believed that somehow this was for the good of the estate. Days passed, days in which the peasants could have fortified themselves, could have been warned of the approaching mob. But no one was warned

and because Alexei trusted the count, he did not even tell
his mother. He packed the silver before dawn and packed
the gold before the next dawn. He personally made lists
and told other servants that their labor would not be
needed. This they accepted readily as a chance to get out of
work and they did not ask questions.

One night, the count himself awakened Alexei and
ordered him to dress immediately and quietly for a long
journey. The carriages and carts had been packed for days.

"I must wake my mother, Your Excellency."

"Don't worry about her," said the count.

And Alexei, trusting the count implicitly, followed his
orders. They left before dawn. When they stopped it was
evening, and they were still on the estate. The count, as it
was explained to everyone, was taking a little trip to
Moscow to confer with the new government. The Czar had
abdicated, a parliament was vainly trying to run things in
Moscow, and the count was headed there to give what help
he could. It seemed just like an ordinary journey with a
few more carriages than necessary. When they stopped,
Alexei looked for his mother. He had been assured, after
all, that he was not to worry about her, therefore she must
have been brought along.

He did not find her. But it was impossible he did not see
her because his work around the carriages kept him so
busy. On the second day he still could not find her, nor on
the third.

By the fourth day, he realized she was not there, and
asked to speak to the count.

"Your Excellency, you said that I should not worry
about my mother. But I cannot find her in this caravan."

"Your mother? Your mother?"

"Yes, Your Excellency, Zemyatin. A maid on the
second floor, Natasha. Somewhat heavy. Not very."

"I don't know. Why are you bothering me about this?"

"Because I do not see her. When you told me not to
worry about her, I was so relieved I could have kissed your
blessed hand."

"I don't know about her. Get back to the carriages,"

said the count. He had tents pitched by the side of the road for his nightly rest.

And then Alexei realized the count had meant she was not worth worrying about, not that she was safely protected. Only his years of training, that perfect control of a Russian servant under a ruthless master, kept him from screaming out his anger.

"Thank you, Your Excellency," he said simply, and bowed away. But outside the tent, he was determined to save his mother. He thought first of stealing a horse from one of the wagons and riding back. But a horse would be noticed. He thought of heading back on foot. But wild rumors already had hundreds of thousands of men looting the countryside. His mother, if she had time, would be smart enough to flee, in which case she wouldn't be at the estate. She might be hiding, in which case he might not be able to find her.

Without even comprehending what was going on, young Alexei Zemyatin was discovering his awesome talent for strategy and tactics. He realized that running hysterically back to the estate was no way to find his mother—indeed, he might be killed by the count, who feared anyone leaving him who knew about the treasure.

In Moscow, Alexei very simply separated the count from his gold by supposedly getting it onto the one train heading to the one open port heading toward the west: Murmansk. The gold crates, of course, were dummies. The count was also assured that Zemyatin would sit with the crates all the way from Moscow to Murmansk.

When the count told Alexei at the train station he would always have a job with him, Alexei knew his plan had worked. He kissed his master's hand and sent him off to a life of racking poverty with a perfect bow and a lie.

"I will be in the baggage cars with the crates," Alexei said.

He didn't bother to board but went to Lenin's Moscow headquarters. Even then Alexei knew he needed people to find his mother. The communists had them. They also had discipline and he had quite coldly calculated they were going to seize the government. They did not believe in democracy. They did not even believe in the proletariat. They believed in winning. That was all the former butler now believed in also.

The day before, he had devised the plan whereby the communists could steal the gold and silver most easily, and thus help finance their rebellion at this crucial time in their history. All he wanted, he said, was to serve the revolution. But he chose to serve in the party's young secret police organization as secretary to Lenin.

He was the only one who had no background or belief in Marxist theory, and that quickly enabled him to become Lenin's confidant. His genius enabled him to become the Great One.

He never did find his mother. Millions died during those first cruel years. Famine spread throughout the land. Wars were fought inside Russia on several fronts, and when Alexei could finally spare the manpower for the search for his mother, the estate no longer existed. So brutal were the conditions that cannibalism reappeared in Russia for the first time in thousands of years.

A junior officer who knew of the search and Alexei's beginnings once asked him if he had planned his revenge of making Count Gorbatov live in poverty to make up for his never finding his mother.

"Revenge?" he asked. He was puzzled by the word. No. There was never an idea of revenge. He had needed the gold and silver to help this new party seize power. He couldn't have cared less about Count Gorbatov. He never sought revenge, or even practiced cruelty. He was, in the hardest of times, the perfect butler, keeping emotions like hunger under control. He did what was necessary.

But shrewdly, he did not let the subordinate think he was above revenge. People who thought you might want to get even were less likely to cross you. Revenge was only worthwhile if you advertised it. The real target was never the person you punished, but the one who thought you might punish him.

Thus, many years later, with the world on the brink of destruction, when a young KGB colonel dispatching a kill team toward Hanoi mentioned that "now we will get him for what he did to us in London," Zemyatin did not discourage this stupidity. He absorbed the messages that made up the pre-kill picture, and asked a simple question.

"Why did they mention that he does not wear a wristwatch?"

"I imagine, Comrade Field Marshal Zemyatin, that San Gauta is a poor country, and most North Americans wear watches. This one did not. It was mentioned."

"Why didn't he wear a wristwatch?"

"I don't know," said the colonel, feeling perspiration form under the neck of his uniform.

"Let's find out. Maybe we can find out. Don't you wonder that here a person functions in the civilized world and does not wear a watch?"

"What do you mean?"

"I mean," said Zemyatin, "that it might behoove us to find out why he does not need to tell time, or whether he is able to tell time without a watch. It could even be that he has a watch hidden somewhere. I don't know. You don't know. Find out."

He did not bother to repeat that an enemy was perfect until he showed you how you could kill him. The young colonel would do as he was told. The young colonel would do exactly what he was told, because he believed that Zemyatin was cruel and ruthless, when the truth was the Great One was only ruthless. He did not trust the young colonel's word. He had never trusted anyone since the count. What he did trust was the colonel's fear.

But as he left the office, something akin to fear in himself emerged. It was not something that halted thought, or demanded that every body function be turned to its service. Rather, it was a question he was asking himself. When was this lone American going to show them all how to kill him?

On the flight to Hanoi on board a Swiss aircraft, Remo allowed himself five minutes' sleep. Kathy tried to make it four. Her hand was on his thigh.

"Have you ever done it in an airplane?" she whispered.

The lights were dim, and the other passengers were asleep. Remo hated the use of the word "it" for copulation. "It" seemed to represent copulation on every stupid car bumper that rolled along on American highways. Divers did "it" deeper. Bridge players did "it" with finesse, and horseback riders did "it" bareback.

"It?" said Remo.

"You know," whispered Kathy as her tongue touched his ear. She could have sworn his ear ducked.

"Yes, of course I know. And the answer is probably. I have done it on airplanes but with people I wanted to do it with."

"Do you find me unattractive?"

"No," he said. "You're beautiful."

"Don't you like women?"

"I like women. I just don't like people who use the word 'it' when they mean copulate."

"It's so unsexy to say 'copulate.' "

"Not to me. Try it," said Remo.

"All right. Remo, let's copulate."

"No," said Remo. "See, isn't that easier than a lot of beating around the bush?"

"I'd rather beat around the bush," said Kathy.

Remo took her hand and gently moved it to her own thigh, where he combined the heat of her body with his, creating a raging urge up the thigh through Kathy's body.

She groaned. A stewardess poked her head out from behind the curtain. She saw two people sitting upright next to each other. The man waved.

"I've heard of people doing it on airplanes, but not in five seconds," she said to another stewardess. "They were just sitting upright a few seconds ago."

Kathy snuggled her head into Remo's arm.

"How did you do that? That was wonderful."

"I didn't do it, your body did it."

"You do so many amazing things," said Kathy. She did not think he would actually go to Hanoi, at least not right away like this. She had thought that it might take him a while to get into that communist country. That would have given her time to get a good change of clothes and, with

some luck, get control of the fluorocarbon beam generator. That wouldn't be hard. It would require all the
corporate maneuvering of rubbing against Reemer Bolt for
a few moments.

But there was no time. As soon as they got out of San
Gauta this man lost no time in getting a passage to Hanoi.
Kathy was sure he worked for some government, probably
her own. He was, after all, very American although he had
some strange eating habits.

In a large South American city outside San Gauta, he
had made a single phone call. And within an hour, a rather
prosperous-looking woman in the back of a chauffeur-
driven limousine pulled up to the phone he was using in a
little kiosk outside a large store.

"Are you looking for Valdez Street?" the woman had
asked.

"Just a moment," Remo had said. And then he had
whispered to Kathy, "Do you remember those words I
asked you not to forget?"

"Yes," Kathy had answered.

"What were they?"

"I am looking for the large groceryman."

"The large groceryman?" said Remo.

"Yes," said Kathy.

Remo winked. "I hate this code pippyding."

"A supermarket," he said loudly to the woman.

The woman tapped her driver on the shoulder, indicating that he should leave.

"He's looking for a large groceryman," yelled Kathy.

"Right," said Remo.

The woman stopped her chauffeur and handed Remo a
small briefcase. Then she drove off. The briefcase had a
simple clasp lock. Remo fumbled with it for a moment and
then simply broke it off. Kathy noticed he only would have
had to slip a bar free.

Inside were two wallets with passports and a plastic
camera. The passports had names but no pictures. There
was also a metal device to make impressions, much like a
corporate seal.

Kathy recognized the camera. It had a picture of two

smiling children on it, with the sun shining brightly behind them. It was called "Insta-Tot," the first instant camera a four-year-old could use. The directions were in pictures and the words were addressed to parents. They said what a thrill a child would get mastering this absolutely simple device. It was so easy to use that words were not even needed. Just follow the pictures. It suggested that the parents let their children figure it out themselves if they had already had preschool experience.

"I don't know where the film goes," said Remo. "Why do they make things like this? Where does the film go?"

"In the bunny's mouth," said Kathy. She pointed to the side of the camera where a smiling bunny's teeth surrounded a square opening. Then she pointed to the film. The film was an oblong square just the shape of the hole. On one end of it was a picture of a bright orange carrot.

"The carrot goes into the bunny's mouth," said Kathy.

"Why didn't they say so?" said Remo.

Kathy pointed to the picture on the Insta-Tot package. There was a click.

"You just photographed your foot," said Kathy.

"Why don't they tell you these things?" said Remo. "I presume these pictures are for our passports."

"Yeah. This will get us both into Hanoi."

Kathy O'Donnell pointed the smiling Insta-Tot sun toward the real sun. Then she put the big blue eye on the camera to her eye. Then she pressed the bunny's nose.

The picture came out in a minute, only somewhat blurred, good enough for a passport.

"You have talent," said Remo. Then she put the camera in his hands, put his fingers on the bunny's nose, pointed the camera at her face, stepped back, and told him to snap.

On the third frame he got her picture.

He crumpled the camera in his hands and gave her the metal seal. She imprinted both pictures into the passport with the seal. Someone had gotten Remo the seal of the United States of America in the course of an hour. He had been instructed to destroy it. He did so quickly with his hands, as though polishing it. He made the seal into a solid block of metal which he threw with a clank to the street.

"How did you do that?"

Even more amazing was his answer. In terms of force and essence, the mystical concepts he explained, came very close to intricate atomic theory.

On one hand, he could do things with his body that were awesome. On the other, he rattled off metaphysical explanations like nursery rhymes. Yet, he couldn't get through the directions for a four-year-old.

She asked him about this.

"I have some difficulty with mechanical things," Remo admitted. "But when they unnecessarily confuse you with directions, then things become impossible."

"What is confusing about pressing the bunny's nose?"

"Well, you see, you're scientific. You understand things like that," said Remo.

"I also understood the carrot in the bunny's mouth," said Kathy.

"Okay, you can be smartass about it, but you were employed for the project in Malden and you do know what we are looking for. You would recognize it if we found it."

"I think I would," said Kathy. She was not sure how they would be able to get out of that Communist capital, but just watching the power of this magnificent man would satisfy her forever, even if she were held in some prison camp. If worse ever came to worst and she was captured, she could trade off what she knew for her safety. Besides, men were men. She would work out something if she had to.

But she did not think she would have to. She would more than likely see a trail of shattered bodies, each one a glorious thrill to her entire nervous system.

She hoped there might even be a problem getting into the group on its way to Hanoi and that he would have to kill to get them out. Just a little killing to make the day bright, to make her feel womanly again.

But the covers were perfect and unchallenged. They were part of the International Media Committee for Truth in Southeast Asia. Their first names were correct, which told Kathy that Remo had informed his superior about her already. It also told her that Remo had to have the highest priority possible with an agency that could get things done quickly.

She thought about these things in the dim light of the Swiss airliner, totally satisfied by the miraculous hands of this wonderful man called Remo. Actually, Reemer seemed like most men to Kathy. But Remo was unlike all the rest.

"I've never met a man like you," she said. "You're so different from other men."

"No, I am not."

"Who are you like?"

"Someone else. Except he doesn't seem to function in the modern world. I don't know. Don't bring up that subject."

"Is he your father?" asked Kathy.

"Sort of."

"I'd like to meet him."

"Go to sleep," said Remo.

Before landing in Hanoi, the International Media Committee for Truth in Southeast Asia had discussed the main draft of their conclusion to their investigation of the truth. It declared that Hanoi had been maligned, that its living standards and freedom should be copied by the rest of the world. It blamed the American media for distortion.

The man reading the communiqué was an actor. He knew the news business as few did. He had played a newspaperman on Broadway and on television.

"We just want to see the truth come out," he said.

"What about the hundreds of thousands of people who are willing to die to get out of Vietnam now that it's liberated?" said Remo. There was no purpose in mentioning this. He wasn't going to change anything. It was just that these people were so sure that their intelligence was superior to the average American's. It had been grating to hear them discuss how provincial the Americans were, how distorted the American news was.

"They're not Vietnamese. They're Chinese," said the spokesman, his craggy face had appeared on many TV commercials announcing his willingness to work for the betterment of mankind.

"So?" said Remo.

"Well, they weren't Vietnamese who were fleeing, but families who had once come from China," said the spokesman for the truth committee.

"You mean they have to be racially pure to have rights?" asked Remo. He had heard this bandied about often in the States when it was obvious that Vietnam had become a bloody concentration camp. Otherwise, why would people flee?

This man, whose every other sentence was about fighting fascism, was unwittingly spouting the fascist line. He could have been a Nazi and not known he wasn't a humanitarian. The last thing in the world of which he could conceive was his own stupidity. By the time the plane touched down in Hanoi it was resolved that the American media grossly distorted the progressive nature of the Hanoi regime.

The news release for tomorrow was to be about the bombing of Vietnamese rice fields that destroyed the ground and created agricultural problems.

The truth committee was still working on the draft denying Hanoi still held American prisoners, but they had to get that cleared first by the Vietnamese military.

When they arrived in Hanoi there were reporters waiting for the leader of the group to read his statement. He tousled his hair and opened his shirt to look like a newsman. He read the statement with a sense of remorse that his own country's media were distorting the nature of a people whose only desire was to live in peace.

The committee had been scheduled to read a statement at the hotel about industrial progress, but they were late. The rickshas had broken down.

The nice thing about communism for this actor was that if the towels were dirty you didn't have to wait for new ones or suffer insolence from the help, the maid was beaten right on the spot by a policeman.

"How are we going to find the beam?" said Kathy. "It's obviously hidden."

"If it is hidden, then someone has hidden it. Therefore, someone knows where it is."

"How do you find that person?"

"Well, if it is not a person but the government, and everything in these places is, you grab the highest government official and get him to tell you about anyone who might know about a new device."

"What if he doesn't talk?"

"They always do."

"But if he honestly doesn't know."

"Too bad for him."

"I love it," said Kathy O'Donnell. "I love it. Start with that guy with the machine gun and the pith helmet."

"I'll start where I want," said Remo.

"Where are you going to start?"

"I don't know," said Remo. The streets were bleak and plain; even the trees seemed to be stripped of bark. Apparently the people had eaten it. No wonder there wasn't any garbage on the streets of Hanoi. The lucky ones had already found it and made it their dinner.

Soldiers were everywhere. Slogans were everywhere. Remo rcognized old Chinese formations of letters. Much of this land had belonged to China at one time. Chiun had talked of insidious rebellions against the Chinese emperors. What differentiated an insidious rebellion from other kinds was whether the emperor had paid a Master of Sinanju.

Often just a few people were behind a rebellion. What they did was work on the grievances of the many and get the people to follow them. The new liberation movements of the world were 3,500 years old at least.

Looking around the streets of Hanoi, Remo noticed that the only fat people he saw were of high officer rank. Everyone else was thin beyond belief.

"Look at how thin the people are," Remo said.

The leader of the truth committee heard this. He was standing in front of his hotel, stuffing a caramel bar into his face.

"Capitalism doesn't encourage them to eat properly," he said. He dropped the wrapper. The doorman fell to his knees to lick it, but was kicked away by the manager of the hotel, who also had the rights to lick the crumbs off the Americans' shirts.

The American actor was told what an intelligent man he was. He was told this often. He was also told how much smarter he was than the average American, who did not know the real truth about the world.

"I owe it to my countrymen," the actor said, "to make them aware of the real world, not some comfortable beer-swilling Formica version of it."

"What is Formica?" asked a Communist minister.

"It's a shiny material that you can spill things on, and it never stains and you wipe it off easily. Always looks new. No character," said the actor.

"Could you get us some?" asked the minister.

The actor laughed. They asked again. He was sure they couldn't want something as bourgeois as Formica.

He asked to be taken to visit a typical Vietnamese family. Remo understood what the two officials were saying, but not word for word because he had only been taught the emperor's tongue. Rather, little snippets of phrases these officials never knew had come from old Chinese lords. The Chinese this committee so casually dismissed as having no rights in Vietnam had been in that country longer than the Normans had been in England.

The words Remo recognized were, "Stall the fat fool until we get the family set up correctly."

"Won't he be suspicious?"

"If that fat pig can think he is intelligent by saying things that people write for him, then he will believe anything."

"Yes, he does have the mind of a wooden puppet." The American actor put on his most concerned intelligent face for the photographers. He also asked to be taken to the scenes of brutal American bombings.

"Americans have a right to know what their government has done in their name," he said.

Remo let the group go off, even though some official was pushing him to follow. He was getting quiet within himself.

Remo walked around Hanoi with Kathy and a guide all morning in what seemed like an aimless pattern. The guide, of course, was not a cultural "enhancement," as he was called, but a Vietnamese police officer.

One building among many, not an especially large building, gave Remo the sense by the way the people walked by it that it was a building of authority.

"You can't go in there," said the cultural enhancer.

Kathy gave Remo a nod. Even she could understand his sign that the building was important.

"How did you do that?" she asked.

"I just did it. You keep looking, that's all."

"Would you teach me?" she asked.

"Teach me how to use that camera?" asked Remo.

"You cannot go there. No, no, no," said the cultural enhancer.

"Remo, you put the carrot film into the bunny's mouth. You point the camera at the person and then you press the bunny's nose."

"I did that," said Remo. There was a tinge of hardness to his voice.

"No camera allowed in liberated country," said the cultural enhancer. "No camera. No talking. You go back to group to get real story of truth of Vietnam. Real truth. Real peasants with real truth. Our truth the good truth. You see. Good truth. Yes."

"I had trouble with the film," said Remo.

"I don't see how," said Kathy.

"Well, I did," said Remo.

"You go. Now," said the cultural enhancer.

Kathy shrugged and looked at the building. The man's real genius was going to show itself now. She sensed an uncontrollable excitement seize her, almost mesmerizing her, making her limbs weak, her body warm. She imagined all the people Remo was going to have to kill in a building like that, the one the guide had confirmed was a security place of the government.

"That place is big enough to house the beam in any one of its many rooms," said Kathy.

Remo moved toward the building. The cultural enhancer grabbed one of his arms, but his hands closed on air.

Inside the building, a Russian with a microphone and a tape recorder commented dryly:

"He is coming toward us. Mark that the subject might be initiating action."

As he spoke another Russian was making notes. Halfway up the page was a comment that positive identifications had been made on the plane and reconfirmed at the airport. The female was Dr. Kathleen O'Donnell. The male was the American.

"We're not ready yet," came a voice from behind him.

The man with the tape recorder looked around with contempt. He was also afraid. The microphone was becoming significantly moist in his hands. He had ordered many people killed in his life, but now he was actually going to have to see the results of his orders.

"It doesn't matter that you are not ready," said Colonel Ivan Ivanovich. Field Marshal Zemyatin had told him to allow no special requests from his execution team.

14

Pytor Furtseva had been primed to kill for so many years that when he was told the target was advancing on him before he was ready, he didn't even mind. He would not have minded if he had to kill the target with his teeth right in the streets of Hanoi. He had practiced with his teeth on cows, and he had made his execution squad do the same.

"Blood faces," they were later called, but rarely to their faces. At one training base in Byelorussia another officer had commented that the chef should throw away his carving knife and let the "blood faces" butcher the cows.

Furtseva killed that officer with his teeth. He killed him in the mess hall where the officer had made that comment and, with the man's throat still in his mouth, he went to every table and stuck his face next to every officer at every place in the hall.

No one peeped. No one left. Furtseva had stood there in that hall waiting to be arrested, to be tried and then hung. He did not care. Eventually one of his fellow officers had the nerve to carefully get up and leave. Then the rest left and he spit out the throat onto the ground. Shortly thereafter armed soldiers filled the hall, surrounding him. He spat blood at them from the dead officer's throat.

As Furtseva was escorted out of the mess hall, his execution squad cheered him. It was the proudest moment of his life. He was ready to die.

The court-martial was held the next day and the execution was scheduled for the following week. The presiding officers were split. Some wanted hanging. The others said he had the right to be shot.

It was unanimous, of course, that he would die.

Pytor Furtseva stood for the verdict. His head was high. He felt a sense of relief, as though nothing mattered anymore. The shame and burden of being trained for something and never used was over. It would all end with a bullet or a rope.

The chief officer at the court-martial read slowly, occasionally adjusting his glasses. The other officers sat with faces passive as sand.

It took twenty minutes before Furtseva realized that he was not being sentenced to death.

"It is the verdict of the defense forces of the Soviet Socialist Republics that you and your entire unit be punished collectively. You will march one hundred miles through the Siberian frost with only knives for protection. You will have minimum clothes. You will have no matches. No food. No water."

"What?" Furtseva said. He could not believe the verdict. The army would never let a recalcitrant officer live. The most important thing in the army was getting along. To bite out the throat of a fellow officer for an insult was perhaps the most extreme example of not getting along.

And then the strange punishment. Why should his unit be punished? He apologized to his men, the only apology he could ever remember making.

They had asked him before he was assigned to the execution squad why he had never apologized to anyone.

"To admit being wrong is to admit weakness. More than anything in the world, I fear weakness."

That answer was scarcely out of his mouth when his Red Army file was stamped:

"This man is never to be allowed near nuclear warheads or to undertake diplomatic missions."

That did not bother Furtseva. He had never met any officer assigned to nuclear weapons he had even mildly respected. They were uniformly phlegmatic, and none of them had ever had even a strange idea, much less a lust for life. Or death.

Still, his actions in the mess hall undoubtedly would get some of his men killed on that hundred-mile starvation trek through the deadly Siberian chill. And it was not his unit's fault. It was his.

So he called them together to explain the punishment. And then came the time for his apology.

"And because it was my fault, I am now saying I am . . ."

The word "sorry" did not come. He gave his pistol to a sergeant.

"If you wish to shoot me, go ahead."

The sergeant stepped back and saluted. The entire unit snapped to attention and saluted. Then they applauded.

"Better to die with you as blood faces, sir, than to live like clerks in the Red Army," said the sergeant. They all had similar psychological profiles. There was something about them Pytor Furtseva liked. At that moment, the liking had turned to love.

Almost half the men died on the hundred-mile trek. They hunted with knives, they burned whatever they could for warmth, they made clothes from elk hides and from the canvas they found. They even stumbled on a stray police unit that was lost. The unit never turned up again,

although somehow they had left their clothes with the
blood faces.

When the hundred-mile trek was over, Furtseva's blood
faces were the strongest unit man for man in the entire Red
Army. Any one of them would have died for him. Every
one of them thought they were the best killers in the world
and were dying to try out their skills, ready to pick fights
with ten times their number.

But also as part of the punishment they were sent to a
base far away from all the other Red Army units. The
sentence was indefinite. The blood faces took it proudly.

The only hard part of their punishment was that they did
not get a chance for combat. Not even during the delicious
invasion of Afghanistan. All over the world assassinations
had become a tool of governments, and Furtseva's unit
remained on their lonely base.

Their leader was told that was part of strategy. Telling
him this was one of those smooth-faced officers who
probably thought a knife was for opening presents and a
gun to hold out in a parade.

The strategy was that the Soviet Union would use its
satellites for assassinations. This would leave Mother
Russia free of terrorism charges and the leaders of the
Communist world free of taint. They would use the Bulgarians and other East Europeans for the dirty work. Who
cared what taint stuck to a Bulgarian when Russia could
remain a socialist beacon of morality?

His unit would only be used as a last resort. It was then
that Furtseva heard the rumor that the man behind that
strategy was an old field marshal from revolutionary days.
The old man—he'd heard the phrase "Great One" used—
had been the one responsible for his strange punishment.

If the commander of the blood faces had been told the
Great One's reasoning he would not have understood. He
was not supposed to understand. It was all part of a very
logical scheme that had brought Furtseva to Hanoi to kill a
lone American while a KGB staff officer looked on.

When news of Furtseva's revolting act in the mess hall
reached Alexei Zemyatin, he inquired rather casually what
the army officers intended to do with the man.

He did not use the word "man." The word he used was Russian for "crazy animal."

"Get rid of him, of course," Zemyatin was told.

"Has any of you thought this through?" Zemyatin had asked.

"You can't keep a crazy animal in the army," Zemyatin was told.

"This man is an executioner, yes? His unit was trained like commandos with all the knives and garrotes and things they use," said Zemyatin. The accent on "things" showed the old man's dictate.

"Yes."

"Then who else would we want for this sort of work but a crazy animal? Who are you going to train for this?"

"We thought someone who would make a better soldier."

"You mean one who would cause no trouble. Who would work well with others."

"Of course. What else would you want of a soldier? He must get along with others, because if he doesn't, you don't have an army. You have a mob."

"Soldiers parade, and soldiers surrender, and soldiers sometimes will not even fire their rifles. I know soldiers. This man Furtseva is a disgusting killer, and sometimes we need just that. So let us not only remove him from the army, but make him an even greater hero to those lunatics in his command."

And so it was then that the "punishment" of the hundred-mile death march through Siberia was determined. The hardships molded the crew into an even tighter unit.

When the commander of the blood faces heard his unit was finally going to be used, his only regret was that it was against one person. He wanted hundreds. He wanted to be outnumbered by ten to one. His unit could tear the throats out of animals with their teeth. They could fell squirrels with knives, and shoot out the eyes of birds with pistols.

"Give us combat," Furtseva had said.

"You will have plenty," he was told by the smooth-faced KGB colonel with the rosebud lips.

He was given only one man.

And not only was that man not going to give him a chase, but he was coming to him. Just one man on those pathetically bare Vietnamese streets of this northern city, Hanoi.

Even worse, the commander of the blood faces had to explain several methods of killing, and promise to use them all. The officer, Colonel Ivan Ivanovich, was also having this entire execution photographed, convincing the commander that the people who ran Mother Russia were lunatics. One one hand they refused to use him because they wanted satellites to take the blame; on the other hand they were taking movie pictures of him, recording him, and making notes.

There were to be three men with knives, followed by an assault with pistols, backed up by snipers on the roof, grenade throwers, and then a three-man team. The KGB colonel had written this down.

"Do you really think any single human being is going to escape my knife fighters?" Furtseva had asked. He had been hoping for perhaps a little war with the Vietnamese, and that way they could fight their way out of Hanoi.

Colonel Ivanovich knew the commander was thinking that absurd thought or something like it. That was what made him so nervous. He did not know if Furtseva would frighten the American, but the commander of the blood faces certainly terrified him.

"He is advancing on us. We won't even have a chase," said Furtseva.

"Subject seizing the initiative," Colonel Ivanovich said into his microphone. His words were written down for backup.

The knife fighters went out first.

Remo saw them coming. They were healthy and moved well on their feet.

"Oh no! They're attacking us," screamed Kathy. She had thought Remo would do the attacking. Suddenly she felt very alone and frightened in this strange Communist capital. And the man she had entrusted to provide magnificent killings had suddenly gone mad. He was whistling.

Remo liked to whistle occasionally while working. Not

familiar tunes, but the rhythms of his body to make everything more harmonious. One of the problems with three people was that they had difficulty moving in unison. So when he caught the first knifer's wrist, he had to make a little adjustment to swing him around like a throwhammer. The stroke was good, accelerating as he brought the first man's feet into the second man's eyes, and then around again to catch the third in the stomach. Precisely in the middle.

The first knifer was good for the following screen of pistol wielders, except that his feet tended to wear out from impact. Remo was through the second screen, and up the walls toward the snipers, before Kathy had a chance to scream in delight. The snipers were duly surprised when their scopes showed the faces too close up, and then showed nothing because eyes whose accompanying brains had been turned to jelly tended not to focus all that well.

Colonel Ivanovich had caught most of it with his microphone. Every crushing death blow had sounded like an explosion before Furtseva's last line had a chance to throw grenades. The commander was running upstairs toward the action while Ivanovich was ordering the cameraman to pack, and everyone else to get out of there immediately.

The commander stopped his grenade throwers from finishing the man because he wanted him to himself. He lunged at the thin American, showing his teeth.

Remo saw the man drive toward him with his mouth open. The man obviously wanted to help, and Remo let him. He offered his throat momentarily, let the man pass, and then caught the back of the man's neck with his chin, driving a neck vertebra out through the man's mouth.

The man had obviously been trying to bite his throat. Chiun had told him that there would be a time when someone would be that foolish.

Remo never understood why anyone would expose himself like that. Chiun had explained that usually people that stupid were white. The man had been white. Remo made sure the grenades did not go off by implanting them through the mouths of the throwers into the cushions of the upper intestines. Then he went on through the building, looking for anyone who knew something about the fluorocarbon beam.

Outside, Kathleen O'Donnell was giddy. "I love you, Remo," she cried. "I love you."

Ivan Ivanovich ran past the laughing woman with his cameramen and note-taker. He thought for a moment that he should seize her, but he was sure from the horrible force of the noise coming from inside the building that he would not be able to get out of Hanoi alive if he laid a hand on her.

And he was going to get out of Hanoi alive. He paused only to make sure of the damage done by the lone American. The entire blood-face team had been dispatched like so much old cabbage. And according to Hanoi security, the American had gone on a killing spree and was still killing as of the phone call from the airport.

Colonel Ivanovich had caused a grave international incident, strained relations between two close allies, and, by his failure to stop the American, had launched a plague upon a capital city. Even now every policeman was looking for the killer, afraid to find him. What had the colonel done?

By the time Ivanovich and his photographers and note-takers reached Moscow, a formal message of complaint and the mounting damages had reached the halls of the Kremlin.

Alexei Zemyatin heard them all, and said when he received the trembling Colonel Ivanovich:

"Good. At least something has finally gone as planned."

15

The man had used another human being like a whip. Everyone saw it.

"He used him like a whip," said someone in the darkness.

"No," said someone else.

"Slow it down. You'll see. He used him like a whip. I swear."

The picture stopped on the screen, and whirred back.

"Who is it? Who is that man? Was this trick photography?"

The picture started again. A single man advancing into three. The three had knives. The single man had no weapon.

The pictures themselves seemed extraordinarily smooth. Everyone in the audience had seen pictures like that. If a top athlete were going to perform internationally, the coaches were allowed to use one very valuable half-hour of that film. It was for shooting at ten times the number of frames per second of ordinary motion pictures. While it couldn't stop a bullet, it could catch the bullet's blur going across a screen.

"Do I have to watch again?"

A voice in the darkness.

"Either all watch this or we watch our cities being destroyed, our farms becoming barren, and a slaughter that none of us who live benefiting from socialism will survive." An older voice in the dark projection room.

"It is so bloody." The first voice.

"Why not soldiers? Why do we have to see these pictures? Don't we have commandos? Judo experts?"

There was silence before the film was run again. The room had a certain pressure to it, as though the very air had been squeezed in. It was not easy to breathe. It smelled of fresh linoleum and old cigarettes. There were no windows, and none of the men were even sure what part of Moscow they were in, much less which building. They had been told that no one and nothing other than they were needed. They had been taken from all over the socialist bloc and brought here to watch these films.

They were all surprised, therefore, when they were given secret information.

"No military man, no KGB expert, has been able to identify what we see here. None."

"When were these pictures shot?"

"Two days ago."

"Are you sure they are real? You know they might have gotten some Western wrestlers or gymnasts and faked all this. You know that Western technology can do wonders."

"It was photographed in Hanoi. And I was right next to the photographer. I saw it all with my own eyes."

"I am sorry, sir."

"No. Nothing to be sorry for. You are here because we don't know what this is. Nobody else who has seen these pictures can explain it. Ask any questions you wish."

"I can only speak for myself, but I have never killed anyone. I am an athletic coach, a gymnast. I recognize other leaders of our socialist sports world here. Running coaches. Weight-lifting coaches. Swimming coaches. What are we doing here? Why us? is the question I now ask."

"Because no one else has figured out what we are looking at. It is not tai kwan do, or judo, or ninja, or karate, or any of the hand-fighting techniques we are familiar with. We don't know. You know the human body. Tell us what you see."

"I see what I have never seen before."

"Look again." The picture began to roll once more and the long man took the knife wielder and, grabbing a wrist, used him like a whip, the feet being the snapping points. It could have been a ballet, the man moved with such grace, if the deaths were not so stunningly real and final.

Once the coaches knew that they were not responsible

for understanding the moves, they could see small things they recognized.

"Look at the balance," said the gymnastics coach. "Beautiful. You can teach that and teach that and maybe one in a thousand learns it. But never like that."

"The concentration," noted the weight-lifting coach.

"Timing," said the instructor who had broken the West's dominance of the pole vault.

Someone asked if it were a machine. The answer was no. Machines had that kind of force, but never the calculating ability to make judgments.

"He looks as though he is hardly moving. Beautiful. Beautiful." This from a skating coach. "You know that he has got the magnificent ability to know where everything is at all times."

Now the mood had been reversed. Admiration replaced horror. Some of the coaches had to restrain themselves from applauding.

Then one of them noticed something peculiar.

"Look at the mouth."

"Right. Look at the mouth."

"It's puckered."

"It might be the breathing. There might be some special method of breathing that unlocks this all."

"Do the sound. Can you get a high resolution for the sound?"

"We already have," said the man beside the projection machine, and turned on the lights. He was the KGB general with the smooth face and rosebuds lips. The new general's pips glistened on his shoulders.

"Gentlemen," said General Ivan Ivanovich, sporting a new medal for combat. "The puckered lips were whistling. The tune was created by Walt Disney, an American cartoon company. It was for their cartoon picture *Snow White and the Seven Dwarfs*. The tune was a happy little melody called 'Whistle While You Work.' "

There was a deathly silence in the room as every man was reminded that they had been watching someone so very casually kill fifteen men. But one of the coaches was not deterred by the carnage. He asked for a copy of the film to use as a teaching instrument for his athletes. He did not even get an answer from the general. Another coach provided it.

"There is no one in the world we know of who could learn what we saw today."

Even better than swearing the coaches to secrecy, something that relied on their characters, young General Ivanovich had them shipped to a lush countryside dacha to wait for a few days or weeks or months, but hopefully not years. In brief, he imprisoned them.

Then he faced Zemyatin. The old man lived alone in a little Moscow apartment one could not tell was for the privileged. He had become almost friendly with the young bureaucrat who had tasted his first experience of combat. And if the young bureaucrat could forget his fear, he was even growing to like the Great One, who would just as soon have a high officer shot as light a cigarette.

When he returned from Hanoi with a tale of how the blood faces, the best killers Russia had been saving, were slaughtered like sheep, Ivanovich had been given those general's pips he had longed for. He had been told that his mission was a success, and for the first time he realized the freedom this old man offered. He was not looking to blame people. He was not looking to claim credit or escape disaster. He was looking to protect Russia.

And Ivanovich had done just that. The mission was two-fold. And entirely different from the disaster in London. In London they had merely lost men. But here, they had learned something, according to the dictum of the old field marshal. You assumed the enemy was perfect until he showed you otherwise.

If the blood faces had eliminated the American agent, all well and good. But if they failed, then Ivanovich's mission with the film and the recorders was to let the man show them how they might kill him.

But even with the field marshal's praises for Ivanovich, the young general felt a bit apprehensive as he rang the doorbell. They had not yet, despite all the films and analysis, found the man's weakness.

A man roughly Zemyatin's age answered the door. He had a big pistol stuck in his floppy trousers. He had not shaved, and smelled of old vodka.

"He's having supper," said the man. Despite his age, General Ivanovich was sure that the pistol would be used more accurately and more often than any glistening automatic in a shined holster on the belt of a smart young officer.

"Who is it?" came the voice from inside.

"The boychik with the cutesy lips."

"Tell General Ivanovich to come in."

"You're eating supper," said the old man.

"Set another place."

"With knives and forks and everything?"

"Certainly. He is going to eat with us."

"I am not a boychik," said General Ivanovich, entering the apartment. "I am a general in the sword who protects the party and the people. I am forty-four years old, bodyguard."

"Do you want a saucer with your cup?" asked the old bodyguard.

"Set a whole place," came Zemyatin's voice.

"A whole place, big deal. A whole place for a pretty little boychik," said the old man, shuffling off to the kitchen.

While there were no grand Western furniture in this apartment as there was in the lush dachas outside the city for men of lesser rank than the Great One, there was enough radio and electronic machinery to staff the most advanced Russian outpost. Zemyatin always had to be informed. Otherwise, it was a simple apartment with a few books, a picture of a young woman, taken many years before, and pictures of her as she grew older. But there was that unkempt feeling in this bachelor apartment; those little things that women gave to the lives of men to create the weather of their lives was missing.

The dinner was boiled beef, potatoes, and a raw salad, with tea and sugar for dessert. The seasonings tasted like someone had just grabbed the first box off the shelf.

"I hate to tell you this," said General Ivanovich, "but

we have had multi-analysis of the pictures, of the reports, of everything. We have not found a single flaw. We may be facing the one man who does not show you how to kill him."

"Eat your potatoes," said Zemyatin.

"But if you are not going to, don't mash them. He'll eat them tomorrow," said the bodyguard. "You wanted the saucer?"

"A full setting for the general," said Zemyatin.

"He may not even want tea," said the bodyguard.

"So he'll leave it," said Zemyatin.

" 'So he'll leave it,' " mimicked the bodyguard. "So I'll clean it up." He shuffled back from the bare table with the linoleum place mats into the kitchen.

"Ivan," said Zemyatin. "The reason I say we must assume that every enemy is perfect is that I am sure no one is perfect. All that has happened is that you have not found the American's flaw yet. So where, we must ask ourselves, have we been looking? This is crucial in our thinking—"

The bodyguard came back into the living room, brushing his shoulder into the conversation.

"Here is your cup. Here is your saucer," said the bodyguard. He banged the saucer down on the table.

"Thank you," said Zemyatin. "Now, Ivan, the world situation is this—"

"The glass on the saucer doesn't even have tea in it, but the pretty boychik has got himself a saucer. You want two saucers for the tea you don't have?"

"Give him tea," said Zemyatin.

"I am not sure about the tea," said General Ivanovich. "I would like to get on with this. We are dealing with a strange new element—"

"Take the tea," said Zemyatin.

"Tea," said General Ivanovich.

"He doesn't want tea. You made him take tea."

"I'll have the tea," said General Ivanovich. His bright, perfectly green uniform stood out like a shiny button in a rag factory compared to the old bathrobe Zemyatin wore, and the floppy trousers with the old lug of a pistol stuck in them that the bodyguard wore.

"Just because he tells you do to something, you don't have to do it. He pushed Russia around. Don't let him push you around."

"He is my commander," said General Ivanovich.

"Bully, bully, bully. We all get bullied by Alexei. Alexei the bully."

By the time the bodyguard got back with the steaming tea, Zemyatin had outlined the situation with brilliant simplicity. Unfortunately, the bodyguard wouldn't leave until General Ivanovich took at least one sip of the tea. It burned his tongue.

"He's not a Russian, Alexei," said the bodyguard. "He didn't put a sugar cube in his mouth."

"He's a new Russian."

"None of us are that new. He doesn't want the tea. Look."

"Would you mind if we defended Mother Russia in the midst of your dinner?" said Alexei.

"Every time you want needless saucers, we have got a national emergency," said the bodyguard.

"You are probably wondering why I keep him," said Zemyatin.

"No," said Ivanovich, who was even now learning to think like the Great One. "Obviously he does the necessary things very well. You can within a doubt trust him to do certain things. In brief, sir, he does work."

"Good. Now, this killer they have. We don't know his flaw yet. All right. Good. Let's put that aside for just a moment. I don't care whether we kill him or not. A few men here or there does not matter."

"There is something else," Zemyatin continued. "The Americans have a weapon we are interested in."

"Would you identify it for me?"

"No," said Zemyatin. "But they were testing it in London, when this man appeared on the scene to snatch away our one lead to it. This extraordinary man. This man whom we don't know how to kill yet. Then he turns up in a South American country. Then he turns up in Hanoi. Why?"

General Ivanovich knew from the way the older man spoke that he was not supposed to answer this.

"Because, as we gather from reports now coming in, he is looking for the same weapon."

"Is it possible they don't have the weapon? Maybe the British have the weapon."

"Logical, but we know everything the British have. We know all their layers of counterintelligence. Now I have told you more than I wanted about other departments. No matter. We must ask ourselves, why are they committing this weapon? As a deception?"

"If it were anyone other than the one I have seen," said Ivanovich, "I would say snatch him and get the information from him."

"What we are seeing on almost every level is an America far more cunning than we ever thought possible. Could I have misjudged, and is there another explanation for all this? I ask because we are approaching a point from where there is no return. A major decision awaits. It will be like a bullet that cannot be recalled. The world will never be the same. Our world. Their world. Never the same."

General Ivanovich thought a moment. "I'll tell you, sir, that before those pictures, before seeing what I have seen both through my own eyes and through the eyes of experts, I would have said yes, you are misjudging the Americans. I had never seen anything the Americans had done, outside of electronics, that would justify our respect."

"And now?"

"And now I know of a man . . . a killing machine whose chin can dislodge the neck vertebrae of another human being. We have tried to put him down twice. And he appears twice. Is he new? Did he come just this month from nowhere? No. He has been around."

"Right," said Zemyatin. "But strangely, they are sending him after this thing we believe they have."

"If they are still looking for it, do they have it?" asked the general.

"Ah," said Zemyatin. "The Americans who never hid things that well before would ordinarily not hide things that well now. But look at this killer they had hidden so well. Who does he work for? We don't know. So they are smarter than we think. What a great deception to make one think one does not have the weapon until it is used, or tested some more."

"The question is, Comrade Field Marshal, are the Americans that cunning?"

"An enemy is perfect until he shows you how to kill him. I never thought we would see the day when I am hearing about one human being who is perfect. There must be something we do not know."

Ivanovich had an idea. His desk had been bothered, of late most intensely, by offers of the North Korean allies to perform services in the international arena. Before devoting all his time to the field marshal, Ivanovich had handled these diplomatic requests himself. Now he had shunted them off to a subordinate.

"Our friends in Pyongyang want to provide a service. They say that we insult them by not making them full partners in the socialist struggle. They have had some success recently and of course have trumpeted it to us. Why not use them on this American?"

"Throwing another piece of dung," said Zemyatin. "What could they possibly have that we don't have? The random purposeless killing for which they have an appetite interests me not at all."

"They have succeeded in killing an SDEC director, a man we couldn't even locate. And now, as a gift of pride, they are going to give us the pope himself. No more meddling in our western Polish border. The pope. The SDEC director dead and the pope about to be dead."

"Let me tell you about the Koreans. There is a saying that when one brings a Korean to wield a knife, one hires not a servant but a master. It's true. Never trust a Korean assassin."

"I am not saying trust."

"This is something you might not know, boychik, but it is an ancient saying. The czars tasted the bitterness. One of the first things we did was to get their records. I was the one who made the decision to employ some of the czar's best policemen. During the fifteenth and sixteenth centur-

ies Mother Russia used special Koreans extensively. Do
you know who got killed as often as a czar's enemy? The
czar. There is a saying in this country that nothing comes
out of Korea but your own death. No to Koreans. No.
Never. I say it. The czars before us said it. And our grand-
children will say it.''

General Ivanovich snapped to attention while sitting.
His back became straight, his heels touched, his chin lifted
to level, and Zemyatin knew the young man was afraid
again. But the old field marshal had not said this to instill
fear. It was something he had trusted over the years, an
order he had given when the KGB first began using satellites. Use anyone but a Korean. The KGB had followed it
blindly like good bureaucrats.

One of the electronic consoles beeped, and the old bodyguard shuffled over and quickly had it going.

Ivanovich looked back at Zemyatin, the Great One, who
gave a small nod. The young general understood that there
had been a question as to whether this information could
be shared with him in the room. Without even a spoken
answer, the field marshal's shrug indicated the exact level
of information that was allowed to be discussed with the
general present.

"They have fired it again," said the old bodyguard.

"Where?" said Zemyatin.

"Egyptian Sahara. An area of one hundred square kilometers. Our people are there already and risking quite a bit
to get us the information. The Egyptians work closely with
the Americans."

"One hundred square kilometers. That's an area any
army would occupy. An entire army."

"And fired in a single second."

"That is their last test. Their last. No more testing.
What would they have to test for?" said Zemyatin.

"Is this the weapon the American is protecting?" asked
the young KGB general.

Zemyatin dismissed the question with a hand. The old
man thought awhile, his face becoming even older, more
grave. Lines of death showed. The eyes seemed to be
looking into hell.

Finally, the younger man asked:

"What is our next step toward their special person? Should we accelerate some tracking operation on him at this point?"

"What?" said Zemyatin as though coming out of a sleep.

"The American."

The bodyguard touched the clean crisp general's uniform. "Leave," he said. The American was of no importance now.

Shortly thereafter reports came in of two more firings in the area. On a map it clearly showed that in a strip of Egyptian desert equal to the size of the Balkans, Russia's soft underbelly, the sand had come under such intense solar heat that it had fused into a hard, slick, slippery surface not unlike glass.

To Zemyatin it was clear why they had chosen the Sahara. The transformation of the sand to glass was the one instant effect observable from a satellite. The Americans could, as he was doing now, plot the range of their weapon. All they would have to do was recalibrate, and lay Russia defenseless. There would be no more tests. The attack, he was sadly sure, could come at any moment. It was time to launch his own. In this moment, Alexei Zemyatin, the man who had only wanted to be a good butler as a boy, would show his true military genius.

He ordered the Premier to immediately inform the Americans that Russia would now share information about the fluorocarbon beam that could harm them all. He did this by telephone because it was faster.

"Tell them there have been certain effects on the missiles. Just certain effects. Do not tell that the missiles are or are not destroyed. Certain effects."

"But, Alexei . . ."

"Shhh," said Zemyatin. It had been suspected but not yet proven that the Americans could bug any telephone line in the world from outer space. "Do it. Do it now. Have it done by the time I get there. Yes?"

His bodyguard noted that the young general had not drunk his tea.

Zemyatin was driven by another old bodyguard to the Premier's dacha. The weather was crisp and hard and there were many soldiers outside. They stood in greatcoats and shiny boots looking formidable. Alexei was still in his bathrobe.

He walked through the soldiers outside, and through the officers inside, and nodded the Premier into the back room. The Premier wanted to take some generals with him.

"If you do I'll have them shot," said Zemyatin.

The Premier tried to pretend he had never been so lavishly insulted in front of his own military. Zemyatin had never done this before. Why he was starting now, the Premier did not know. But there were certain formalities that should be observed.

"Alexei, you cannot do this to me. You cannot do this to the leader of your country."

Zemyatin did not sit. "Did you contact the Americans?"

"Yes. They are sending their Mr. Pease back again."

"Good. When?"

"They seem to be as nervous about this as they say we should be."

"When will he be here?"

"Fifteen hours."

"All right, we will have some technical people add to what we know to stretch out our information. Figure eight hours for the first conference, then we all sleep. That should get us another twelve hours. We will stretch this for two days, forty-eight hours. Good."

"Why do we give them faulty information for forty-eight hours?"

"Not faulty. We just won't give them the fact that their beam totally destroys the electronics in our missiles until the second session, and in that session we keep them locked up with us until the forty-eighth hour has passed."

"Why are we giving them the truth about our missiles being useless?"

"Because, my dear Premier, it is the one thing they don't have yet," said Zemyatin. "Look. At this moment they have everything they need to launch an attack with this weapon and do it successfully. Everything. We would be through. They could sit in Moscow tomorrow and you could throw stones at them."

"So why give them the last thing they do not know?"

"Because it is the only thing for which they might delay. The only thing they need now is absolute assurance that our missiles—not their own, which I am sure they have tested this weapon on—but ours, do not work when hit by the unfiltered sun's rays. They will delay because we will give ourselves up on a silver platter."

"Do we want to do that?"

"No. What we have done is past the point of no return. While they are delaying for the last thing they need, our new missiles will go off."

"You mean in two days?"

"Within two days."

"When exactly?"

"You do not need to know. Just talk peace," said Zemyatin. He did not, of course, trust the head of the Russian government with this information now that the top bureaucrat had given him permission to launch the missiles in their very building. That was the reason for the time data given to every commander who perilously trucked the huge cumbersome death machines into the new Siberian sites. Alexei Zemyatin did not trust all of them to fire at once, given a sudden order. The trigger on the gun had already been pulled. Two days from now the holocaust would come out of its barrel.

In Washington, McDonald "Hal" Pease was told that the Russians were willing to share secrets now. They had realized that they shared a fragile planet with the rest of the human race.

"I'll believe it when I see it," said Pease.

16

If there was a remote chance that Alexei Zemyatin might call off the attack on the suspicion that America might not itself be really planning its own attack, a simple cassette would smother that faint suspicion with brutal finality. Actually there were twenty little cassettes in a cheap plastic case with a colorful brochure. The packages cost three dollars each to manufacture, and sold for eight hundred.

They promised to bring out the leadership potential in every man. What they did was hypnotize people into ignoring reality. On his steady corporate rise Reemer Bolt had bought many such self-fulfillment programs. Their basic message was that there was no such thing as failure.

There were facts and there were conclusions. One had to separate them. When Reemer Bolt looked at a field of useless cars, it was not a fact that he was ruined, his cassette program told him. The fact was that fifty cars had been ruined. The fact was that he had notched his company one step closer to ruination. But Reemer Bolt himself was not ruined.

Look at Thomas Edison, who, when he had failed in ninety-nine different ways to make a light bulb, said he had not failed. He had really discovered ninety-nine ways not to make a light bulb on his sunny road to success.

Look at General George Patton, who had never let ideas of failure bother him.

Look at Pismo Mellweather, who had produced the cassette tapes. Mellweather was a millionaire many times over, even though he'd been told as a child he would never amount to much. Teachers had even called him a swindler. He had spent time in jail for extortion and embezzlement. But now he had homes in several states because he had dared to face his own self-worth. The key to succeeding

was not succumbing to the false notion that you had failed
in some way.

Failure, the tape said, was a state of mind just like
success. One only had to accept the fact that one was a
winner and one would become a winner. Pismo Mellweather had sold three hundred thousand of these cassette
programs with the astronomical markup, and had made
himself a success for life.

Reemer Bolt had bought one of those programs and had
listened to it so many times that at moments of despair he
would even hear Pismo Mellweather's voice. And so while
he now looked at a field of disaster, by nightfall he was
able to see the car experiment not as a failure, but as just
another way the miracle device should not be used.

"Reemer," he was told by an assistant, "we blew it."

"Little men blow things. Big men create success from
what others call disasters."

"You can't manufacture anything with an electronic
part in it," said the assistant. "You can't use the rays here
in the world. The world is electronic. Good-bye. Good
night. Do you have the employment section of the paper?"

"No," said Bolt, with the gleam of a true believer in his
eyes. "We have discovered that we must manufacture non-
electronic products."

Many products were not electronic, the assistant pointed
out, but none of them lent themselves to cheaper manufacture by exposure to the unfiltered rays of the sun.

Bolt's leadership kit solved that problem. Its message
was that every problem had a solution if only a person
unlocked his leadership power through a simple and tried
method. One should think about a subject very hard, the
tape advised, and then put it out of one's mind and go to
sleep. In the morning, the answer would come.

In this hour of trial for Reemer Bolt, he did just that and
the answer did come to him in the morning.

An assistant phoned him with a suggestion. Heated sand
made glass. Glass was not electronic. Glass was still used.
Why not make glass at the source? Undercut the price of
even an Oriental laborer.

Thus was conceived the experiment that convinced a

nuclear power that it was going to be attacked. The Sahara was chosen because it had the most sand. If the process worked, you only had to send your trucks out to the desert with a glass cutter and haul back the cheapest and perhaps the most perfect glass in the world.

"Why most perfect?" Reemer Bolt was asked.

"I don't know. It sounds good," he said. When the results came in he was so ecstatic he called a meeting of the board to announce an even great breakthrough. Indeed, the initial survey showed that the glass was perhaps as clear as anything this side of a camera lens. And they had just made several hundred square miles of it. They could produce a million square miles of perfect glass every year. Forever.

"Forever," screamed Bolt in the boardroom of Chemical Concepts of Massachusetts, Inc. And then, in case anyone with a remaining eardrum had not heard him, he yelled again. "Forever."

"Reemer," said the chairman of the board, "what happened to that wonderful car-painting procedure?"

"A minor problem, sir. We are going to wait for that to come to its full fruition. Right now I am going to get us all our money back and then some. Once that is done we'll push ahead with the car-painting process."

Several of the members were puzzled. No one seemed to be agreeing.

"I will tell you why I asked," said the chairman of the board. "While the glass concept is good, by creating several hundred square miles of glass in Egypt you have just ruined the glass market for the next sixty-five years according to my calculations."

"Can we cut the price?"

"If they don't need as much as you have put on the market, you already have. No profit from cheap glass."

"I see," said Bolt. He felt something strange and warm running down his pants leg.

"Reemer, have you just wet your pants?" asked the chairman of the board.

"No," said Bolt with all the enthusiasm of a man who

understood his leadership potential. "I have just discovered a way not to go to the bathroom."

It was a night of exhaustion. Delirious, delicious exhaustion, with every passionate nerve aroused and then con-
tented.

That was before Kathy made love to Remo. That was in
Hanoi, going from one government office to another.
From one military base to another. That was in the dark
alleys while a city went mad searching for the killer among
them.

Several times the police would have gone right by if
Kathy hadn't knocked over something. And then she saw
them come against this wonderful, magnificent, perfect
human being, and die. Sometimes their bones cracked.
Sometimes death was as silent as the far edge of space.
Other times, those special times when they came roaring
down upon them, the bodies would go one way and the
heads would go another.

It was before dawn when Remo said, "It's not here.
They don't know where it is."

"That's too bad," said Kathy.

"Then why do you have that silly grin on your face?"
asked Remo.

"No reason," purred Kathy. She nestled into his arm. It
didn't feel very muscular. "Are you tired?"

"I'm puzzled. These people don't know where the
fluorocarbon thing is. They never heard of it."

"That's their problem."

"What else do you remember about it?"

"Just that awful man in San Gauta."

"I dunno," said Remo. They were in a warehouse
marked "People's Hospital." It had been labeled that way
during the Vietnam war so that when the Americans
bombed the warehouses they could be accused of bombing
hospitals. The reporters never mentioned that it stored
rifles, not wounded.

It still stored weapons, Remo and Kathy saw, but now
they were for battles in Cambodia or on the China border.

So much for the peace everyone had predicted if America left.

"Are you ready to move?" asked Remo.

"No. Let's just stay here tonight. You and me." She kissed his ear.

"Are you tired?"

"Yes, very."

"I'll carry you," said Remo.

"I'll walk. How are we going to get out of here? We're white. It's a police state. Are we going to walk out through Indochina? That will take months."

"We'll go out through the airport."

"I know you can get us through any guard, but they'll shoot down any plane you get to. There are no alleys to hide in. It's flat. You might make it somehow, but I'll die," said Kathy. She was still wearing the suit and blouse she had arrived in. The shoulder was ripped, but she felt this only made her sexier. She knew her own deep satisfaction had to be sending out signals to this man, making him desirable as well. After all, hadn't he suddenly taken her here into this warehouse when the killing was over?

"Would you mind if I died?" asked Kathy. She wondered if she were acting like a little girl. She grinned coyly when she said this.

"Sure," said Remo. She was the only one who knew anything about this mysterious device that could end life on earth.

"Do you mean it?" She hated herself for asking that question. She'd never thought she would. She'd never thought she would feel like all the other girls in school had felt, giggly all over, fishing for any little compliment from the man she loved.

"Sure," said Remo. "Don't worry about the airport. People only see what they're trained to see."

"You can make us invisible?"

"No. People don't look."

"I thought Orientals were more sensitive to their surroundings."

"Only compared to whites. They don't see either."

She was amazed at how simple and logical it all was, so natural. The human eye noticed what startled it, what was different. It noticed what it was supposed to notice. The mind didn't even know what it saw. People thought they recognized others by their faces, when actually they recognized them by their walk and size and only confirmed the identification by face.

This Kathy knew from reading. The way Remo explained it, it sounded more mystical but still logical. He said the mind was lazy, and while the eye really saw everything, the mind filtered out things. It filtered out twenty men and blurred the message into a marching column. Remo and Kathy easily joined a line of marching guards, and by being part of the mass, just moved with it. If she had dared, she would have moved her head to look into the faces and see them actually staring through her and Remo. But Remo had told her to listen to her own breathing and stay with him. That way she would remain part of the natural mass of the moving column. He told her to think of his presence.

For Dr. Kathleen O'Donnell that was easy. She was ready to stay with this man forever. She listened to her breathing as she sensed the choking odor of burning jet fuel and felt the ground tremble with the big engines revving up. She knew she was boarding an airplane because she was climbing up. But the miraculous thing was that she did not feel as though she were climbing.

Then they were in the aisle and there was a fuss over seats. The problem was that two other people did not have seats. They did not have seats because she and Remo were sitting in them. Remo settled it by showing the others two seats even the flight attendants weren't aware of in the back. The people didn't return.

"Where did you put them?" she whispered.

"They're okay," said Remo.

When the flight was airborne it was discovered that a stockbroker and a tax lawyer had been stuffed into the lavatory seats.

It was a British airplane. They had to find someone who

could determine what had gone wrong, why there were two extra people for seats that did not exist when the extra people had tickets.

Since there was a new labor contract with the British airline, a crew member who was also practiced as a mediator took charge. Remo and Kathy sat comfortably all the way across the massive Pacific to San Francisco. By the end of that flight, the mediator had formed a committee to establish who should be blamed for the failure to provide seats. The stockbroker and the tax lawyer stood the whole way, massaging where they had been pressed into the lavatory.

At the airport, Remo dialed Smith's special number.

"It ain't there, Smitty," said Remo. "Not even remotely there."

"We have found one in the Northeast but we can't locate it. I am sure the Russians are going to attack. I am alone in this, Remo, but I know I am right."

"What do you want me to do, Smitty?"

"We have got to make the Russians trust us."

"Do they trust anyone?"

"They think we are behind the fluorocarbon beam. They are sure of it. They are sure we are using the beam to destroy them."

"That doesn't sound like they are going to trust us."

"They may, if we do something."

"What?"

"Stay there. Right on that line."

Kathy waited contentedly by the baggage-return racks. Every once in a while she blew Remo a kiss. Men glanced at her longingly. They always did that. She had never met a man she couldn't have if he liked women. But she had never met a man until this one whom she wanted. "Wanted" was too weak a word. This was a man who was like air to her lungs and blood to her cells. This man was hers, part of her, beyond separation.

She blew him another kiss. She knew her clothes were dirty by now. She was penniless. She had lost the sole of one shoe in Hanoi. Her undergarments had ceased to be comfortable in San Gauta. And she did not care. Kathleen O'Donnell, whose dress had been regal armor all her professional life, did not care. She had everything she needed, especially for her secret desires.

Her only thought at that moment was whether Remo wanted children. He had mentioned something about his friend wanting him to get married and have children. Kathy could give him children. She could give him everything. And more.

She wanted to trot over and kiss him. She wondered what people would say if he took her right there on the baggage rack. Would she mind? She would enjoy it, of course. But she wondered if she would mind what people would think.

No, there was only one person whose opinion she cared about, and that one person was no longer herself. He had just hung up the telephone and was coming over to her.

"You need money or anything?"

"No. I don't need anything, Remo," said Kathy. "It's strange, I used to think I needed things before. But I don't now. I have everything."

"Good," said Remo. " 'Cause I'm leaving."

Kathy giggled. "I love your sense of humor."

"Bye," said Remo.

"Where are you going?"

"I'm leaving," said Remo. "Gotta go. Business."

"Where?" said Kathy, suddenly realizing that he was actually leaving her. She shivered under the shock, her hands tight and trembling.

"Gonna save the world, sweetheart. So long," said Remo.

"What about saving the world from the destruction of the ozone shield? That's saving the world."

"That's number two. Disasters nowadays have to wait in line."

"How can it be number two? It can make the entire world unlivable."

"Not right away," said Remo. He gave her a kiss on the cheek and headed for an Aeroflot office. The way Smith had set this up, there was a chance, a fair chance, that even Sinanju might fail. In his effort to save the country, he had all but told Russia that he was sending a man in.

"Thanks a lot," Remo had said when he heard the plan the President of the United States had approved. "But how do you expect me to come out of this alive?"

"You can do anything, it seems, Remo."

"Except what you set up for me. You're going to get me killed."

"We have to risk that."

"Thanks."

"Look, Remo. If you don't make it, none of us will make it."

"Then kiss your bippee good-bye."

"You'll make it, Remo," said Smith.

Remo had given a little laugh and hung up. That was before he kissed Kathy good-bye and before he went to the Aeroflot office. He had looked at a picture of the crude Aeroflot jet, remembered how many men Russia was willing to lose in the Second World War, and then slowly backed away. Very slowly. He could not use that plane.

Dr. Kathleen O'Donnell watched Remo leave. She waited, believing that he would return. She told herself that he was playing a joke on her, a cruel joke. He would come back and she would insist that he never play that joke on her again.

Do anything he wanted to her, she would plead, but not that. Never leave her like that again. Several men stopped to talk to her, seeing she was alone. A few pimps at the airport offered her work.

When she let out a scream that halted everyone at the baggage racks, she acknowledged that he had done it. He had actually left her.

Someone tried to quiet her. She poked her nails into his eyes. Airport police came running. She poked them, too. They wrestled her into a straitjacket. Someone gave her a sedative. With the chemicals heavily drugging her mind, she felt only a roaring, all-consuming hate. Even drugged, she was planning her revenge.

Someone found her passport on her body. They wondered how she had just gotten a British entry stamp, without the debarkation stamp from their customs.

She told them a story. She told them several stories. She got Reemer Bolt on the telephone. Bolt's voice cracked as he was trying to explain that everything was not lost.

Kathy told him to contact the lawyers of Chemical Concepts of Massachusetts. She told him to contact her banker. She told him how much money to wire. She told him to get her out of there. She told him the magic words:

"Everything is going to be all right, Reemer."

"Of course, but how?"

"I am taking over," she said.

"Your project? Your responsibility?"

"Of course, Reemer."

"You are the most wonderful woman in the world," said Reemer Bolt, realizing there *was* a way out of this mess.

Thus when the technicians started complaining later that day that Dr. O'Donnell was going to destroy the world, Reemer Bolt had little sympathy for them.

Kathy, returning on the first flight back east, had stormed into Chemical Concepts of Massachusetts and, without even a change of clothes, begun ordering the technicians around.

Bolt happily endorsed everything. But soon the technicians began sneaking out of the beam generator station with tales of what was going on.

"Mr. Bolt, did you know that she has placed a locked wide arc on the beam?"

"No. Frankly, I don't care," said Bolt. "It's Dr. O'Donnell's project, and what she does with it is her business. I tried to save it with marketing directions, but I don't know if I can do anything now."

Then another technician entered Reemer Bolt's office.

"Did you know she is building a second beam generator?"

"Thank you for telling me," said Bolt, and promptly began preparing a memo from him to Kathy with another copy to the board of directors. That memo would suggest

that they first make one beam generator feasible before
they invest in another.

All the technicians came in on the next one:

"Did you know that she is doing a central eclipse with a
locked perpendicular arc on the second generator?"

"No, I didn't," said Bolt with great thoughtfulness.
"But I do resent your coming to me with tales about
another officer of this corporation. Underhandedness is
not the way Reemer Bolt likes to do business."

"Well, for one thing, if she turns on that second generator, none of us is going to be able to get out alive."

"What about the radiation suits?"

"They're only good for standing near it. And the arc
she's going to set up for that second one can wipe out all
life from here to Boston."

"Keep up the good work," said Bolt, who immediately
set about establishing a Rhode Island branch of the
corporation, something he was going to have to do before
she turned on the second beam.

In the laboratories Kathy O'Donnell heard all the com-
plaints. The technicians' objections became increasingly
shrill. And she cared not a whit for any of these people.
She hardly even heard them. She didn't even enjoy the
obvious suffering of one of the technicians as he described
the horror she could inflict on the world with these changes
and additions to the program.

Kathy O'Donnell did not care.

Remo had left her.

Everyone was going to pay for it, especially Remo.

17

Ironically, it was Chiun's understanding of Russia that might get Remo killed. Smith had no choice. That was the horror of these great events. Everyone was really helpless to do anything but try to avoid the megadeaths they all faced.

Smith had wanted Chiun to penetrate Russia. Even now he would rather have launched Chiun into Russia than Remo. But Remo was all he had. No one knew where Chiun was or what he was doing. Smith reviewed what Chiun knew about Russia. Smith had made the correct move. The rest of the government was wrong.

Chiun, in some strange way, read the Russians like children read comic books. It was all clear to him. Every move that seemed baffling and threatening to the West was like a colorful, unmistakably simple design to Chiun.

"Russia is not an enigma wrapped in a riddle. You are the enigma wrapped in the riddle so that simple imperial logic seems strange." Smith rarely understood the Master of Sinanju.

Chiun, of course, did not approve of wars, cold or warm, because the art of the assassin in such a conflict was always replaced by hordes of amateurs. Wars were also unjust, especially the modern ones among conscripts, because "your eighteen year olds die instead of your kings and generals." The implication was that if an assassin were hired instead of an army, justice, not mass murder, would be done.

What Chiun had seen so simply, and what had at last explained that the world had little time left, was the Russian manner of fighting. He had explained it in terms of ying and yang, fear and not-fear, strength and not-strength. It was, in brief, Oriental mishmash. Except

Chiun always seemed to be able to tell what Russia would do when he was asked.

So Smith himself had taken all Chiun's ideas on Russia and translated them into mathematics, a subject he knew well. It was called the Russian mode. He had done it for himself, and had once offered it to the government but was refused. Frankly, Smith couldn't blame them because many of the terms to feed into the formula were things like "face" and "spine."

"Face" was what the Russians showed you and "spine" was what they were really doing. As in the body, the spine showed where everything was really going. The face could look anywhere. But the spine was where a person was. And so when this latest incident had begun, Smith had fed the moves of the "face" into the Russian mode designed from Chiun's mystical formulas. They actually weren't so mystical if you read everything as a never-ending fight for life. Sometimes the Russians were stupid. But more often than not they were brilliant.

It was Chiun's formula that had first suggested a possible link between the opening of the ozone shield and the building of the irresponsibly dangerous new missiles. The link was fear. And every move America made only worsened that fear, because the Russians believed, had to believe, according to Chiun's explanation, that America had a weapon that could easily destroy them and was planning to use it.

Chiun's formula said that when the Russians built their first-strike missiles they already felt that all other armor might be or was definitely useless.

The trust of mutual terror that had kept the countries in a nuclear stalemate had been broken because Russia was sure that America was about to win it all. That's where Russia's spine really was.

The face showed hostility. The spine showed fear.

When the American special negotiator went to Russia with a gift of showing defenses as food faith, it had only confirmed that America had something so strong it would make ordinary Russian missiles useless. Spine.

When Russia invited the special negotiator back, it wanted to show peace by its willingness now to share the reports on the damage done to Russian missiles by exposure of electronics to unfiltered sun. The face was reasonable. The spine, according to Chiun's formula, showed they had really decided on war.

All of this became ice clear with the last Russian move, the suddenly reasonable face after hostility. The last Russian move unmistakably completed the entire formula. They were going to use those new missiles soon. A day maybe, two days, and they would be on their way.

There was no way to explain this to a harried President because the unmathematical translation was that after strong bitterness, sudden sweet was the sign of the steel spine. America could not launch a nuclear war because Smith had seen a computer translate a mathematical formula back into a term called "steel spine."

But if there was hopelessness on one hand, there was a chance on the other. If Chiun's understanding was correct, and Smith was sure it was, there was one way to show Russia that opening the ozone shield was not an American weapon.

America had one slim chance before the missiles went, probably from both sides. The opportunity to prove that the machine that destroyed the ozone shield was not an American weapon was gone. What they had to do now was show they had a greater weapon that they did not use.

To be brief and Western about it, America had to show the Russians that anytime they wanted to, they could take apart the Russian government, but had chosen not to do so.

America's word was not good enough for that. America had to do it for the benefit of the person who really ran Russia. The negotiator had indicated that there was another person behind the Russian Premier because the Premier had run out of the room and come back with a different answer. This was not a surprise because the Premier was the face. It was the spine that was hidden. The spine ran Russia.

When McDonald Pease had returned to Russia for the supposed cooperation, Smith had asked for and received permission to include a special message. It read:

"To whoever really runs your defenses: We know we cannot prove to you that we do not open up the skies with a secret weapon. So be it. But know this as a sign of our intentions not to conquer you: at any time we wish, we could take apart your Politburo and make your leaders prisoners in their own land. But we have chosen not to do so. Why? Because we really do not wish to conquer you. The weapon is just one man." And then there was a brief description of Remo so they would know where all the hell came from, and that his was really a peace move, not a search-and-destroy mission in the heart of Moscow.

Smith had told the Russians Remo was coming. He had taken away what was perhaps Remo's most valuable protection: surprise.

And Remo accepted this with a wisecracking thanks. But Remo's signal was ringing now.

"I can't take the Aeroflot," said Remo.

"Why not?"

"If you were expecting some sort of superweapon and you were willing to get thousands of your people killed just to win a war, wouldn't you shoot down the plane that brought him in?"

"We'll fly you over at high altitude," said Smith. "But the parachute won't work from that far up."

"I'll work it."

"Remo, I know you know what this means. And you know I am not sentimental. But good luck."

"You're going to get me killed and the big-deal emotional pitch is 'good luck'?" said Remo. "Don't break down in tears all at once."

The last flight allowed to land at Moscow carried the American McDonald Pease. Shortly thereafter, the air-defense command received a strange order. No flight was allowed to land, including Russia's own civilian aircraft.

Any flight that did not attempt to land was to be shot down immediately, no matter who was on board.

In the whole tragic business, Alexei Zemyatin had one bright note.

"They have finally showed us the flaw in the perfect enemy," he said, showing young General Ivanovich, KGB, the note from the American peace mission. The old field marshal knew this sharp young man whom he had been training to think had connected the major problem of war with the minor one of this single agent. That there was going to be a nuclear war within forty-eight hours he did not tell Ivanovich, who did not have to know about it at this point. The young general already had more facts than Zemyatin liked to trust any single person with. He showed Ivanovich the note brought by the special American envoy, McDonald Pease.

"So the man himself was the awesome weapon. That explains it. So America means peace," said Ivanovich.

"No, of course not. They want us to delay because they want to figure out a way to finish us off. Apparently someone over there has seen through our agreement to negotiate, and is willing to sacrifice this 'weapon.' "

"Are you sure?"

"As sure as I can be," said Zemyatin. They were in his apartment. Zemyatin had a cup of brandy and had poured one for the general. The bodyguard was asleep, snoring loudly.

"They sacrifice the lesser weapon to protect the greater."

"Unless, of course, what they say is true."

"No. They have sent that man to his death. We know he has incredible speed. He has incredible strength. But he is one man. Maybe he can dodge one bullet, but he cannot dodge a thousand. He is one man and he has shown us his flaw. We have films of him. A sergeant could figure out what to do," said Zemyatin.

Ivanovich's face had lost its smoothness. His eyes narrowed. "Yes, we will kill him, because he is one man. But what is his flaw?"

Zemyatin swirled the brandy around in the teacup. The years, the dead, the wars, had left him tired, tired beyond his years.

"His faw is his commanders. They have sent him to us on a platter. And if they are that kind, we will eat from it. There will be much death in the coming days. It would be nice, boychik, if the world were butlers and pantries, yes?"

Then they toasted each other, draining the imported brandy and putting their cups down on the table. There was work to be done and the drinking was over.

The bodyguard was awakened by a message from the Kremlin negotiators that the American McDonald Pease had just discovered he was a prisoner, and that they were not really negotiating. Pease was giving them an alternative.

"Shoot me or let me go. And you'd better shoot me because I'm leaving."

"All right," said Zemyatin. "Give him what he wants."

A guard and an officer entered the negotiating chambers. The guard put a bullet into the brain of McDonald Pease and left him in the locked room with the Americans, who suddenly lost any possible hope that the Russians were interested in peace. Pease's body was left where it was to remind the Americans not to try to escape to their embassy.

They all remembered what Pease had said on the plane coming over:

"I long for the day when it will be a crime in the world to shoot an American. When people know they are going to be punished good if they mess us over."

The Russian missile command spotted the American plane first, high above missile range. It was the familiar CIA recon plane, but this time it dropped a load—too small for a nuclear bomb, however. It appeared to be a stick, roughly six feet long, and two and a half feet wide. Five miles up, everyone at radar control realized it was a person.

"That's the one," said a staff officer. "Got to be him."

The whole defense structure of the city was waiting for him. No one knew, of course, why everyone should be so anxious to kill one person, but the rewards were going to be great. It was hoped, but not demanded, that his head would be intact for identification purposes.

"Shoot when the parachute opens," came the order. KGB cars were dispatched to retrieve what was left of the corpse. As backups, local police units were also alerted to pick up the body. Both groups had orders, if the person was still alive, to finish him off carefully.

At four miles up, the order to hold fire was given. At three, then two miles, there was muttering about firing so low in the city. He might slip out.

At two hundred feet there was only a puzzled chuckle of contempt. There was no need to fire. The parachute wouldn't have time to open at the speed the man was falling. Hopefully, some skin would be left intact so that he could be identified.

The radar did not pick up a sudden jerk of the body at 120 feet. Remo had pulled the ripcord.

If he'd had time to think about it, he probably would have gotten himself killed. He never intended it to float him down like a normal chutist. That would have given him too much time up in the air being hung out for bullets.

Remo simply broke his fall with the parachute. He did that by slowing his descent to the speed of a drop off a ten-story building. He met the earth with his center in control. He met the earth moving. He knew certain places in the city where the men he wanted would be.

The parachute was found within four minutes of Remo's landing.

General Ivanovich, in charge of this elimination, was informed immediately. He had bunkered down at 2 Dzerzhinsky Square in his old KGB office.

There was no body attached to the chute. Ivanovich made a note: "Possible decoy?" If so, where was the body? On the other hand, he himself had seen what this man had done in Hanoi. It was possible that the American had such good control of his body that he could survive a fall that would kill others. Not, of course, a fall from five miles up. But a lesser one.

"Was the parachute opened?" asked Ivanovich.

"Yes, it was, Comrade General, but at two hundred feet . . ."

Ivanovich hung up. All right, the American had landed alive. But they were ready for him. They had been given special orders for this very special single person. The blood faces had shown which tactics were useless. Now all personnel were told never to wait for a clear field of fire, but just to fire, filling the entire area with flame and bullets. One could not expect to hit this man aiming. Blanketing was the only answer.

It was 11:15 P.M. Moscow time. By 11:30 there was a report from the Rossiya Hotel that the entire top floor of the building had been penetrated. The top floor was allocated to the director of state information, who was hysterical and accusatory.

The Rossiya was the finest hotel in Moscow.

"General. Your men attracted him. He got through your men. He got through my men. Stop him. This is Moscow. Stop him."

"What did he do?"

"He made a mockery of your men. Not a scratch on them or him."

"Did he do anything to you?"

"He created lies."

"What lies?"

"I am in charge of truth. I give no credence to anything Americans say."

"So you spoke with him. You know he's an American. What lies are you talking about?"

"Under duress I was forced to sign a statement which is an obvious lie."

"What was the lie?"

"That we are defenseless against him, and that I would be a dead man if I didn't sign. And you know, he was right."

"Thank you, director," said Ivanovich.

At the apartment house atop Lenin Hills, overlooking Moscow on Verobyevskoye Way, the supreme commander of the KGB refused to sign any paper. He paid for it with his ribs. They were torn out of his body.

Again, none of the officers or enlisted men guarding him was hurt.

Report:

"We only knew he was in the apartment complex when the body was discovered."

Report:

Dacha near Kaluga just outside of Moscow invaded. Again, none of the enlisted men injured. Admiral murdered for strangest reason. Did not write fast enough.

Report:

Minister of Defense crushed to death in the Kremlin complex while eating a light snack of cheese and crackers.

And so on through the night. Through every secured place, into every trap. Occasionally the guards saw someone enter and got off a few rounds. It was hoped that by morning, this invader would be more vulnerable. But in the morning, the crushing truth came home.

The Premier's complex had not only been successfully invaded in daylight, but the Premier had written out several prayers and promised, in writing, to build a shrine to the gods of a small fishing village in North Korea. The invader was now waiting to speak to "the guy who really runs things."

"You win," said Ivanovich. He notified Zemyatin. They had failed. They had not found the flaw.

"This person—this thing—has taken apart our government."

"I will talk with him," said Zemyatin. "Tell him where I live."

"Should I bring him to you?"

"Boychik, this may surprise you, but I have never killed or ordered killed anyone I did not have to. And I am not going to start now. You stay there. Let's not lose anyone else to this crazy animal. Maybe America is telling the truth. Eh?"

"Maybe we can slip someone close to him when he

enters. Maybe we can use the North Koreans. They have something as awesome as . . ."

"This front has collapsed, boychik. But I tell you, son, that you have done well. You will be a field marshal sooner than you think."

"But we lost."

"Both of us have seen that you can make the right decisions. That is the kind of man Mother Russia needs, not someone who is lucky because two hundred thousand men somewhere suddenly do something better than expected. I am ordering you now, young bureaucrat with the smooth face, to coordinate everything should I not live."

And then, by hand messenger because he wanted to take the greatest precaution about the missiles, Zemyatin sent the message that could not be listened in on by American electronics to the young general who could think. The message explained about the simple, crude, and malevolently dangerous new Russian missiles now ready to fire.

Ivan Ivanovich was going to replace the Great One as adviser to the leaders of Mother Russia, but strangely this young man with so much ambition did not rejoice in the promotion. Because he realized while working with the Great One, Field Marshal Alexei Zemyatin, that the thrill was not in wearing more buttons on one's shoulders, but in winning.

Without being told, Ivanovich stationed men at a distance from the old man's apartment house and ordered them to do nothing. He was almost tempted to shoot one of the guards to wake them up. Zemyatin might have done that.

Zemyatin did not see the guards and would not have cared about them anyway. He saw this young American stride into his apartment without knocking and began giving instructions.

The American, strangely, could speak an old form of Russian dating back to Ivan the Terrible, but not too well. Zemyatin's English was rusty but better than the American's Russian. The American was under the impression that he had showed he could conquer Russia.

"So you see you can trust us. We don't control that fluorocarbon thing, or whatever it is. So put down your new missiles, and let us work together in getting this beam thing."

"Are you done?" said Zemyatin.

"I guess," said Remo. "Do you want me to kill some more?"

"No. You have done enough of that. You may even be able to destroy our government. But you alone cannot conquer Russia. You can kill but you cannot rule."

"I don't want this dump. Nothing works right here."

"You did not perform that demonstration around our capital because we don't have something that works."

Remo glanced at the bodyguard. He was an old man, but there was a way he carried his body around the big pistol in his belt that showed he had used that weapon. It was obviously not an ornament.

"You want to win an argument or do you want your gizzard on the floor?" asked Remo. He waved some of the signed statements in front of Zemyatin. The old man flipped through them, amused at who had buckled and who had not.

"I do believe your people would believe that you might be a superior weapon to that fluorocarbon beam that lets in the deadly rays of the sun. Which means you may be telling the truth."

"You must know what America is like. Who would want your place when we have ours?"

"Son, I have seen the workings of the minds of counts and commissars, so do not bring something so absurd to my table as the dish that governments act rationally. You have earned a degree of my trust."

"Then put down your missiles," said Remo.

"There is a problem with that. You are going to have to think now. We created those missiles because we were sure at that time that America was responsible for the device and that it was a weapon. Further tests conducted in your country, young man, appeared to confirm our original estimate. We had to create a missile you could not damage. Not to say that such a device could put out our missiles.

But it would place them in a category of unreliability we
could not accept. Are you following me?"

"We showed we could knock out all your missiles so you
had to build new ones."

Zemyatin controlled an acknowledging nod. It did not
shock him that the man looked so average. The most
dangerous things in the world were the commonplace. The
bodies around Moscow were proof enough. He did not
have to see muscles.

"These new missiles have two orders that can be delivered. Go and no-go. That is exactly why your intelligence
agency correctly called them 'raw buttons.' "

"So tell them no-go."

"Without burdening you with details, the deployment
system across a nation larger than yours was necessarily
cumbersome. We do not have some electronic command
that maneuvers the missiles in series of calculated change-
able firings. If we say 'no-go' it would take weeks to get
everyone organized again, to get the orders out again. In
effect, in this missile age they would have to be put down
forever."

"I am not against that," said Remo.

"We have a designated firing time, soon to be upon us.
If you kill me there is no way to put down those missiles. If
you torture me, you will get a wrong command that will
tell them not to listen to the right command if it should
come next."

Remo noticed the electronics against the wall, the dishes
yet to be cleared from the table, and the old bathrobe this
man confidently wore while discussing the gravest matters
of state. This was the one, he was sure, he was to look for.
The one who made the deals.

"In brief, young American, it is either war or no war,
the rawest of raw buttons. To tell them to stand down
means virtually abolishing the system. And for that, I must
have more proof than your showing off. I am sorry."

"So it is war."

"Not necessarily," said Zemyatin. "We have time. I will
not tell you how much. But we do have time."

"If there is a war, you are not going to survive it. And

tell your friend over there not to bother with that blunderbuss he has stuck in his pants."

"Another death, American?"

"I don't keep score anymore," said Remo. "If those missiles go, I will spend a lifetime in this mess you call a country evening things out. I want you to know that no chairman or commissar or king will live one night. I will make your country into desert, a body without a head, a dung heap among nations. I don't want conquest. To win Russia is to win nothing."

"For you. But for me, it is everything."

The bodyguard whom Remo knew wanted a chance with the gun suddenly turned to the electronics. Remo caught only vague words of the language, but he knew that something horrible had happened.

"American," said Zemyatin, "I now believe your government has been telling the truth about that weapon. Unfortunately."

Remo waited to hear what the Russian leader meant by "unfortunately."

"Your government may be stupid, but it is not completely so. The beam has been directed toward your northern pole with the largest arc yet, on a continuous scan parameter."

"Wonderful," said Remo. What was he talking about?

"In brief, the ozone shield is being punctured continuously above the polar ice cap."

Remo eyed the Russian suspiciously. So what? he thought.

"Terrible," he said.

"Yes," said Zemyatin. "Unless that machine is stopped, the entire polar ice cap will be turned to water. So large is the polar ice cap that the oceans will rise many, many feet. Low-lying areas of the earth will be flooded, and that means most of Europe and America. Civilization as we know it will be doomed."

"That machine can really get you so many ways," said Remo. "What is the source?"

"Your America. The beam has been on long enough now for us to get a fix on it. Your northeast corridor."

"Good. If you can get a fix on it, we must know exactly. Anything in that electronic junk on the wall that can get an American phone number?"

"Yes," said Zemyatin. And Remo gave Smith's secret number to the Russians for dialing.

While the bodyguard was dialing, Zemyatin asked, "Are you part of the CIA?"

"No. Internal, mostly."

"Secret police?"

"Not really. We don't want to control anything. We just want to keep the country from going under."

"We all say that," said Zemyatin.

"But we mean it," said Remo.

"Of course," said the Great One of the Russian Revolution.

Smith's voice came over the transatlantic line surprisingly clearly.

"This line is being eavesdropped on, Remo," Smith said. There were gadgets in his office, Remo knew, that could tell that, but he had never heard Smith say that before.

"I would be surprised if it weren't, Smitty. This is a KGB line."

"Doesn't matter. We have located the beam. You will not believe what it is doing!"

"Continuous parameter scan on the polar ice cap. Low-lying areas are going to be flooded," said Remo.

"Right," said Smith, wondering if Remo had suddenly learned to deal with technology. "The source is located just ouside of Boston on their high-tech Route 128."

"Then you can put it off now, and we can show their leader. I found him. His name is Zemyatin, Alexei. He has a stupid bodyguard."

"Can't do that. Not that simple. There are two of those beams. One of them, we've been told, is called the doughnut. In its center, perhaps two hundred square feet, everything will be all right. Outside of that center, in a ring two hundred miles wide, everything will be exposed to the unfiltered rays of the sun. Washington, New York. Everything. It will be a disaster of enormous proportions."

"Ask him how he knows," said Zemyatin.

"How do you know?" asked Remo.

"That is the key, Remo. She has told us about it. If the government takes one step toward her machines, the doughnut goes off. Remo, she knows you and she wants you. That woman you were with is behind all this."

"Dr. Kathleen O'Donnell?" asked Zemyatin.

Remo nodded. He didn't have to ask Smith.

"She wants you. She will settle for no one else. I am glad you called."

"You mean she would destroy a world just to get another date or something?" Remo asked.

He saw Zemyatin signal his bodyguard. Another phone was produced. Zemyatin spoke hurriedly. He was getting that psychological profile he had ridiculed before. He presented the facts to the nervous KGB officer in charge of the British desk.

The answer was horrifying.

"That is precisely what she would do," came back the voice from the other end of the phone. "One death or a million deaths means nothing to her. She might even enjoy them."

"Tell your commander, American, we are coming. You and me," said Zemyatin.

On the way out of the apartment, Remo slipped the pistol from the bodyguard's belt and crumbled it in his hands.

"It wouldn't have worked, sweetheart," he said to the old warrior clutching at space.

He also warned Zemyatin to give the command to stand down the new raw-button missiles, because Remo did not trust planes.

"I mean, what if something happens to you?"

"I am sure that with your awesome protection, American, nothing will. When I see the beam destroyed, then I will tell them to stand down. Trust is too rich a meal for an old man who has supped on the chicanery of international politics. Not at my age. Not now."

"I don't care. You want us all to go up in a nuclear cloud if you have a heart attack? Fine with me. I think all you Russians are crazy."

Alexei Zemyatin shrugged. It was not his country that had allowed something like the fluorocarbon beam to be produced.

18

It was said of those who fought closely with the Great One that they began to think like him. So, too, was it with General Ivanovich.

Traditionally, the North Koreans had been dismissed as gloating barbarians, too ruthless and crude and incompetent to even consider using a joint exercise.

This time, their intelligence chief, Sayak Cang, was not humored and dismissed; this time, General Ivanovich stepped in, for even as Zemyatin and the American monster were boarding the plane for the flight to America, Ivanovich knew he had taken charge. He was not seeking how to appear well no matter what happened. He was looking to make this dangerous world work in Russia's favor. That was the secret of Zemyatin's brilliance. And the Great One knew Ivanovich understood that now.

That was why Zemyatin had told him about the American discovery of the device in their own territory and the Russian missiles ready to go like a timer on an American coffeepot; without an order, just a date. Even now Ivanovich could hear the Third World War clicking away with all the mindlessness of a mechanical clock. He did not panic. He thought. And when the North Korean boasted about finishing de Lyon himself, Ivanovich did not wait to get some superior to join him in this new bold move he was taking upon himself.

He had remembered Cang from a visit to Moscow. The man's only weakness was cigarettes and a sense of inferiority which he hid well. There was no reason for North Korea to eliminate a Russian problem in Western Europe, but Ivanovich understood immediately the North Korean action. Instead of laughing at the North Koreans for doing something seemingly not in their direct self-interest, Ivanovich ordered a direct salutation sent to Kim Il Sung with a request for advice from their genius in special action work abroad.

What Ivanovich did, in effect, after all these years, was to have his country answer the North Korean's call. Sayak Cang was on a line immediately inside the Russian embassy, an access Ivanovich, too, had risked ordering. But now, thinking like Zemyatin, he understood that retribution at home did not matter, especially since the American monster had personally crippled the great government of the Soviet Socialist Republics.

Ivanovich held an entire country in the palm of his hands as he talked to the once lowly Sayak Cang.

"We stand in awe of you, and seek your protection," said Ivanovich. "You are the leader of the socialist world."

"I have lived my life to hear those words," said Cang. His voice cracked. Was it the emotion? It sounded so much like fear.

"We had failed so many times with our problem in Western Europe that we called it insurmountable. You solved it."

"You see we are a great nation."

"Great nations have burdens, Sayak Cang. We have sent one of our leaders with a monster of a man, a killer you could not fathom, to America to seize a weapon that will destroy the Eastern world," said Ivanovich, shrewdly playing on Russia's Asian connection.

"We not only can fathom any American killer, we can crush him like a leaf," said Cang. Cang cleared his throat. He sounded nervous.

"There is a man whom we must have killed," said Ivanovich. "We have failed. There is an object we must have. There is a great game America is playing against us, and we are losing."

In an almost stuttering voice, Cang asked what the game was. Ivanovich gave him the location of the American device near their city of Boston in their northeast province of Massachusetts. The general also gave Cang a description of the American monster and the Russian whom he wished saved. What Russia wanted was the device taken, the American dead, and the Russian, his name Zemyatin, taken out of the country, safely if possible.

"We can do that. We can do all of it."

"But it must be done now. Your experts who have shown us the way must take off now. Immediately."

"Perfect. I really don't have much time now either way," said Cang. "Give all the glory to Korea because I will not be here."

"Are you all right?"

"I must build the only door our greatest sun cannot pass through. The door is death. In that I will control him."

Ivanovich did not explore that. He gave the North Korean intelligence chief his salutations, and then tried to reach the plane Zemyatin was on to let him know what he had done. There just might be that flaw in the American after all. For the way the French SDEC director was killed, according to reports from the Paris embassy, was virtually identical to the way the American monster killed.

Fire was going to be fought with fire.

Cang could not feel his arms or legs, or even the last breaths in his throat. Good, he thought. I am lucky. The timing is perfect.

He ordered the Master of Sinanju to be informed of where he was. Cang had been hiding for days now, trying to figure out exactly what his country could do. He knew he was a dead man. He accepted that. But how could his country use his death? And then the Russian gave him the perfect way to use a life any reasonable man had to admit would be over soon.

Chiun had figured out who had stolen the treasure of Sinanju and why.

He had told Cang in their last meeting:

"Pyongyanger, dog. The treasure will be restored to the

House of Sinanju. And I will sit here to receive it. I do not carry burdens like a Pyongyang dog."

Cang did not protest. He bowed and left, and went into immediate hiding, warning the President for Life to stay out of the country at all costs until this disastrous corner could be turned. He had not even asked Chiun how he had figured out who had stolen the treasure. Now he would know that, too. He was using the door even Chiun and all the Masters of Sinanju were defenseless against.

When Chiun entered Cang's rock-deep office, Cang was lying on a mat with his head on a pillow and smiling inwardly because his lips were hard to move.

"I am dying, Chiun."

"I have not come to witness the disposal of garbage," said Chiun.

"The poison I have taken robs me of almost all sensation. I cannot feel, therefore you cannot make me tell you where I put your treasure. I am about to pass through the only door that can withstand an assault by a Master of Sinanju: death, Chiun. Death." Cang's fading eyes saw that Chiun remained still. He did not talk. Good. He did not wish to waste time. Cang had ordered what he wanted to be written out in case the poison acted too quickly. It was all the descriptions the Russian had given him, including the location of the machine. Chiun was to bring the machine to Russia and then he would be told where the treasure was. And incidentally, there was a presumptuous American he was to kill, and a Russian he was to save.

"I am to trust you now?"

"Trust or not. Do the task or not. I am leaving you and you cannot follow through the door of death. No one here knows where the treasure is, and you can kill for a hundred years and never find it."

Chiun read the note again. He knew where Boston was. He had spent so long in America, wasting the best years of his life in one country serving the insane emperor who refused to take the throne. He knew Boston. He knew whites. He was perhaps the foremost authority on whites in the world.

"Tell me, O Great Master, how did you fathom I had

stolen the treasure? Tell me that, and I will give you one piece now."

"The Frenchman told the truth. He didn't know who had sent him the coins. This I know. And the great theft by the pope was impossible."

"How did you know that?"

"The popes have not shown any skill since the Borgias. To steal the treasure of Sinanju, maybe, only maybe, could have been done by a Borgia pope who sought conquest and land. But for the one decent period, the popes have been as useless as their founder, caring not for the glory of gems, the power of land, but for fanatic and useless things like prayer and their Western cult manners of charity and love, and whatever other peculiarities are endemic to their kind."

"You truly know whites, don't you?" said Cang.

"They are not all the same. But Pyongyangers are. They are dogs without the virtues of courage and loyalty," said Chiun. "Where is this piece of treasure you are willing to return?"

"Underneath me," said Cang.

Chiun rolled him over with one foot and found a minor silver statue taken as tribute by a minor Master, Tak. Tak was always the Master Chiun used to forget when memorizing the cadences of the history of the Masters of Sinanju.

Chiun ordered one of the flunkies to return the statue to the village of Sinanju and let the villagers place it on the steps of his house in tribute.

Cang now faced the floor after having been rolled over. No one dared roll him back in the presence of the Master of Sinanju. But with his last breaths, Cang explained what Sinanju meant to Korea, and that all Koreans should now work together. He had not desired to touch such a treasure but he knew of no other way to induce service from a Master of Sinanju now working in the white lands. Cang's last words were of his admiration for Sinanju, and his love of Korea, and his plea that Koreans work together as the true brothers they always had been. Only in that way could the land they all loved be free of foreign domination.

These were Cang's last words as he passed through the

door even the Masters of Sinanju could not penetrate to harm him. He spoke them into the hard floor of his office. The floor heard the plea much better than the Master of Sinanju.

Chiun had left for America after seeing which piece of the treasure had been returned for an answer to the question.

It was Ivanovich's competence that led to the great battle of America's high-tech Route 128 just outside of Boston. He knew the last moment that Zemyatin could call off the missile attack. He found out the speed of the airliner headed toward Boston carrying the Korean detachment. He had only one element to control, and he did that to perfection.

He slowed down the Russian aircraft. Zemyatin apparently understood because there was no complaint. They did pick up conversations ground America to air Russia between the American monster and a man named Smith. Smith was asking what on earth kind of game the Russians could be playing now. Even his computer couldn't figure that out.

Famous ports around the world began noticing the strange new tide licking ever so slightly at their piers and wharves.

Scientists around the world were tracking the phenomenon over the polar ice cap. The ozone shield was thinning, opening and threatening to collapse, bringing with it the last gasp of life on earth.

And General Ivan Ivanovich controlled it all with the simple speed of an aircraft headed toward America. He played it perfectly. Chiun's car and the car bearing Remo and Zemyatin arrived at the barricades outside of Chemical Concepts of Massachusetts virtually at the same time.

Remo and Chiun cried out:

"Where were you?" And each answered with his own version of: "I am here now. All right?"

The paratroopers, state police, national guard, and local police had all received orders to seal off the building, but they didn't know why. They were all ordered now to pass the barricades and not to let anyone through until otherwise ordered.

What they could not be told from above was that they were only constituting a pitiful holding action. Their barricades would not protect them, would not stop the madwoman from incinerating everyone around her in the northeast corridor. They had orders to let only one person through: the one she wanted.

When three men tried to get through—one Oriental, one American, and one Russian—the guards reacted swiftly.

"I just want one, the handsome one," screamed a beautiful red-haired woman from the flat building of CCM.

"Remo isn't bad-looking," said Chiun, wondering where in that ugly building the machine was.

"The young white. Remo. Get in here."

"You know her?" said Chiun. "You've been hanging around with whores."

"How do you know she's a whore?"

"She's white, isn't she? They all do it for money."

"My mother was white," said Remo.

"Gentlemen," said Zemyatin. "The world, please. It is coming apart in a multitude of ways."

"You don't know for sure who your mother is. You told me you're an orphan."

"She had to be white. I'm white."

"You don't know that."

"Gentlemen, the world," said Zemyatin.

"Remo, you get in here now," screamed Kathy O'Donnell from the factory window.

"He is not white. Don't believe him," said Chiun. "Ungrateful as a white, yes. Slothful, yes. Cruel, yes. Shortsighted, yes. But he is not white. He is Sinanju."

"Remo, that is the woman," Zemyatin broke in. "She has got the machine. You get the machine to stop. I will put through the stand-down order of the missiles, the polar ice cap will stop melting, and we may all live to see tomorrow."

"Am I white?" said Remo.

"You are as white as snow," said Zemyatin. "Please. In the name of humanity."

"Not white," said Chiun, moving through the guards.

"White," said Remo, pushing Zemyatin through also, and leaving a couple of guards trying to disengage their weapons from their jumpsuits.

"Asking another white? Ask me," said Chiun. "You couldn't do the things you do and be white. Yes?"

Inside the building, none of the typewriters were working. None of the bookkeepers were pounding on computer consoles. Only a few terrified technicians and a man named Reemer Bolt huddled in a corner.

"You've got to stop her," said Bolt. "I can't even get out of here. I've got to establish a Rhode Island branch office."

"You, Remo," called out Kathy. She had a bullwhip in her hands. She raged with venom. "Are you sorry now? Are you sorry you left me?"

"Sure," said Remo. "Where's the machine?"

"I want you to apologize. I want you to suffer the way I suffered."

"I'm suffering," said Remo. "Where's the machine?"

"Are you really?"

"Yes."

"I don't believe you. Prove it."

"What can I say? I'm sorry. How do I turn off the machine?"

"You love me, don't you? You have to love me. Everyone loves me. Everyone has always loved me. You came back for me."

"What else?" said Remo.

"Do you really love me?" said Kathy.

"Where's the machine?"

"It's underground, in the basement. It's firing contin-uously," screamed Bolt.

Kathy O'Donnell thew herself in front of a locked steel door. She thrust out her magnificent bosom. She allowed her soft lips to smile. She knew that Remo loved her. She knew he had to want her. She couldn't have been that physically excited by someone who didn't crave her also.

"Over my dead body," she said. "That's the only way you get to the machine."

"Sure," said Remo, and obliged her with a simple stroke into her beautiful forehead as he opened the lock to the machine's basement bunker. The technicians followed, along with Zemyatin.

Remo and Chiun looked at the console and the glittering chrome tanks in amazement.

"There should be an Off button somewhere," said Remo.

"She locked the arch parameters," said Bolt. "You've got to power them down or ruin them."

"I go for ruin," said Remo.

"No," said Chiun. "We need it. We have got to deliver it to the Russians. Destroy that machine and we will never get back our treasure."

Zemyatin did not know how General Ivanovich had managed to arrange this, but he had known something was happening when the young general had slowed down the plane. So this was it. Brilliant.

Zemyatin saw Remo move toward the machine, but it seemed only like the jerk of a finger, for the Oriental had done the same. Slowly, ever so slowly, they appeared to turn and face each other and then remained immaculately still.

They did this for ten minutes on Zemyatin's watch before he realized what he was seeing. When top boxers fought each other, they felt each other out. To the person who knew nothing about boxing it looked as though the fighters were doing nothing, when actually the most important part of the fight was happening. The American monster had apparently met his equal, and their movements were so quick as to be beyond the human eye, like a bullet.

Zemyatin checked his watch again, and the crystal cracked. Vibrations tickled his toes through the soles of his feet. The American technicians, who would be needed for the future use of the machine if the Oriental won, stood back. They were still horrified by their earlier domination by the beautiful redhead and then by her sudden death.

If they are so evenly matched, Zemyatin reasoned, then a small help to the Oriental might turn the tide. But as he tried to get behind Remo, he felt a vibration so strong it almost liquefied his ligaments. Then he knew for sure that this great battle he witnessed was as far beyond the human eye as the first great cataclysm of all creation.

Then the white spoke. He was breathless.

"Little Father, the world is flooding. If nothing else, we will lose to waters all the great ports of the world. All the great cities on rivers will go. New York, Paris, London, Tokyo."

But the Oriental did not break contact, nor did he break off the awesome fight now beyond the eyes of those who watched.

"And Sinanju is a village on a bay. It will go before Paris."

Suddenly the room was filled with shattered console, broken drums, parts resembling shrapnel. In a smoking heap, the beams were done for.

The American monster was gasping for breath. The Oriental's kimono was wet with perspiration.

"Good-bye, treasure of Sinanju. Thank you, Remo," said Chiun.

"Stand down your missiles, Russian," said Remo.

"Of course. Why not? We never wanted a war."

"You did well enough for someone who didn't want one," said Remo. But he insisted on waiting for verification that the missiles had been stood down.

"I am trusting you not to build another one of these weapons."

"Big deal, trust," said Remo. "Why would we want to destroy ourselves, too?"

"For me, it is trust. You are the first one I have ever trusted, monster. And I trust you because you know no fear. You have no need to lie to me. So be it."

When verification came from the American satellites and was transmitted through Smith to Remo, Remo allowed as how the deal was done, and hoped they would never fight again.

"Not with those missiles. They are so crude that, once stood down, they can never be used again. It was a very raw button," said Zemyatin.

"You mean on that order, the new missiles are down forever?"

"Forever," said Zemyatin.

And on that, the American he trusted said softly:

"Thanks, sweetheart. And I am the first you ever trusted?"

"The first since I was a young man. Yes," said Zemyatin at the irony of that first person being an American enemy.

"You lose," said Remo, taking out Zemyatin's frontal lobe with a simple precise backhand that left the front of the face work for the wax embalmers of the Kremlin if they ever wanted to stick what was left in a museum alongside Lenin and Stalin.

Zemyatin could not in the least have improved America's position anymore by living.

"Done," said Remo.

"Not done," said Chiun, who understood the move Remo had made against the Russian to be correct.

The important thing was that the treasure of the House of Sinanju had been lost, lost because Remo had failed to join Chiun in favor of running after white interests. The least Remo could do to partially make up for that lack of gratitude was to write in his own hand a small sentence saying that he very well could have had a Korean mother because he didn't know who his mother was, being an orphan.

"I can't do that, Little Father," said Remo. "I am who I am. And that's it."

"Only a white would be so ungrateful as to not admit he was a Korean," said Chiun.

THE END

* * *

Aftermath: Reemer Bolt went on to become president of a major corporation on the strength of a résumé that showed he had been responsible for a fifty-million-dollar project with international ramifications both scientific and commercial. Guy Philliston, of the top-secret British intelligence organ called Source, was called in to handle another problem. According to the Americans, the Russians had placed a mole high up in British intelligence. The man was of a better British family, believed to be homosexual, and of course a total traitor to his country and the whole Western world. Philliston's only comment on getting the assignment to ferret out this blighter was:

"Hardly narrows it down, you know."

Mystery and Adventure from Warren Murphy's Trace Series